# A HOME OF OUR OWN

*Recent Titles by Gwen Kirkwood*

FAIRLYDEN
THE MISTRESS OF FAIRLYDEN
THE FAMILY AT FAIRLYDEN
FAIRLYDEN AT WAR


THE LAIRD OF LOCHANDEE *
A TANGLED WEB *
CHILDREN OF THE GLENS *
HOME TO THE GLEN *
SECRETS IN THE HEATHER *
CALL OF THE HEATHER *
WHEN THE HEATHER BLOOMS *
DREAMS OF HOME *
A HOME OF OUR OWN *


*Writing as Lynn Granger*

THE LAIRD OF LOCHVINNIE
LONELY IS THE VALLEY
THE SILVER LINK
THE WARY HEART

* *available from Severn House*

# A HOME OF OUR OWN

Gwen Kirkwood

severn House

This first world edition published 2010
in Great Britain and in the USA by
SEVERN HOUSE PUBLISHERS LTD of
9–15 High Street, Sutton, Surrey, England, SM1 1DF.
Trade paperback edition published
in Great Britain and the USA 2010 by
SEVERN HOUSE PUBLISHERS LTD

British Library Cataloguing in Publication Data

Kirkwood, Gwen.
  A Home of Our Own.
  1. Farm life–Scotland–Fiction. 2. Rape victims–
Fiction. 3. Single mothers–Fiction. 4. Scotland–Social
conditions–20th century–Fiction. 5. Domestic fiction.
  I. Title
  823.9'14–dc22

ISBN-13: 978-0-7278-6861-9    (cased)
ISBN-13: 978-1-84751-215-4    (trade paper)

Severn House Publishers support The Forest Stewardship Council [FSC],
the leading international forest certification organisation. All our titles that
are printed on Greenpeace-approved FSC-certified paper carry the FSC logo.

**Mixed Sources**
Product group from well-managed
forests and other controlled sources
www.fsc.org Cert no. SA-COC-1565
© 1996 Forest Stewardship Council

Typeset by Palimpsest Book Production Ltd.,
Grangemouth, Stirlingshire, Scotland.
Printed and bound in Great Britain by
MPG Books Ltd., Bodmin, Cornwall.

# Acknowledgements

I would like to thank Betty Tindal and Janet Stewart for supplying the factual information I required.

# One

'We've had a good year together, haven't we, Meggie?' Steven Caraford mused, watching the firelight flicker over his wife's red-gold hair. He had always loved its rich colour and shining abundance. 'Have you any regrets?' he asked softly as they listened to Big Ben strike midnight on the radio, heralding the New Year of 1951.

'Not one,' Megan smiled, clinking her glass of ginger wine against his. 'I think I'm the luckiest girl in the world. I'm happily married to the man I love . . .' Her green eyes sparkled as she looked at him over the rim of her glass, '. . . and we're blessed with a lovely baby boy. What more could a girl want?'

Steven knew there were a great many things most women would ask for; things Megan could have had if she had continued her career in teaching, or married Doctor Lindsey Gray, but she had chosen him. His heart swelled with love.

'We've been lucky. No one but the McGuires would have allowed us to farm their holding as well as our own.'

'They're a lovely old couple. I'd still think so, even if they hadn't given us this opportunity to expand. I hope the land agent never finds out they're subletting to us, though. I'd hate them to get into bother.'

'Mmm, so would I. They're not the only ones who would be in trouble either. We'd all be out on our ears.' He held up his glass. 'Here's to the good health of the McGuires. And may our own good fortune continue.'

'I'll drink to that,' Megan agreed. 'We'd have to sell at least half of our animals if the McGuires couldn't let us farm their land, wouldn't we?'

'Yes, but we'll cross that bridge if we come to it,' Steven said. A frown creased his forehead. 'You could have had security and a much better life than living in a chilly old farmhouse and getting up at the crack o' dawn every morning to help me with the milking, Meggie.'

'So long as we have each other, Steven, I have all I need in life,' Megan said firmly. 'I nearly lost you once and I know how terrible that felt. Money isn't everything.'

'It is to some people.'

'Well I'm not one of them, as you should know by now, my love.' She slid on to the hearthrug and laid her head on his knee, staring dreamily into the fire. 'It was no hardship to give up teaching, and I never did want to marry Lint, or any other doctor. I love it here at Schoirhead, farming our own wee smallholding, looking after the animals, living and working together every day. Truthfully, Steven, I don't want anything to change.'

Steven stroked her auburn tresses soothingly and murmured endearments, but in his heart he knew things couldn't stay the same indefinitely. All it needed was for their landlord to discover the McGuires were subletting their holding to him and their world would be turned upside down. But this was a New Year, a time for optimism. He set aside his glass and drew his lovely young wife into his arms.

'I promise I'll give you a better life than this one day,' he murmured huskily, 'but for now let's go to bed?'

'Mmm, I'm ready if you are.' Her eyes gleamed mischievously.

'I can't believe you were so shy less than a couple of years ago, Meggie.' He stood up, drawing her with him, holding her close. 'It's morning already and we shall have to be out at the byre again in a few hours.' He grinned. 'I doubt if Joe will be fit for much work by the time he and Jimmy Kerr return from "first footing" the neighbours.'

'Poor Johan, it must be hard for him living in a foreign country, even though he's no longer a prisoner of war. I'm sure he must miss his family, especially at this time of year. I've heard the Germans have great celebrations at Christmas. I'm glad Jimmy invited him to celebrate Hogmanay with him and his pals. We can't begrudge him one night of drinking himself silly.'

'No. He works hard,' Steven agreed. 'I don't think he has any family left in Germany, or at least he's not been able to trace them. He says he's grateful to have survived the war and to have a home with us now.' He grinned. 'But I don't envy him the sore head he'll have tomorrow, or rather today.' He drew Megan close as they went towards the stairs.

Shandy was lying on his favourite mat in the hall. He lifted his head a little, opened one sleepy eye and thumped the floor approvingly with his tail. Steven bent to pat his head.

'You, my good friend, should be sleeping in your kennel. I'm not the only one who has been spoiled since I got a wife.' Shandy thumped his tail again as though in agreement.

'I haven't spoiled him,' Megan said with a smile. 'He appointed himself as Samuel's guardian from the day he was born. He's never far away, except when he's working with you or Joe.'

'I know. He's a grand wee dog. He could have been jealous of a new baby.'

Moments later they stood side by side gazing fondly down at their sleeping son in the cot which now occupied a corner of their bedroom, then they tumbled together into the big bed, snuggling close to keep each other warm.

'It's hard to believe Samuel will be a year old next month,' Megan murmured sleepily.

A few hours later, Johan Finkel looked very green when they met him coming home as they were making their way across the farmyard to the byre to begin the milking.

'I come quickly to work,' he said anxiously. 'First I change clothes.'

'Happy New Year, Joe,' Steven grinned, shaking his hand vigorously. Joe winced as pain shot into his head.

'Happy New Years to you, Boss, and Mrs Boss.' He blinked as he tried to focus on Megan.

'I think you'd better get some sleep, laddie,' Steven advised him wryly. 'You don't look so good. Megan's parents will be here by midday, as well as my mother. Megan is cooking a huge dinner,' he added wickedly, his eyes glinting with laughter as the younger man clutched his stomach and groaned before he darted away.

'You shouldn't have mentioned food,' Megan said. 'That was cruel.'

'I know.' Steven grinned. 'I couldn't resist. Come on, we'd better get cracking. There's a lot to do with one man less this morning. As soon as we've finished the milking, I'll feed the pigs while you go in and make breakfast and attend to Samuel. Don't worry,' he said, silencing her protest. 'I'll help you with the hens and things after breakfast. We'll manage for once. Mother promised to come early to help with the dinner or to keep an eye on Samuel, whichever you prefer.'

'She's so good to us, your mother,' Megan said as she settled herself against a cow in the next stall to Steven's.

True to her word, Hannah Caraford turned up at Schoirhead as Megan was washing the breakfast dishes.

'I've brought the roast of pork as we arranged, Megan. Shall I pop it in the oven?'

'Yes please. We're a bit behind this morning. Johan is under the weather after celebrating Hogmanay with Jimmy Kerr and his friends.'

'Jimmy Kerr? That's your neighbour's son, isn't it? The one who is a mechanic in Annan?'

'Yes. He's the one who persuaded Steven to buy a van. He's very good at helping us with repairs to the tractor in his own time.'

'Is there anything I can do for you? Peel the potatoes perhaps?'

'I prepared the vegetables last night and made the stuffing and apple sauce. Mum said she would bring one of her Christmas puddings. It would be a help if you could dress Samuel, and keep an eye on him while I see to the hens.'

'Looking after Samuel is always a pleasure, isn't it, ma wee man?' Hannah smiled broadly as she lifted her grandson from the highchair which had once been his father's. She adored children and her first grandchild had a very special place in her heart.

'What time do you expect your mother and father, Megan? I expect they have to do the milking at Martinwold whatever day it is?'

'Yes, I'm afraid there are no days off when you're a self-employed dairy family,' Megan said. 'I thought Dad might move and settle for a smaller herd now they only have themselves to consider. They'll need to leave here by three o'clock to start the afternoon milking so they're as tied as we are. At least we are working for ourselves and not putting the profit in someone else's pocket.'

'They have worked for Mr Turner for many years. I suppose it would be a big change for them if they moved.'

'Yes, that's what Dad says, and mother says "better the devil you know". Mr Turner is a good boss. He keeps things modern and as easy to work as possible.'

'It must make a difference having a milking machine, I suppose?'

'It does. Three people couldn't milk sixty cows without one and there's not so many young men, or women, wanting to milk by hand seven days a week since the war. Steven would have liked to install a milking machine here before next winter now that we have twelve milking cows, but we would need to get permission from the official who deals with the tenancy leases for the smallholdings. It would be awkward because we're using the McGuires' byre as well as our own. Did Steven tell you he has opened up a door between the two byres to save us carrying the milk all the way round?'

'I didn't know that. Steven would be in big trouble if the land agent found out, wouldn't he?' Hannah said anxiously.

'He would, but he says we have to take a risk sometimes. The McGuires say the agents hardly ever inspect the buildings when they come to review the rents, so we're hoping they'll never find out. We keep some loose hay nearby so that we could camouflage the door if we knew they were coming. It has made a tremendous difference to the work. We only need to use our own dairy and equipment now so there's less washing and steaming to do as well as not carting the milk round about to get to our own dairy.'

'Yes, I can understand that,' Hannah nodded, 'but I can't help feeling anxious in case anyone finds out. Steven is taking a big risk. It would be terrible if they put him out of Schoirhead for farming his neighbour's holding without permission.'

'Mr McGuire says Steven makes a better job than he ever did, even when he was younger. He thinks they should be glad he's taken over. But we know the land agent wouldn't see it like that. Subletting is strictly against the rules,' Megan admitted. The situation worried her sometimes too, but she had faith in Steven's judgement and she knew how grateful the McGuires were. While Steven did the work and paid the rent to them it allowed them to stay in their house and keep their poultry and an odd pig in the wee paddock at the back. They trusted Steven to pay the rent to them on time so that they, in turn, could pay it as usual.

Joe did not put in an appearance for dinner, but it was a happy affair with both Granny Oliphant and Granny Caraford sitting on either side of Samuel, both eager to help him eat his meal now that he could sit up at the table.

'We have a bit of news for you,' Chrissie Oliphant announced while Megan was serving the pudding. 'Natalie Turner has announced her engagement.'

'Oh? Who has she managed to ensnare?' Steven asked with a grin.

'Just you be thankful she didn't snare you, laddie,' John Oliphant winked. 'She got her eye on you as soon as she saw you in your army uniform.'

'Don't tease him, John,' Chrissie remonstrated. 'Steven only had eyes for Megan and she only had eyes for him.' She looked at Megan. 'Natalie is engaged to that young doctor who often comes to stay at Martinwold. I think he has qualified as a surgeon now, so he will be Mister Gray, I suppose. She will need a man with deep pockets and they say his parents are quite well off.'

'Did they have an engagement party?' Megan asked.

'They're having it next weekend so his parents can come to stay. They live in the south of England – Gloucestershire, I think. Mr Turner says they are going down there to visit at Easter, to meet the rest of his family.'

'I wonder if Mr Turner is disappointed his son-in-law will not be taking over Martinwold Farm?' Steven mused.

'I would be if I was him,' John Oliphant declared. 'Martinwold is his life's work. But Natalie has never had any interest in the farm. The doctor laddie shows more interest than she does. He often comes for a walk round the stock with Mr Turner. Sometimes he comes on his own now that he's familiar with the farm boundaries and the farmyard and buildings. He asks a lot of questions and he seems keen to learn. I reckon he's too decent for the likes o' Natalie Turner, even though she will be a wealthy woman some day.'

Steven had known Megan's parents since he started school and became friends with their son, Sammy. He got on well with Megan's father. When the meal was over they went to look around the cows and pigs while the women cleared away the dishes. John Oliphant took a great interest in his son-in-law's wee farm. The two of them had a lot in common and he enjoyed his discussions with Steven, especially since he had lost his own son during the war.

'We'll pop round to the McGuires to wish them a Happy New Year while we're outside,' John called to his wife.

All too soon it was time for Chrissie and John to leave for home and their own work at Martinwold, the farm where Megan had lived most of her life until her marriage to Steven.

'You'll not need to go home yet, Mother?' Steven prompted. 'You've no cows waiting to be milked now.'

'No-o, I don't need to go yet,' Hannah said, chewing her lower lip. It occurred to Steven that she had been unusually quiet all day and he had noticed the way she twisted her wedding ring round and round on her finger. He always used to think she did that when she was agitated or worried about something. 'My neighbour, Angus Paterson, promised to shut in my hens and feed Sally, my sow,' she said. 'If it's all right with you, Megan, I'll stay and look after Samuel while you two are at the byre.'

'That would be a great help,' Megan smiled.

They were getting ready to go outside when Joe came slowly downstairs. His face still had a green hue.

'How do you feel now, Joe?' Steven asked sympathetically.

'My head, it feel like a bruised apple,' he said with a wan smile, 'and here . . .', he clutched his stomach, 'I think do not belong of me. No more I drink Scotch whisky.'

'We'll manage the milking without you tonight,' Steven said. The lad did look ghastly. 'You feed the pigs and make sure the hens are all shut in so the fox doesn't get them. A bit of fresh air might help.'

'Thank you, Mr Steven. Then I go back to bed? I no eat tonight.'

'Whatever you wish, Johan,' Megan said. 'But do drink plenty of water,' she called over her shoulder as she followed Steven across the yard to the byre.

'It's a great help having Granny Caraford to look after Samuel instead of having to wrap him up and bundle him in his pram to come with us,' Megan said happily as she settled on her stool to begin milking. 'I think she enjoys being with Samuel, but I have a feeling she's uneasy about something.'

'So you noticed too?' Steven frowned. 'I wondered if she's missing Willowburn. It's a big change from running a farm to running a shop. She's never complained, but I feel sure she has something on her mind.'

'That's what I thought.'

'She always loved animals so I thought she would be all right when she could keep a sow and her hens. The shop seemed an ideal solution when she had to move from Willowburn after Father died. There's not many places with such a large orchard and two pigsties, as well as enough ground for all her hens. Then there's the old stable. I suppose the shopkeeper must have kept a pony and trap for deliveries at one time.'

'I think she does enjoy her house and her bit of land, keeping her hens and a pig or two, but I'm not so sure about the shop,' Megan said thoughtfully. 'I'm not sure I would like a shop either, to be honest.'

They went on with the milking in silence, each lost in their own thoughts. Steven never forgot how generous his mother had been, handing over her own savings, even before he knew he would get a tenancy for a government smallholding. She'd always had faith in him. None of them had anticipated that her own life would be turned upside down so soon. First there had been their father's death, then Fred, his half-brother, taking off for Canada without warning. Giving up the tenancy of Willowburn where both he and Fred had been born must have been a wrench. Neither he nor his mother had relished the prospect of a farm sale, so he had taken out a loan from the bank and bought most of the Willowburn stock himself, paying the prices the auctioneer had used for the valuation. He had no regrets about that. He knew their father had always kept good, healthy cattle and it had proved a wise move because they were producing well for him here, at Schoirhead. The proceeds had allowed his mother to buy the shop business with the house and land attached. It would be a problem if she gave up the shop now as it would mean she had very little income.

'Steven?' Megan interrupted his thoughts. 'Why are you looking so troubled? Are you seriously worried about your mother?'

'Not worried exactly, but if she doesn't keep the shop on I'm thinking she will need the money she gave me when I started up here. I haven't finished paying off the bank loan I took out to buy the Willowburn cattle yet. We are progressing well and I was looking forward to clearing it by the end of May. I hoped we'd be able to modernize things a bit here then. We ought to have a milking machine and we can't go on relying on Jimmy Kerr to find us machines to hire to fit our old tractor, especially now he's working for a different firm. We need to buy a plough of our own, as well as a seed drill. Later on we'll need a mower for the hay.'

'And a binder if the government insists we must go on growing cereals,' Megan nodded agreement. 'Yes, I see why you're worried.'

'But if Mother needs her money I shall have to find it somehow.'

'There's no use worrying until we know for sure,' Megan said in her matter-of-fact way. 'We may have jumped to the wrong conclusion.' She gave him a wicked grin. 'What would you say if your mother wanted to marry again?'

'My mother? Marry again?' Steven got up from the cow he was milking and stared down at her.

'I was only teasing, but she is still an attractive woman and she keeps herself trim and fit. Angus Paterson seems very keen to help her with odd jobs. I'm only saying we could be worrying about all the wrong things. The most important thing is good health. It would be awful if she was worried about something like that and couldn't tell us. Money is insignificant beside good health. Look at the McGuires. We're young. We'll find a way to manage.'

'Yes, you're right, Meggie. You usually are. I'll milk the last cow and clean up the byre if you'll wash up in the dairy.'

'All right. It's a shame the McGuires couldn't join us for a meal tonight, but Mr McGuire can barely manage to get to the bathroom lately and he never ventures outside.'

'I know. I expect Mother will have taken Samuel round to wish them a Happy New Year and have a chat. Annie McGuire and my mother have got on well ever since I moved into Schoirhead.'

'If there's something really worrying her she may confide in Mrs McGuire. They are the same generation after all.'

'Maybe, but I'd like to know what's troubling her too.'

They did not have long to wait. Hannah had bathed Samuel and given him his supper so he was ready for bed when they returned to the house.

'That's wonderful,' Megan said gratefully. She picked up her small son and hugged him. 'Much as I love my fine fellow, it's good to find you all ready for bed for once.'

It seemed quiet when Samuel was in bed and Joe had gone back up to his room. Steven could see his mother's agitation increasing.

'Are you going to tell us what's wrong, Mother?' he asked at last.

'There's nothing wrong,' Hannah denied too quickly. She took a drink of tea and swallowed hard. 'B–but I do have some news and – and I'm not sure you'll approve.' She lifted her chin. Steven knew that sign. Whether he approved or not, his mother had already made up her mind about something.

'So, what's the news?'

'I've decided to give up the shop.'

'You mean you want to sell it and move somewhere else?' Steven asked cautiously.

'No, I like living there. I love the garden and the orchard with plenty of space around me, but I hate the shop with people coming in all day, expecting me to provide them with everything they want, even things which are rationed and which they've already had. Some of them seem to think I can conjure things out of a hat.'

'Don't upset yourself, Mother,' Steven said soothingly. 'There's always some people who are unreasonable.' He spoke cheerfully, but his heart was sinking, knowing how much she had helped him get a start at Schoirhead. His conscience wouldn't allow him to stand aside when she had no money coming in.

'It isn't just me who feels constantly under pressure,' Hannah said defensively. 'The butcher was telling me the government are in dispute with Argentina and they've cut the ration by another two pennyworth. He says rump steak is two shillings and eight pence a pound and it would take three ration books to buy a pound, and rations from thirteen people to buy a leg of lamb.'

'Then we should be thankful we were allowed to kill your pig,' Steven said. 'The pork we had today was delicious.'

'Are you trying to change the subject, Steven? It won't work. I've made up my mind.'

'I don't think I would like having a shop either,' Megan said quietly. 'It must be impossible to please all of the people, all of the time, especially when such a lot of things are still in short supply. Surely the rationing can't last much longer?'

'I'm glad you understand, Megan,' Hannah said with relief.

'How soon do you want to close the shop, Mother?' Steven asked resignedly.

'As soon as I can sell most of the stock I have in. I need to do it without delay,' she added on a note of urgency. 'But I wanted to explain to you first.'

'Why is there such a hurry?' Steven asked. 'I will speak to the bank manager and explain that I need another loan to repay the money you gave me when I started up, but it may take a while to arrange it.'

'I don't want your money, Steven! That's not the problem at all.'

'It's your money, Mother. I must repay you now. When you gave it to me none of us knew Father would die so soon or that Fred would take off for Canada and you would have to leave Willowburn. You will need something to live on.' Steven's tone was sharper than he intended. He was tired after the late night waiting up to welcome in the New Year, and he'd had a long day; now he was worried. Things had seemed to be going so well for him and Megan, but this would be a big setback.

'That money was a gift, Steven, not a loan. It was to help you get your stock and the start in farming you deserved,' Hannah said firmly.

'But you'll need something to live on.'

'I shall still have my eggs to sell. Also, I shall have a small income once I carry out my plans,' Hannah said quietly. She looked anxious and Megan noticed how she twisted her wedding ring round and round on her finger. 'That's what I wanted to explain.' She lifted her chin and her mouth set in a firm line. 'I'm going to take in a lodger.'

'A lodger?' Steven echoed in surprise. 'A—a man? Is it this Angus Paterson you keep mentioning?'

'Angus? Goodness me, no!' Hannah chuckled at the thought. 'He has a lovely house of his own, and I'd say he has plenty of money too.' She grew serious again. 'Do you remember I once told you about one of the land girls we had during the war who left suddenly? She was a really nice person. Her name was Ruth Vernon.'

'I remember,' Steven said slowly. 'At least I remember you

telling me about her leaving. You were upset at the time because
you believed Fred had assaulted her, didn't you?' He had suffered
many a nasty beating from his half-brother himself, but he hadn't
really believed Fred would hit a defenceless girl. 'Was that the
one whose father was a vicar?'

'Yes, that's Ruth. We've kept in touch – on and off,' Hannah
said quietly. 'I really did like her, but I–I felt I owed her that too.'

'What do you mean – owed her that?' Steven asked warily.

'She had a baby. A wee girl. Fred is the father . . .'

# Two

'Fred has a child?' Steven stared at his mother incredulously. 'I remember you told me he gave her a black eye and her face was badly bruised, but he said she'd fallen off a cart, didn't he? Are you saying he . . .' He stared at his mother in disbelief. 'Surely you don't think he raped her?'

'Yes. I didn't know for sure at the time, but Ruth was terribly distressed. She was incoherent. She couldn't speak, even to me. She rushed upstairs, stuffed her things in a holdall and left the house.'

'Poor girl,' Megan said, her eyes wide with horror.

'I didn't realize how dreadfully Fred had behaved, nor did I understand the full consequences of his actions until fairly recently,' Hannah sighed. 'We did correspond, but only a card at Christmas and an odd letter now and then. Ruth didn't tell me she'd had a child until I told her that Fred had emigrated to Canada and explained why I was leaving Willowburn. She really loved the farm you know, and the animals.'

'You're sure she – she never encouraged Fred?'

'Oh no. She was quite shy and she was always tense and on edge whenever he went near her. I should have guessed the reason, but I never thought Fred would force himself on a girl. She was only seventeen and it was so obvious she'd had a sheltered upbringing. I've always felt I should have been more vigilant, protected her in some way. I shall always feel I let her down.'

'You couldn't have watched over her twenty-four hours a day, Mother. Besides, Fred was not a child and he was always sly. I remember how he bullied me, and Sammy. He always took care not to let you or Father see him. Sam told you what he was like, didn't he, Megan?'

'Yes, my brother was no coward, but he was no match for Fred. He was so much bigger and heavier than either of you. Sam said he used to hide and then jump out at you.'

'A girl wouldn't stand a chance against him,' Steven said with contempt. 'He should have been made to answer for his crime, but you can't be responsible for what he did, Mother.'

'Maybe not, but he has ruined Ruth's life. She says she could never bring herself to marry any man now. She went home to her father. Her great-aunt lived with them. Ruth's letters were very vague; I thought she must be suffering from nerves, what with the war and her experience with Fred and everything. Now I know it was because she discovered she was expecting a child. Her father employed a girl to help her great-aunt look after the baby when it was born while Ruth attended college and trained as a teacher. Her great-aunt died just before she qualified so she moved back to the vicarage and lived with her father and her wee girl.'

'I see . . .' Steven frowned, wondering where all this was leading.

'Her father died in November,' Hannah said flatly. 'The vicarage went with his work. Naturally Ruth was very upset as they'd been very close and he had stood by her when she needed him so badly. I invited her and Avril, her wee daughter, to visit. They came the week before Christmas and stayed two nights.'

'Stayed two nights? You never mentioned that.'

'No. I wanted to see how we got on after all this time.'

'Are you sure the child is Fred's?' Steven demanded.

'I never doubted Ruth's word,' she said reproachfully. 'Even if I had there was no doubt at all when I saw her. She reminded me so much of my cousin Eleanor, Fred's mother, when she was a girl. Before Ruth agreed to visit she made me promise I would never tell Fred he was the father of her child. She doesn't want him to know or to see her – not ever. She's adamant about that.'

'I can understand how she feels,' Megan said quietly.

'Anyway, the long and the short of it is I have invited them to live with me and I intend to—'

'Live with you? But Mother you don't owe—'

'Hush, Steven,' Hannah said. 'It is not a case of owing anything. Ruth is fiercely independent. She has a little money which her great-aunt left her, and she is looking for a change now her father has died. She has taken temporary lodgings until Easter, when she will leave her present teaching post. She has been offered a job at a school in Annan.'

'But surely . . .'

'Please, Steven. I knew you might not be happy about the

arrangement, but I have thought it all out carefully. The shop has its own entrance, the two store rooms will make suitable bedrooms for Ruth and Avril, and the main shop will make a lovely sitting room, all quite separate from my own living quarters.'

'Yes, I can see the possibility,' Megan nodded. 'And there's a toilet and wash-hand basin in the back, isn't there?'

'That's right.' Hannah flashed Megan a grateful smile. 'The passage which leads to the rest of the house will make a small kitchenette. They will need to share my washhouse and my bathroom, but otherwise we can each have our privacy. Ruth insists on paying a fair rent. She understands I shall need to spend money converting the shop to living accommodation.'

'Well, I don't know . . .' Steven frowned.

'I have thought it all out,' Hannah insisted. 'I love children and I'm sure I shall get on well with Ruth. She's not the type to take advantage and she will have the same holidays from school as Avril, so please try to understand, Steven.' She looked at him pleadingly.

'We do understand,' Megan said softly. 'Is this what has been troubling you?'

'It has rather, but I made up my mind to tell you both today. I know it is a big decision, but I'm looking forward to it now. I've missed your father's company, especially in the evenings, Steven. People coming in and out of the shop are not the same as the company of someone close.'

Much later as they lay in bed, Megan took Steven's hand in both of hers. 'I can tell you're worrying about your mother's plans, Steven, but think how much worse it would have been if she'd told us she had a serious illness, or something equally bad.'

'Yes, I know, but I can't help wondering if this Ruth is taking advantage of her. How can we be sure the child is Fred's, and even if it is, it's not Mother's responsibility.'

'Your mother is a sensible person, Steven,' Megan said gently. 'She seems sure the wee girl is Fred's. I think we should wait until we have met them before we judge.'

'I suppose you're right,' Steven sighed. He turned towards her and drew her into his arms. 'I don't know what I should do without you, Meggie.'

\*    \*    \*

February was seriously wet and Megan trudged around in mud, trying to arrange her work so that she could dash out to attend to her poultry while Steven ate his meals and kept an eye on Samuel at the same time. He was almost walking now and difficult to watch; he missed not being able to go with Megan round the hens or to gather eggs. Joe had temporarily taken over the pigs and Steven fretted about the field still waiting to be ploughed. The river had flooded over the meadow again, but fortunately they had no cattle outside.

Annie McGuire caught an exceptionally nasty cold which laid her low, and Megan did her best to repay some of the older woman's past kindness by taking round pots of home-made soup, a few scones or a fresh loaf whenever she had time to bake. Mr McGuire's spirits were low and Megan guessed he felt himself to be a worse burden when his wife was not well herself and he could do nothing to help her.

'Just keep warm and well yourself.' Megan smiled at him. 'It would be worse if you tried to do things and had a fall. In spite of this dreadful weather the snowdrops are nodding gaily under the hedge and beneath the apple trees, and I saw some primroses on the bank beneath the hedge yesterday. It will soon be spring, then you'll be able to sit outside again.'

'Aye, I suppose so,' he nodded, making an effort to respond to her cheery smile. 'Ye're a grand lassie, Megan, aye a smile for an old man. I kenned ye'd make a grand wee wife for Steven. He's a lucky fellow.'

Annie McGuire was making a good recovery as March brought the longer, brighter days and the weather began to improve. Steven got on with the ploughing at last and Joe made a start on spring-cleaning the McGuires' buildings. Each year Steven insisted all the buildings were cleaned out and disinfected and the outsides were whitewashed. He made sure the McGuire sheds were done before their own. It was usually around this time that the Scottish land agent made his annual inspection. They always felt a sense of relief each time the visit passed without awkward questions, although Megan felt it must be obvious that Mr McGuire couldn't possibly be doing his own cultivations when they saw how crippled he had become. Steven was always tense until he had the seasonal work done, the cereals sown, and the agent had completed his review.

The changes to Hannah's premises were going ahead at speed, far quicker than Steven had anticipated, and he realized his mother must have had everything organized before she even mentioned the changes to him. Ruth Vernon and her daughter had arranged to move north when the school term ended just before the Easter weekend at the end of March. Hannah knew Steven was still wary about Ruth's motives in moving to Scotland, so the sooner he and Megan met her and Avril the better, she decided.

It was Megan who answered her telephone call.

'I wondered if you and Steven would come to lunch with me on Easter Sunday,' Hannah said. 'I would like you to meet Ruth and I'm sure Avril will be enchanted with Samuel. Although she will be seven in April, children usually get on together.'

'We'd love to come,' Megan said. 'Steven is not in just now, but I'm looking forward to meeting Ruth and I think it will set Steven's mind at ease when they have met.'

'That's exactly what I thought, Megan,' Hannah said with relief. 'I'm hoping the two of you will get on together as well. You're similar in age and you both trained as teachers.'

Steven was startled by his first sight of the girl who had aroused such tenderness in his mother's heart. She looked much younger than he had expected. Megan would soon be twenty-three, and Ruth looked about the same. The two were similar in height and build, but there the resemblance ended. Ruth Vernon had wide brown eyes, thickly fringed by dark lashes and well-marked brows. Her hair was as dark and glossy as a raven's wing, curving slightly against her heart-shaped face. Her mouth was too wide for beauty, but as she extended her hand to Megan with a tentative smile there was a hint of a dimple in each cheek. There was no doubt she was an attractive woman, but there was a dignity and a reserve about her which Steven guessed would have irked someone like Fred. Steven was carrying Samuel, but as he extended his hand in greeting he saw the wary expression in her eyes. She lowered her glance. He frowned, realizing she was as wary about meeting him as he was about her. Samuel held out his chubby arms, clearly asking to be greeted too. Her eyes flew open in delighted surprise and he saw the golden flecks which surrounded the black irises; a smile lit her face as she took Samuel into her arms and held him close for a few moments before carrying him to the settee to introduce him to Avril.

The child was another surprise. She bore no resemblance to Fred, with his thin mouse-brown hair and coarse features. She was delicately boned and her long golden-brown hair and sweet smile reminded him of photographs he had seen of his mother with her cousin Eleanor when they were young. She had her mother's dark-brown eyes and heart-shaped face, but not her dimples. Steven was unaware that he was staring intently at the pair of them until his mother touched his shoulder.

'Please try to make them welcome, Steven, for my sake if not for theirs,' she said softly. 'Ruth is already nervous about meeting you, although I assured her you were not the least bit like Fred, although you share the same father.'

'Like Fred? God I hope not!' he scowled. He paused, seeing this encounter from the girl's point of view. How was she to know he and his half-brother were as different as chalk and cheese. Samuel came toddling drunkenly towards him, throwing himself into his arms as he reached down to catch him. Avril giggled with delight.

'Would you like to see the alterations, Megan?' Ruth asked diffidently. 'Our belongings only arrived on Friday afternoon and I haven't managed to unpack everything yet so you will need to excuse the muddle.'

'Och, I know all about muddle.' Megan laughed. 'But I'd love to see how the alterations have turned out. We both would, wouldn't we, Steven?'

'Er . . . yes, of course.'

'You can leave Samuel with us,' Hannah said. 'Avril will look after him, I think.'

The little girl gave her an eager smile. 'Can I show him the big picture book?' she asked.

'He'd love that,' Megan assured her warmly. 'He loves looking at pictures.' She followed Steven and Ruth through to what had been the front shop.

'Gosh it's made a lovely sitting room,' she exclaimed involuntarily 'What an excellent idea to make the big window into a glass door with windows on each side. It's so light and airy.'

'It was Mr Paterson's idea,' Ruth said. 'Eventually the builder is going to make a small patio outside. I want to encourage Avril to grow some flowers. We brought an ancient stone trough from the vicarage. It belonged to my mother.'

'That's a splendid idea.'

'Mr Paterson is a retired architect, I believe, though he looks more like a retired farmer with his round ruddy cheeks. He drew up the plans for Mrs Caraford.'

'I didn't realize he was an architect,' Steven commented.

'Oh?' Ruth looked at him uncertainly, then turned back to Megan. 'I've brought a pair of long curtains from the vicarage. I think they will go right across.'

'What colour are they?' Megan asked.

'Dark-red velvet. I'm afraid the edges will be a bit faded, but I shall turn them end for end so it shouldn't show so badly, do you think?'

'I'm sure they'll look lovely. Red velvet is so cosy in the winter,' Megan said. 'Don't you agree, Steven?'

'What? Oh yes, I suppose so. What about the kitchen?'

'It's better than I thought possible,' Ruth said stiffly, wondering whether he disapproved of his mother spending money on the conversion. She lifted her chin. 'I did offer to pay towards the conversion, but – but Mrs Caraford wouldn't hear of it. She said Mr Paterson had drawn up the plans in return for her help when his wife died a few months ago. And he knew all the right tradesmen to employ. He supervised them. To be honest I had thought it would take twice as long.' She went through a door. 'This is the kitchen.'

'Oh . . .' Megan was surprised. 'It looks different somehow. Wasn't that end where the toilet and wash-hand basin used to be?'

'Yes, I must admit making so many alterations worried me . . .' Again she lifted her chin defiantly and glanced at Steven. 'It was Mr Paterson's suggestion, but I was afraid it would all cost too much. He incorporated the area which was the toilet and wash-hand basin and used the extra space for a cooker and the kitchen sink. It's stainless steel instead of the usual white sinks I'm used to. He says they'll all be stainless steel in a few years' time.' She ran her fingers over the gleaming surface of the draining board. 'He got it from one of the plumbers he knows.'

'It will be a lot cleaner than the wooden draining boards,' Megan agreed.

'He has had a small bathroom built on next to the bedrooms so it makes a completely self-contained flat now. I–I've insisted I must pay a market value rent,' she added defensively. 'I'm truly grateful to get such good accommodation, especially when I have Avril to consider. Don't think I don't appreciate it – or that I shall take advantage of Mrs Caraford's generosity,' she said, lifting her chin proudly and throwing Steven a challenging glance.

'Of course we don't think that,' Megan assured her swiftly, but Steven remained silent.

'Mr Paterson thought it would be better to make what he calls "a right job of it" so that it's completely self-contained. He said I might want to move out sometime and Mrs Caraford could end up letting it to strangers.'

'I suppose there's always that possibility,' Steven said. 'If you were to move to a different job, or get married, or . . .'

'I shall never do that!' Ruth declared vehemently. 'Never.' She couldn't suppress a shudder, and Megan was relieved when Hannah called them through for dinner. Steven went ahead and Megan touched Ruth's shoulder gently and smiled.

'I think it will be lovely when you have all your own posses-sions around you. I hope you will be very happy here.'

'Thank you,' Ruth said in a low voice. 'I pray I've made the right decision – coming back to Scotland, I mean.' She shud-dered again. 'I–I couldn't bear to m–meet that – that monster again.'

'I can understand that,' Megan said with sympathy, 'but I think it's unlikely Fred will ever return from Canada after the way he left. He didn't care that he was leaving Steven's mother in the lurch, even though she had done her best to be a mother to him all those years. Mind you, I think she was glad to see him go.'

'I didn't realize until he went to Canada that he was not Mrs Caraford's son.'

'Oh no, Fred's mother died when he was born. Did you think Steven might be like Fred?'

'Well I er . . . , yes I did.'

'They're not the least bit alike,' Megan declared. 'None of us have heard from Fred since he left with Edna Wright. We don't even know if they're married. He was a horrid character. My brother, Sam, was killed during the war. Fred was five years older and he bullied him and Steven cruelly when they were boys. I hope he never returns.'

'But we can't be absolutely certain, can we?' Ruth asked, badly needing the reassurance which Megan could not give. They both knew Fred was idle and greedy. What would he do if his money ran out and he hadn't found himself an easy way of earning a living?

# Three

Megan was busy getting the brooder ready for the arrival of a batch of day-old chicks. She was determined to make a better job of rearing them this year. Last spring Samuel had been only a few weeks old and she had been tired and preoccupied, anxious about the tiny scrap of humanity she and Steven had brought into the world. The responsibility had seemed enormous and she had concentrated all her attention on her new baby. Consequently she didn't notice one of the oil heaters was not properly trimmed, and twenty-three of the young chicks had suffocated with the fumes during a single night. She had been in tears over them and she vowed it would never happen again.

As the days lengthened, Steven and Joe turned the cows out to grass once more.

'It's like watching them being released from prison the way they gallop round and round the field like wild things until they realize they're there to eat the grass and not trample it under-foot,' Megan said with a chuckle as she leaned against the gate with Steven while Samuel waved his chubby arms and crowed jubilantly, as though he understood the cows' joy at being free after being tied by their necks in their stalls all winter.

While Steven and Joe mucked out the sheds and started the limewashing, Megan began her own spring-cleaning in the house, washing the blankets and heaving the mattresses out to air in the sunlight along with the feather pillows and eiderdowns. Steven helped her roll up the sitting-room carpet and lift it on to a cart rope strung between two apple trees. Joe volunteered to take a turn at beating the dust out during his midday break and again in the evening. He fitted into the household as though he had lived with them all his life, and he was always willing to lend a hand or keep an eye on Samuel. Earlier in the day Megan had scrubbed the floor and washed all the paint and the windows so everything would be dry before Steven helped her bring the carpet inside again. Samuel had found the bare floor and echoing

room a novelty and had done his best to hinder the work by
spreading his bricks and a wooden horse and cart around, and
she was thankful when evening arrived and he was secure in
his cot.

'We must lay the carpet the opposite way to last year,' she
instructed Steven hastily, 'so it wears evenly and not just at the
door or in front of the hearth.'

'I'm glad I've got a thrifty wife, Meggie.' He grinned as he
patiently refolded the carpet to turn it the opposite way. 'Did I
ever tell you about Natalie Turner coming to look at the house
before I moved in to Schoirhead, and how much money she
thought I should spend, buying a brand-new carpet and a new
moquette suite?'

'You didn't tell me, but my father did,' Megan said darkly. 'I
was really miserable when I knew you'd brought her to see your
first wee farm. If you'd had Natalie for a wife you wouldn't have
needed to help me beat the carpet or move the furniture before
we could lay it again.'

'You wouldna be fishing for more compliments, would you,
Megan?' Steven asked with a laugh, pulling her into his arms to
steal a kiss before Joe came back carrying one of the armchairs.

'I was not fishing for anything,' Megan denied indignantly, her
green eyes sparkling. 'I thought perhaps you regretted not marrying
Natalie and benefiting from her father's money.'

'No, sweetheart, I've no regrets about that. I never fancied
Natalie Turner anyway, but even if I had, the price would have
been much too high. She would have expected to own me –
body and soul.' Megan smiled up at him, well satisfied with his
reply. She had been painfully aware that Natalie Turner had set
her sights on Steven, and she had had more to offer a struggling
young farmer than Megan would ever have. 'Anyway, speaking
of regrets, Meggie, what about you? You wouldn't have had to
work like a slave if you'd married the brilliant Mr Lindsey Gray.
Natalie wrote specially to tell me about him taking you home
from the dance.'

'That was Natalie doing her best to stir up trouble between
us.' She smiled and hugged him tightly. 'I've no regrets, but I can't
help wondering if Lint knows what he's letting himself in for
when he marries Natalie. He seems such a nice person and he

really cares about his work, but she's so spoiled and selfish she doesna care about anyone else.'

'Lint? Oh yes, I'd forgotten that was the good doctor's nickname. Your father says he's interested in the cattle and what they need. He reckons animals and humans are not so very different when it comes to their health. Perhaps it's the farm he's interested in?'

'I think his parents are fairly wealthy. According to Natalie they have a big house and a bit of land down south somewhere. I suppose he might take an interest in the farm as a sideline, a sort of hobby?'

'He wouldna be the first to treat a farm as a hobby and earn plenty of money from something else,' Steven said with a touch of cynicism.

'I imagine Mr Turner will be pleased if his son-in-law takes an interest in Martinwold for whatever reason. Lint could probably keep it going if he had a trustworthy manager to run things.'

'I'm sure he could so long as your father and mother are managing the dairy herd the way they do,' Steven agreed. 'That's the major part of Martinwold's income.'

'That's praise indeed for Mum and Dad! I shall have to tell them what a big compliment you paid them.' Megan grinned, and then her expression sobered. 'They'll not be there forever, though. I keep telling Dad he should go for a smaller dairy but he says it would be three steps backwards. He's used to organizing things his own way at Martinwold – well, most of the time anyway. Mr Turner doesn't interfere so long as things are running smoothly, except when he's wanting to expand or modernize something. Even then he usually discusses his plans with Dad first.'

'I can understand your father's point of view,' Steven nodded. 'The owner of a small herd couldn't afford to employ a contract dairyman to take charge of it. He would probably work beside him and expect him to do other work as well, as we do with Joe.'

'I hadn't thought of it that way,' Megan said slowly. 'I suppose you're right, but I often think it's hard on Mum. It would have been different if Sam hadn't had to go to the war. He would have worked with them, but she has to have a boy living in the house, feeding him and doing his washing, as well as helping with the milking and washing the dairy equipment.'

'You do the same here, Meggie, with Joe living in the house, and you help me with the milking,' he said slowly. 'Do you ever feel—'

'That's different!' Megan interrupted and hugged him tightly. 'We're doing it for us, and for our children . . .'

'Children?' Steven chuckled. 'How many are you planning to have?'

'Oh, I don't know, but certainly more than one. Don't you agree?'

'Mmm, I certainly do . . .' His arms tightened around her and he lowered his head, kissing her with passion, until a cough from the door interrupted them and Joe staggered in with yet another chair.

'I not able to carry the chair for two persons myself, Mr Steven,' he said.

'The sofa? No, no, of course you can't, Joe.' Steven lifted his head, enjoying the blush on Megan's cheeks. They had forgotten all about Joe. 'I'll come and help you lift it back into place.'

Although it was not part of his job, Joe liked to help Steven and Megan when they worked in the garden on spring and summer evenings.

'I learn to grow vegetable,' he said. He had dug and planted the McGuires' garden with a little instruction from McGuire himself, sitting on his wooden bench in the evening sunlight. Annie McGuire had a beehive at the bottom of their garden and she persuaded Joe to help her with that, too. Steven knew they paid Joe for his help and he helped him open a bank account so that he could save his money.

'You'll need plenty of cash one day when you meet a nice girl and want to get married,' he said, half teasing, half serious, but Joe's blue eyes clouded.

'I German. How I meet girl in Scotland who marry me.' It was a statement, not a question. He looked so sad that Megan's tender heart ached for him. She knew, and understood, why many people were still bitter and prejudiced against all Germans, but surely there must be plenty who realized boys like Joe hadn't wanted to fight, any more than her brother Sam had wanted to go to war and die fighting. Johan had been only eighteen when he was taken prisoner.

'You're a handsome young man, Joe,' she told him. 'One day you will meet a girl and fall in love and she will not care where you were born.'

Joe shook his head.

Steven frowned. 'You get on all right with Jimmy Kerr, don't you, Joe? Didn't you enjoy being with his friends at Hogmanay?'

'Och aye, aye,' Joe laughed, trying to imitate Grandfather Kerr's Scottish accent, 'but I not want Jimmy, or Jimmy's friends for wife!'

'I know that.' Steven grinned. 'But I expect some of them have sisters and sisters have friends?'

'Oh yes.' Joe nodded. Jimmy's cousin had been staying at the Kerrs' over New Year. He liked her very much and she had been kind to him, but that was his secret and he kept it in his own heart. He had thought about her a lot, but he might never see her again.

When there was a pig killing they all shared the liver and other offal. This time it was the turn of the Schoirhead pig to meet the butcher and Megan decided to invite the family for Sunday dinner. She included Ruth Vernon and her young daughter in Hannah's invitation.

'Are you sure we should be inviting them?' Steven said irritably. 'She is only mother's tenant after all.'

'I think your mother considers her a bit more than that,' Megan said. 'Anyway, Avril is really your niece, although she will probably never know that. Ruth doesn't want her to know who her father is.'

'I hadn't thought of it like that.' Steven frowned. 'But I suppose she is. Even so . . .'

'It would please your mother if we make her welcome. She has no family of her own now and she's a stranger to this area.'

'Did the two of you get on all right?'

'Yes, I like her. I think we could be friends when we get to know each other better, and Ruth has accepted my invitation so I hope you'll be nice to her.'

'How nice?' Steven's eyes flashed wickedly and his eyebrows quirked.

'Not *that* nice!' Megan said darkly. 'Friends.'

Chrissie Oliphant liked Ruth on sight. There was something sincere and earnest about her and she liked the way she offered to help.

'Mum and I catch up on the family gossip over the washing up,' Megan smiled, declining her offer. 'And you've obviously made a conquest with Samuel. Why don't you take him and Avril to see the wee chicks. I must warn you, though, don't let him pick them up or he'd squeeze the life out of them in his efforts to love them.'

'I'll come too,' Hannah offered. 'It's a lovely day for a stroll outside and I do miss seeing the cows in the field and the young calves.'

'Dad and Steven are down the cellar checking to see whether Steven has cured the bacon and hams properly,' Megan said, 'but they'll be going for a walk out to see the cows. Joe is getting ready to go with Jimmy Kerr for a run on his motorbike. I don't know where they're going but Joe seems excited and he's sprucing himself up.'

'It sounds as though they're expecting to see some girls.' Chrissie chuckled knowingly. 'Have you rendered the lard from the pig yet, Meggie?' she asked, changing the subject.

'Yes, do you want some? I've saved Dad plenty of crisp scraps. Steven doesn't like them much but I remembered Dad loves them with a bit of salt.'

'He does, but don't send him too many. I'm sure they can't be good for him, even if you have rendered most of the fat out of them.'

'If that's me you're talking about,' John Oliphant interrupted, 'the fat scraps have never done me any harm yet. You send me as many as you have to spare, lassie.'

'Joe wouldn't even try them when he realized they were the pieces of fat that were left after I'd rendered all the lard out of them,' Megan laughed. 'He wouldn't try a pig's trotter either, but he likes the brawn I made.'

'You've been busy,' Chrissie sighed. 'I'm sorry I haven't had time to come and help you a bit. I know Samuel takes a lot of watching at this stage.'

'Oh, he's not so bad. I still strap him in his pram while we're milking and he talks to the cows, but he'll not fit in it much longer. He toddles along behind when I'm feeding the hens or collecting the eggs. He has a wee basket of his own now and I pretend I've found some eggs in a nest for him, but they're a couple of china eggs I keep in my pocket. Mrs McGuire has some bantams this year and she gave him two tiny eggs and told him they were specially for wee boys so he ate them up without a quibble.'

'You do love it here, don't you, Meggie?'

'Yes, Mum, I wouldn't change my life here with Steven for anything. I've no regrets about giving up teaching.'

'I'm glad the pair of you are happy,' Chrissie said. 'Steven's a grand man. The McGuires think so too.'

'I know they do, but we think we're the ones who are lucky. Renting their land as well as our own has allowed us to keep twelve cows milking all the time and still have stalls for four in-calf cows. That's twice as many as we could have kept if we only had our own byre. Steven thinks we ought to have had a milking machine by now, but we daren't install it in the McGuires' byre in case the land agent notices. We have a few in-calf heifers this year too, and the milk cheque comes in regularly every month – not like cereals or lambs, or even poultry. The eggs are always scarce in the winter so there's less money coming in from them. We're doing all right. You and Dad have no need to worry about us.'

'I don't think John does worry. He's delighted to have Steven for a son-in-law and he looks forward to having a walk round the cattle and the fields with him. They have a lot in common, and I think Mr Turner envies him. He would have been happier if Natalie was marrying a farmer, although he does get on well with Mr Gray. I suppose he wonders what will happen to Martinwold when he has to give up. It would be hard for him to see it sold to strangers.'

'They never brought Natalie up to take an interest in the farm,' Megan protested, 'so how could they expect her to marry a farmer. Anyway, I thought Lint was showing quite an interest, according to Dad. He might decide to live at Martinwold and be a hobby farmer.'

'He might, I suppose,' Chrissie agreed doubtfully. 'He probably earns a good salary so maybe it wouldn't matter if he didn't make much profit from the farm.'

'I don't think you need to worry about changes, Mum. Mr Turner seems hale and hearty. He'll probably be the boss for as long as you and Dad want to work at Martinwold.'

'Yes, you're right there. He's five or six years younger than your father and he always says he'll never give up his farm until they cart him off in a box.'

After that first visit Ruth and Megan met fairly often. When Megan took Samuel to visit Granny Caraford they often had tea together, or Ruth would come to Schoirhead with Avril, even without Hannah. Sometimes Megan's parents were at Schoirhead at the same time and Chrissie was pleased to see how well the two young women got on together.

'Everyone needs friends and Ruth is not afraid to help, is she?' Chrissie remarked.

'Oh no. Now that she knows me well enough she volunteers to stay with Samuel while I'm at the milking and she and Avril get him bathed and ready for bed, and she always has the supper ready for when we finish work outside. Avril is a proper wee mother. She has started calling Steven's mother Granny Caraford, the same as Samuel.'

'What does Hannah say to that?'

'She seems happy about it.' Megan frowned. 'She is a sort of grandmother to Avril anyway, or at least a step-grandmother.'

'Yes, I suppose she is. It's a strange world, isn't it? Ruth is welcome to join you and Steven when you come to us for dinner next Sunday.'

'I think she would like that, if you're sure, Mum?'

'Of course I'm sure. I like her, and Avril is a lovely wee girl. I notice Steven has accepted her now.'

'Yes. She doesn't know many men so she's still a bit shy with him, but she's so eager to learn about everything that I don't think Steven could help but like her. Samuel adores her, of course.'

'Are you sure your parents will not mind me coming with you to Martinwold?' Ruth asked diffidently when Megan told her of the offer.

'They'll be pleased to have you. Mother insisted. Anyway, I reckon Dad can't wait to show you how many cows he has to milk.'

'Yes, I'm really looking forward to seeing the farm. Mr Paterson says Martinwold is one of the biggest and most modern farms in this area.'

'I suppose he's right about that, but how does he know? I thought he used to be an architect?'

'Yes, he had his own business in Dumfries, but he takes an interest in all sorts of things.'

Both Avril and Ruth were mesmerized by the length of the Martinwold byre when the cows were tied in their stalls, waiting patiently to be milked. Only Samuel was impatient to toddle away as fast as he could, so Megan followed him outside with Avril close on her heels. Ruth was so busy examining the cows and their stalls and the pipes and taps for the milking machines that she didn't notice they had left her alone. Nor did she realize she had other company until a deep, amused voice greeted her.

'Fascinating, isn't it?'

Ruth spun round in shock. 'Who – who are you?' she asked abruptly. The man's dark brows arched in surprise at her tone, but his grey eyes surveyed her calmly.

'I might ask you the same question.' He glanced at her ring-less fingers. 'Miss . . .?' Ruth glanced down the empty walkway, but there was no sign of Megan or the children.

'I–I'm visiting the Oliphants.' She made to move on but her path was blocked and she looked up. 'And you are?' she asked coldly.

'Lindsey Gray. Are you a friend of Megan's?' He held out his hand but Ruth ignored it.

'Yes.' She chewed her lower lip, anxious to get past him and join the others, but her reluctance to speak to him, or even look at him, intrigued Lindsey Gray. Without conceit he knew he was not a bad-looking fellow and he had no difficulty attracting more than his fair share of female attention, but this young woman seemed almost afraid of him. The doctor in him wondered what lay behind her tension and the terror in her dark eyes.

'Amazing, isn't it,' he said conversationally, 'all these animals standing so quietly in their stalls. John Oliphant tells me every one knows its own place and refuses to stand anywhere else.'

'Y–yes, I know.' Ruth remembered the cows at Willowburn

had been the same, although there were relatively few of them compared to this herd.

'So, Miss . . . What did you say your name was?'

'V–Vernon. Ruth Vernon. I must g–go . . .'

'Mummy? Oh, there you are,' Avril giggled with relief. 'We thought we'd lost you, and Megan's daddy said maybe you'd fallen in the midden.' She screwed up her face.

'I–I'm just coming,' Ruth said, and looked up at Lindsey Gray, indicating he should let her pass. He smiled his attractive smile and turned to walk beside her to the end of the byre.

'Hello, Lint,' Megan greeted him easily as she held a squirming Samuel in her arms. 'Have you two met? Ruth, this is Doctor Gray, or I should say Mr Gray now, I believe. He is Natalie Turner's fiancé. Lint, this is a friend of mine, Ruth Vernon. Ruth teaches in Annan.'

'I see, and this little girl is . . .?' But before Lint could say any more, Natalie called impatiently. He sighed and walked away as John Oliphant and Steven appeared.

'I see the good doctor is being called to heel,' Steven grinned wickedly.

'Mmm, I think I should take a lesson or two in calling you to heel,' Megan threatened, but laughter glinted in her green eyes. John Oliphant didn't smile.

'She'll try calling him to heel once too often if she doesna watch,' he said darkly. 'I canna imagine why an intelligent man like that let himself be drawn into an engagement with Natalie Turner. He doesn't strike me as the type to let a woman like her tell him how to run his life. He's a man who commands respect.'

It took some time for Ruth to feel inwardly calm again after her encounter with Lindsey Gray. She knew now she'd had nothing to fear from him, but sometimes she wondered if she would ever feel at ease when she was alone with a man. Even Mr Paterson, who was old enough to be her father and had a fatherly manner, made her feel uncomfortable and ill at ease if he gave her a hug.

'Avril loved visiting your parents and seeing all the cows at Martinwold,' Ruth said the next time she visited Schoirhead. She and Megan were enjoying a quiet cup of tea together while the two children played outside. 'She told her teacher at school she had seen "hundreds" of cows, and a machine that made sucking noises and sucked their milk into big cans. Mind you, I had never seen so many cows in one place myself, and I'd never seen a milking machine working either.'

'You really do enjoy the countryside and the animals, don't you, Ruth?' Megan remarked quietly.

'Yes I do.' She chewed her lower lip. 'B—but sometimes I still wonder whether I was wise to come back up here . . .' She never talked about the past or even about her home life in the vicarage, but Megan sensed there were times when it would help her if she could forget her reserve and talk freely to someone. Although there seemed to have been an instant bond of friendship between her and Hannah, Megan could understand there might be some personal topics that would be impossible to discuss, especially in relation to Fred.

'Did you live in the country when you were in the Lake District?' she asked gently.

'It was not far to the hills and fields, but the vicarage and church were part of a small town community, maybe more of a large village really – a very close community.'

'I suppose you must miss being part of that.'

'No! Well, I mean I miss some of the people, but . . .' She drew in a deep breath. 'Have you noticed, Megan, how one bad or cruel person can influence a whole group?'

'You mean like one rotten apple can turn the whole barrel bad?'

'Something like that. After I returned home, or at least once I discovered I was expecting a child, many of the people I had known all my life – people I thought were friends, or friends of my family – turned out to be so cruel. My father said they spoke with forked tongues and I should ignore them, but I suspect their judgement of me and my situation caused him some distress too.'

'Some people are like that, especially in a small community, and yet others can be so kind and understanding,' Megan said sympathetically.

'Maybe.' Ruth sounded sceptical. Then, in a rush, she added bitterly, 'I couldn't go round proclaiming "I am not wicked! I was raped! I hated the man! I didn't want this baby!", but I wanted to shout it from the roof tops.' She gnawed her lower lip and blinked furiously to prevent the tears falling.

'I'm so sorry,' Megan whispered and bent forward to clasp Ruth's agitated fingers. 'Fred was a beast to do that to you against your will. He was always a bully to those less strong than himself. He couldn't bear opposition.'

'He tried to bully his own father and he knew I couldn't bear to be near him. I hated when he touched me.' The words came pouring out. 'He was so brutal!' She shuddered. 'I–I thought I was going to suffocate. Even now I still have nightmares about being shut in that loft with him and being unable to get my breath, or get away from his cruel clawing fingers. I screamed and he – he shoved his filthy handkerchief in my mouth and tied it with the binder twine, th–then he did it again. He was so strong! The more I struggled, the more he – he . . .' She began to tremble. 'When he tried a third time he c–couldn't do it and he was furious. He blamed me. He slapped me across the face. He wanted me to – to . . .' She shuddered and hid her face in her hands. 'When I refused he hit me with the back of his hand several times.' She began to cry in earnest and Megan moved to the arm of her chair and held her close in silence. She hoped the tears might wash away some of the memories. After a while the tears stopped and Ruth blew her nose and wiped her face. 'I–I'm so sorry, Megan. I–I don't know why I'm telling you this – this . . .'

'Hush, Ruth,' Megan said softly. 'Don't be sorry. I'm glad you've told me. I think you were needing to unburden yourself to someone and I feel privileged you chose me.'

'Thank you.' She summoned a watery smile. 'I–I didn't mean to . . . It just came out. I've been so fortunate. Hannah has been so good to me and I truly value your friendship, Megan.'

'Yes, I know you do, because I feel it is mutual.' She smiled. 'Now I shall make a fresh pot of tea. My mother believes it is the cure for all ills.'

'Like Great-Aunt Ruth then,' Ruth said. 'Although she had never been married and she was very strict and Victorian, she never once blamed me or said a cruel word. I–I wouldn't like you to think everyone was bad. I loved Avril dearly from the moment she was born. I wouldn't part with her for the world, but I do worry when she asks about her daddy. I don't like to lie, but so far I have managed to be vague and distract her. My greatest fear is if Fred should return and realize he is her father.'

'Even if he did I don't think you need to worry,' Megan said. 'From what I know of Fred he is more likely to run away fast if he thinks he has any responsibilities.' Megan was speaking the truth, but even as she uttered the words she knew in her heart that Fred was evil enough to do the opposite of what Ruth wanted. They could only pray he would never return to Scotland and that he would never learn he had a child.

# Four

It was a Friday at the end of August and Steven and Joe had been cutting corn all day with the binder while Megan did her best with stooking the sheaves until they were free to help her. When Samuel was tired of toddling after her he curled up and went to sleep in the shade of the hedge with Shandy, their beloved collie dog, lying on guard beside him. The two were inseparable.

They all stopped work in the field to bring in the cows and milk them, but as soon as that was finished and they had eaten their meal they returned to the field, anxious to set the sheaves into stooks in case the weather should change overnight and soak them if they were lying flat on the ground. This time Megan pushed Samuel in his pram, knowing he was ready for bed and would soon fall asleep.

'I wish I could fall asleep where I'm standing,' she said, smothering a yawn as they set the last of the sheaves in place.

'Aye, we'll all be glad to get to bed,' Steven agreed. 'It's been a long day, but a satisfying one. You've worked hard, Joe. I'll try to see you're free on Sunday afternoon.' He grinned knowingly. 'Are you and Jimmy Kerr planning to go off on his motorbike again?'

Joe's fair skin flushed. 'I – we go see Jimmy's Aunt,' he stammered.

'Oh yes?' Steven queried innocently. 'Is that the aunt who has a daughter called Evelyn, who has a friend called Fiona?'

'Y–yes,' Joe nodded, his face growing redder.

'Stop teasing the poor boy, Steven.' Megan laughed. 'Take no notice of him, Joe. He's jealous.'

'No!' Joe exclaimed seriously. 'He not jealous when he got you for his loving,' he assured her earnestly.

Steven chuckled and put his arm round her, drawing her close as she pushed the pram with their sleeping son, who was oblivious to the bumpy ride over the stubble.

'Quite right, Joe. I have all I need right here,' he said, squeezing

Megan's shoulder. He raised his eyes to glance over the field as they made their weary way back to the house. 'It's a good crop this year,' he remarked, eyeing the rows of neat stooks with satisfaction.

'Let's not count our chickens until it's safely gathered in,' Megan warned. 'Aren't we supposed to leave oats in the stooks for a fortnight to harden off before we bring them in to the stacks?'

'Aye. We'll pray the weather stays fine, but we'll be lucky to get two weeks without rain in this area.'

They were all glad to tumble into bed early that night and sleep claimed them instantly.

It was the shrill ringing of the telephone which wakened Megan from a deep slumber. She groaned and glanced at the luminous hands of the big alarm clock which ticked away beside the bed. It was not quite midnight.

'The McGuires . . .' she murmured, and struggled out of bed.

'What's wrong? Where're you going?' Steven asked sleepily.

'It's the phone. Mr McGuire must have had a fall or something.' She dashed downstairs in her bare feet. The persistent ringing seemed terribly loud in the silence of the night and she snatched up the receiver.

'Dad!' Megan exclaimed in shocked surprise. She recognized her father's voice in spite of the distraught words tumbling from his lips. Steven followed Megan down the stairs, pulling on his trousers, expecting to dash round to help his elderly neighbours, knowing the McGuires would never phone at this time of night unless it was an emergency. He stopped dead on the bottom step as he heard Megan's exclamation. He saw the blood drain from her face.

'B–but what did the doctor say? Surely he must have seen Mum was in severe pain?' She was listening intently. Apparently a relief doctor had visited in place of Doctor Burns.

'That's ridiculous.' Megan bit down hard on her lower lip, struggling to stay calm and to think. She had never known her father to be so shaken and out of control. He was almost weeping over the phone. She felt Steven's arm around her shoulders and leaned into him gratefully.

'Listen, Dad, I'm coming up to you right now, as soon as I'm dressed. Are the lights still on at the Turners'? They never go to bed early.' She waited for his reply. 'Right, then telephone Mr Turner. He needs to know Mum will not be able to do the milking in the morning anyway, and he is friendly with Doctor Burns. He might persuade him to visit tonight, even if he is supposed to be on holiday. Will you do that? I'll be with you as soon as I can.' She put the phone down and turned briefly to Steven.

'I have to go to Dad. He says Mum has terrible pain in her stomach. The relief doctor says it could be colic. He prescribed bicarbonate of soda in water about eight o'clock, but Dad says she's getting worse. The pain is so bad she's barely conscious. It's not like Dad to panic, Steven.'

'I know that, sweetheart. You get dressed. I'll start the van and bring it to the door. I wish I could come with you but we can't both leave Samuel.'

'I know, and I don't know how long I shall be.' Megan was already running up the stairs to pull on some clothes. When she came down Steven was standing by the van, his bare torso gleaming palely in the darkness.

'You go back to bed, Steven. I can rest tomorrow . . .'

'No, love. I'll bring a blanket and a pillow downstairs so I shall hear the phone. Let me know what's happening as soon as you can.' He kissed her firmly on the mouth. 'Chin up, Meggie,' he said gruffly, wishing with all his heart he could accompany her. Every instinct told him Chrissie Oliphant must be seriously ill. She was not a woman who complained about trivial things.

He crept upstairs and collected his clothes and the alarm clock. He didn't think he would sleep, but if he did drift off he wanted to be sure of getting up earlier than usual in case Megan didn't get back for milking time. He would need to get the cows in from the field then call Joe. He would have to put Samuel in his pram and take him to the byre. He might have to milk all the cows himself while Joe carried the milk to the cooler in the dairy. They would have to leave the other animals until after breakfast.

He prayed Chrissie would be all right. He realized he had little idea about all the things Megan did with such quiet efficiency. Samuel still wore nappies at night. Did she change them when she lifted him from his cot early in the morning? Or did she wait until they came in for breakfast? Would the wee fellow cry when his mother wasn't there? His mind buzzed with plans and questions, but until he heard from Megan he knew it was pointless.

As Megan turned into the drive to Martinwold she was surprised to see so many lights on, both at the Turners' large house and at the old farmhouse where her parents lived. Her tension increased. As she reached the fork in the track that lead into the farmyard she saw a figure vault over the wall at the bottom of the Turners' garden and run across the yard towards her parents' house. Her headlights illuminated Lindsey Gray, still in his evening suit. They arrived at the door of the house together.

'Hello, Megan. Natalie and I have been out for the evening. Mr Turner says your mother is ill. He can't get Doctor Burns. Do you think it would be all right for me to see her?'

'Y–yes, I'm sure Dad will welcome your reassurance. H–he sounded terribly worried.' He followed her inside and up the stairs. John Oliphant was kneeling beside his wife, holding her limp hand in both of his, but as Megan entered he brushed a hasty hand over his eyes and face and Megan was dismayed to realize he was brushing away tears. She had never seen him so distressed, not even when they heard Sam had been killed in action in France. When she saw how grey and drawn her mother looked, and the film of perspiration on her face, her own heart seemed to freeze. Chrissie didn't even open her eyes at the sound of Megan's voice, and she was lying with her knees curled up tightly like an embryo in the womb. Megan glanced up at Lindsey Gray and saw his pleasant expression change. His mouth tightened. His eyes flashed, but he assumed a professional mask as he quietly asked if he might examine Chrissie. It did not take long before he ushered them downstairs.

'Your wife needs attention immediately, John. It may be acute appendicitis, but I suspect it is a twist or blockage in the bowel. She needs to get to hospital. I may be wrong, but it's my opinion she needs an operation without delay.'

'Oh God . . .' John Oliphant sank on to the bottom step, his head in his hands. 'I knew that bloody doctor was talking nonsense.' He looked up, his eyes pleading. 'What shall we do?'

'Trust me.' Lindsey Gray put a firm hand on his shoulder. 'Martinwold is as near to the infirmary at Carlisle as it is to Dumfries.

I can telephone Carlisle. They will have the theatre prepared for an emergency operation by the time we arrive. I shall ask them to contact Mr Higgins. He is the senior surgeon and one of the very best for this sort of thing. If he cannot be located I shall operate myself.' His mouth was set. 'Or we can send for an ambulance to take Mrs Oliphant to Dumfries?'

'I'd like her to be in your hands,' John Oliphant said simply.

'Right. I'll get my car. It will be quicker than waiting for an ambulance. There's no time to lose.' He gave Megan instructions to bring pillows and a blanket. 'It would help if you travelled with us, John. Will you be all right to drive yourself, Megan? Your father will need your support.'

'I'll be fine,' Megan said, already on her way back upstairs to collect things for her mother. She was unaware that her eyes were like deep green pools in her pale face. Her stomach was churning, but she was determined to keep calm for her father's sake.

'Good girl. You should both be prepared to spend the night at the hospital.'

Megan was standing at the door, her arms full of bedding by the time Lindsey Gray brought his car round to the door, but Natalie had cut across the garden. She arrived breathlessly at the same time. If he saw her he gave no sign as he opened the doors of the car and arranged the seats and the pillows, to make his patient as comfortable as possible.

'I told you, Lint! It's not your place to go! You're on holiday,' Natalie yelled. 'We're supposed to be spending time together.'

'For God's sake, Nat, I've spent years training to *save* lives. It's my job.'

'Not when you're supposed to be with me, it's not!'

'This is an emergency. Now please keep out of the way. There's no time to lose.'

'Send for an ambulance. It's not your affair.'

'When a person's life is in danger it *is* my affair, and when that person is someone you've known all your life I'd say it was your affair too – or don't you care?'

'No, I don't care! You're spoiling everything.' She glimpsed Megan's white face above the blanket she was clutching. 'You wouldn't be doing this if it wasn't for her!' she screamed viciously. 'You've always been taken in by her big green eyes. She's—'

'You're in the way, Natalie,' Lindsey snapped impatiently. He turned to take the blanket from Megan's arms. 'I'll help your father carry her down,' he said gently. 'Try not to worry.'

'Dad is bringing Mum now.'

'Good. I'll settle her as comfortably as I can. We shall have to drive steadily. You'll follow us?'

'Yes,' Megan nodded numbly.

'If you go with them we're finished,' Natalie screeched, heedless of her father's approach. 'Do you hear me!'

'I came to see if there was anything I could do?' Mr Turner said, addressing Lindsey.

'No thanks, not here. I'm taking Mrs Oliphant to Carlisle Infirmary to operate.'

'It is serious then?' Murdo Turner asked gravely.

'Very. She'd have stood a better chance four hours ago.' Lindsey's voice was terse and there was a pulse throbbing in his jaw. He was anxious to get away. He ignored Natalie's mulish expression. 'You'll need to make other arrangements for the milking.'

'Of course,' Mr Turner nodded. 'I'll have a go at milking with the machine myself and I'll call one of the other men up in the morning. The Oliphants' student will carry the milk to the dairy as usual. I'll ask Mrs Richards if she will give him board and lodging until we see how things go. Tell John not to worry about anything at this end.'

'Thanks, I'll tell him.'

'Lindsey Gray!' Natalie gave his sleeve a furious jerk to demand his attention. 'We're supposed to be making plans for our wedding while you're on holiday! If *you* put my father's workers before *me,* then you needn't come back,' she said harshly. 'Do you hear me?'

'Nats? What are you talking about?' Mr Turner turned to look at his daughter in surprise.

'He knows what I'm talking about. It's them or me.'

'You get into the car, John, and we'll be off,' Lindsey said quietly as he closed the door on his patient. He ignored Natalie. In a temper she yanked off her engagement ring, an expensive solitaire diamond, and flung it at him as he bent to get into the driver's seat. The ring fell on to the ground. Lindsey Gray left it where it lay.

'Goodbye, Natalie. One day I hope you'll learn not to be so utterly selfish.' He let in the clutch and drove away smoothly.

Megan decided to drive her father's car. It would be quicker than the van and she knew her father always kept plenty of petrol in the tank. She went towards it.

'Megan, Megan, lassie . . . ' Mr Turner hurried after her. 'I hope all goes well. You'll let me know? And if there's anything, anything at all I can do, you've only to tell me.'

'Thank you,' Megan said huskily, grateful for Mr Turner's sincerity, especially after Natalie's outburst and obvious resentment, but she was anxious to be off. She knew the way to the hospital, but she had no idea where to go once they were in the grounds and she didn't want to lose sight of Lint's car. She was troubled that her family might have caused a rift between him and Natalie. She didn't believe Natalie meant what she'd said, but having glimpsed the distaste on Lint's face she was not so sure he would forgive and forget the unpleasant scene.

The problems of Natalie Turner were rapidly forgotten as she parked the car and followed her father into the hospital behind the stretcher which now bore her mother away from them. Fear filled her, but she knew she had to be strong when she saw the lost look in her father's eyes. He looked so forlorn she could have wept for him as well as for her mother, who seemed barely aware of where she was or what lay ahead.

The nurses all treated Lindsey with deference and addressed him as Mr Gray, reminding Megan he was a fully qualified surgeon.

'We managed to contact Mr Higgins,' Sister informed him. 'He was visiting his sister in Kendal but left immediately. He said he realized the case must be urgent but you would know how to proceed. He will join you in the theatre as soon as he can.'

'Thank you, Sister,' Lindsey said with a note of relief. 'I'll go and get scrubbed up right away.'

Sister Jardine had overheard Megan address him as Lint and she had noted the gentle expression on his face as he tried to reassure her, without making promises he might not be able to keep. The Oliphants must be friends of the young surgeon, she surmised, as well as relatives of the patient. Before Mr Gray could ask she offered to send one of the junior nurses for tea and said she would take care of them.

'It–it's very kind of you,' Megan said gratefully, 'but I really need to find a telephone. My husband will be anxious. I forgot to let him know what was happening before we left. It is all such a sh–shock.' Her voice shook. She was trying hard not to think of her mother looking so small and helpless on the stretcher.

'That's all right, my dear,' the sister said kindly. 'You can telephone from my office, then nurse will show you both where to wait. She will bring you a cup of tea.' The young nurse was astonished. Sister guarded her privacy and was regarded as an ogre who might snap the heads off junior nurses at any moment.

Back at Schoirhead, Steven lay wakeful on the settee, which was too short for his long length. He had left the door to the hall open to be sure of hearing the first ring of the telephone, or any cry from Samuel if the toddler should waken. Time passed and still there was no call from Megan. Unable to bear the suspense he telephoned the Oliphants' house but there was no reply. Steven fretted more than ever. Where could Megan and her parents be if they were not answering? Could they have gone to hospital? Surely Megan would have let him know?

Steven must have dozed because he was startled by the shrill ring of the telephone. He listened to Megan's trembling voice in shocked silence.

'Oh Steven, Lindsey Gray was so good with Dad and Mum and he has called in the chief surgeon. I–I'm so afraid. Lint was honest with us. He says Mum's condition is serious and – and it would have been better if she had been admitted earlier.'

'Oh Meggie,' Steven said gruffly. 'I wish I could be there with you . . .'

'I know. I wish you were here too, but we both know that's not possible. I'm so terribly worried about Mum,' her voice shook, 'and I can't leave Dad on his own. He looks so lost. It's as though his world has crashed around him.'

'I suppose it has, Meggie. I know I'd feel like that if it was you. You must stay with him. Don't worry about things here. When I've brought in the cows I'll come back in to call Joe up and I'll put Samuel in his pram as usual. I'll telephone Mother. I'm sure she'll come and look after Sammy as soon as she's attended to her own livestock. Thank goodness she doesn't have the shop any more.'

'I've left the van at Martinwold. I drove down here in Dad's car.'

'That's all right, Meggie. I'm not needing it and I can borrow Mother's if I need anything. Please tell your father I'm thinking of him and praying for your mother. Phone me when you can, Meggie.'

'I will.'

Steven guessed she was near to breaking point. 'Chin up my brave lassie.'

'Bye, Steven,' Megan whispered huskily as the young nurse came in to show her where her father was waiting.

# Five

The next few hours seemed like a lifetime to Megan and her father. They were thankful they had each other for comfort. They alternated between anxious murmurings and pensive silence, each of them lost in their thoughts and memories, and regrets for the things they wished they had done.

'I should have listened to you, Megan,' John Oliphant said out of the blue. He got up and paced restlessly around the small room. 'I should have moved to a smaller dairy. Chrissie wouldn't have needed to be at the milking twice every day; maybe she wouldn't have needed to work in the byres at all.'

'Oh Dad, it wouldn't have made any difference. This could have happened whatever Mum was doing. You mustn't blame yourself.'

'If only Chrissie can pull through this I don't care what changes I have to make, so long as we have each other,' he added brokenly. He sank on to a chair and put his head in his hands. Megan went over to him and laid her arm around his bowed shoulders.

'I've never known Mum to be ill. I'm sure she will pull through this if Lint managed to operate in time.'

'He said leaking would be the danger if it caused infection . . .'

'He also said Mum's physical condition was excellent and it would help her,' Megan reminded him, trying to sound positive. She felt drained and exhausted and sick with worry herself. She hadn't expected anything so serious as this when she had left Steven with Samuel and all the work to do at Schoirhead.

'I pray Mr Gray is right,' John Oliphant said fervently. 'They seem to treat him with a lot of respect here. Thank God he was at Martinwold. He came to see Chrissie of his own accord. He was having a few days' holiday.'

'He and the other surgeon will do their best. I'm sure Mum couldn't be in better hands.'

'Aye, I dinna care if it costs me every penny we've got so long as they can save her.'

'It won't cost you anything, Dad, not now we have the health service.'

'Oh aye, I'd forgotten old Bevan had got all that through parliament. We've never needed doctors much before.' He was silent for a little while, chewing his lower lip. 'This will mean a big change in our lives . . .' he reflected. 'We can't carry on at Martinwold now. Mr Turner will have to look for another family to manage his dairy herd. We shall have to move out of the house. He will need it for the next man.'

'Don't worry about that now, Dad,' Megan said gently. John looked up at her and squeezed her hand where it lay on his shoulder in a gesture of comfort.

'You're a good lassie, Megan, and Steven is a fine man. I'm not worrying about Martinwold or Mr Turner. We've worked hard for him and aye done our best, but he's done well by us. He paid well and your mother has always been thrifty. We've a tidy wee sum put by . . . Oh God, please help her get through this . . .' His voice shook.

'Try not to think about the future, Dad.'

'It helps if I can think of something else . . .' He shuddered. 'I canna bear to think o' Chrissie in such pain and looking so helpless on that stretcher.'

'No, I know what you mean.' Megan realized he was right. It was better for them both to think of other things, even though their minds were on her mother.

'All her life Chrissie has had to live in a tied cottage, and make do with second-hand furniture, but she never grumbled.'

'That's because she was happy for you to do the work you loved and because she enjoyed being able to work beside you, Dad.'

'Aye, I never wanted to do anything else but work with cattle. But Megan, if your mother pulls through this I shall do whatever *she* wants to do and I'll not care if I never see another cow.'

'Oh Dad, you don't really mean that.' Megan summoned a watery smile.

'As far as your mother is concerned I do. I can't have a dairy that's big enough to merit a dairyman taking charge without your mother to help, so I'd rather do something else. I'll come to visit you and Steven when I get a hankering to see some cows.'

'Mmm . . .' Megan chewed her lower lip. She prayed fervently that her mother would come through the operation, but Lindsey had warned them it was major surgery. Whatever happened it was true her mother would not be able to work in the byres as she had done before; she would be unable to lift heavy buckets or wash the milk churns. She was glad her father realized that. 'You know you'll always be welcome to come to us, Dad,' she said at last, 'but you'd be lost without some kind of work.'

'Oh aye, I ken that, lassie. I'm only fifty-one and I never felt my age until tonight. I didn't mean I would stop work myself. I meant we should look for a wee house for the two of us. Now that you're settled a two-bedroomed cottage would be enough. It will be easier for Chrissie to keep. She'd never need to worry about moving again because our house was tied to my job. It would be her own wee nest. I'm tired of knowing our home depends on my work.'

'I can understand that, Dad,' Megan said slowly, her thoughts only half on what he was saying, knowing he was talking to stop himself thinking of her mother and what was happening in the theatre two floors below.

'I'd need a cottage with a good size garden, though,' John Oliphant chattered feverishly. 'We have always liked gardening, your mother and me. I could travel to work now we've got a car. I could find some other kind o' work, or maybe I could do relief milking when a farmer wants a holiday or when somebody is ill . . .' He broke off as the door opened.

Both Lindsey Gray and Mr Higgins came in. Their faces were grave and they looked exhausted. Megan and her father jumped to their feet. Tension radiated through the small room.

'We believe the operation has been a success, Mr Oliphant, but your wife's condition is critical. She will need constant nursing during the next few days and—'

'C–can we s–see her?' John Oliphant pleaded earnestly.

The two surgeons exchanged glances. 'I leave it to you, sir,' Lindsey said. 'It is crucial that we avoid any infection. Even the slightest thing could kill our patient in her present state. She is unconscious so she would not know you were there. She is in a room of her own and a nurse will remain at her side at all times.'

'Please, I need to see her . . .' John Oliphant pleaded desperately.

'I suggest you look through the window. Then I think you should go home and get some rest yourselves . . .'

'I canna go and leave her here,' John said emotionally.

Lindsey Gray looked pensive. 'I will have a word with Sister and see if she can find you a cubicle, but you must rest, John. You look exhausted and there is nothing you can do to help your wife at this stage.'

'I'd feel better if I can stay near her. I'll sit in this chair, Doctor . . . er, Mr Gray.'

'Very well. Sister will take you to look through the window of her room. Don't be alarmed by the appliances. We are monitoring her condition carefully and the tubes are to assist her.' He turned to look at Megan. 'I think you should go home, Megan, at least for a few hours. You will want to see your wee boy and you must try to get some rest. Maybe you could return this evening and relieve your father?'

'Y–yes, I ought to go home for a little while to see how Steven is managing. Is that all right with you, Dad? When we've seen Mum?'

'Aye, lassie, you've been a grand support. You go and attend to your bairn now.' He turned to look at the two surgeons. 'I know Chrissie has a long way to go yet,' he said seriously, 'but you've seen her over the first hurdle. I canna tell you both how grateful I am . . .' His voice was gruff and he broke off, blinking back tears of relief and exhaustion.

'You need some rest, my man,' Mr Higgins said briskly. 'Lint, you have a word with Sister while I take Mr Oliphant and his daughter to see our patient. Oh, and Lint – you did a good job tonight. There's no doubt your swift diagnosis and prompt action has gone a long way to saving this patient's life.'

'Thank you, Sir.'

The world was awakening and early workers were setting out as Megan drove carefully home. It had been a terrible shock to peer through the window and see her beloved mother lying so helpless and unconscious in the hospital bed. She had felt tired and frightened, but Lint had accompanied her to the hospital entrance afterwards.

'Try not to worry too much, Megan. The nurses will give her every attention and Mr Higgins will be checking regularly during the next few days. He is going to persuade your father to take a couple of pills and have a sleep. It is obvious, even to him, how deeply attached your parents are to each other. It isn't always the way, you know.'

'No, I suppose not,' Megan said, swallowing over the lump in her throat.

'I promise to look in on her myself, and to keep in touch with the hospital, but I'm supposed to be off for another two days.'

'Oh gosh, yes! I'd forgotten you were on vacation at Martinwold. I'm so sorry. If you're going back there now would you tell Mr Turner how things are? I promised to let him know.'

'I will keep him informed.' His mouth tightened. 'But I shall not be returning to Martinwold.'

'Oh Lint, I'm sure Natalie didn't mean to cause a scene. She didn't understand Mum was so ill. We shall all feel terrible if her illness causes a rift between you two.' She looked up at him, her green eyes wide and troubled. He swallowed hard as he looked down at her pale face. He could have loved Megan Oliphant. He'd known that the first time he had met her at the village dance, but even then her heart had belonged to Steven Caraford and there was no doubt that he loved her in return.

'Natalie's outburst was nothing new. Almost from the minute we got engaged she has been making more and more demands, many of them quite unreasonable. I knew she was spoiled, but she can be good company when she forgets to be petulant. I get on well with Mr Turner; he's a man I could respect as a father-in-law. I believed Natalie would mature when we began to make serious plans for the future.'

'I'm sure she will,' Megan murmured, but without conviction.

'No. This time she has gone too far. A man in my profession cannot be subject to the selfish whims of a woman who acts like a child in a tantrum. If I'm honest it is a relief that Natalie has broken our engagement. There is no going back,' he added firmly, 'so don't even think of trying to mend things, or believe your family are to blame.' He turned to face her as they stepped outside together. He gripped her shoulders and looked down at her. 'I mean that, Megan. I've had no time to think of my own affairs until now, and all I feel is a sense of release – and great relief.

That's not how a man with a broken heart should feel, now is it?' he asked with a rueful smile.

'I suppose not,' Megan said slowly. 'What will you do for the rest of your time off if you're not staying with the Turners?'

'Don't worry about me, my dear. I don't want to be too far away. I care about all my patients, but especially when it is someone I know and like. I have friends up near Lockerbie. As a matter of fact, Katherine is my half-cousin. She met Douglas Palmer-Farr when they were at university. His family own a sort of dilapidated mansion house called Langton Tower.'

'Oh! You do move in exalted circles. The Palmer-Farrs are local gentry, aren't they?'

'I wouldn't know,' Lint said with a smile. 'There's nothing very gentlemanly about Doug when he's had a drink or two, and the house is almost falling down around their ears. That's not strictly true. They have modernized one wing for their own use and it's very comfortable. They are modernizing the rest as and when time, money and materials are available. I think it was full of evacuees during the war. I imagine the grounds would have been lovely at one time, but they've been badly neglected. They are planning to turn it into a non-residential hotel to make it pay for its upkeep. Katherine is excellent at organizing and she's a good cook. She enjoys that sort of challenge. Meanwhile they always make me very welcome, even if they do set me to work.' He smiled down at Megan. 'So now you know there's no need to trouble your head about me, or the Natalie Turners of this world. Go home and get some sleep. I think your father will need your support over the next few days. Drive carefully, Megan.'

'Thank you, Lint. Thank you for everything,' Megan said huskily, and to her dismay she had a struggle to blink away her tears.

As Megan drove into the yard at Schoirhead she saw Joe was putting the cows out to the field so she knew Steven must have finished the milking. Wearily she made her way into the house. Hannah had seen the car draw up and she went to greet her. One look at Megan's white strained face was enough to tug at her heart strings and she opened her arms. To Megan's dismay she fell into them and wept.

'I–I d–don't know why I'm crying,' she hiccoughed. 'Mother

has had her operation and th—they say she's holding her own, b—but . . .'

'There, lassie,' Hannah comforted her. 'What you need is a good sleep. You look exhausted.'

'I must see to Samuel and find out if Steven needs me first.'

'Don't worry about Steven, lassie.' Hannah patted her back soothingly. 'He telephoned me early this morning so I came straight away. I hope you don't mind, but Ruth offered to come with me and collect Samuel. She thought it would be easier if he was out of the way until we knew what was happening.' Hannah sounded anxious. Maybe Megan wouldn't like her wee boy being taken away?

'You're all so kind and thoughtful. I feel so guilty and torn in two. We were supposed to be cutting the other field of corn today and now . . .'

'Don't worry about any of that, Megan. You need a good sleep. Shall I cook you some breakfast first?'

'No thanks. I couldn't eat anything, but I do feel very weary. I must see Steven, though.'

'You get into bed and settle down. I'll send Steven up as soon as he comes in.'

'All right, if you're sure. I—I really want to be here and yet I hate leaving Dad at the hospital on his own. Mother looked so — so very ill,' she whispered fearfully.

'I understand, Megan. We all do. You try to get some rest while you can.'

Megan didn't think she would be able to sleep, but she had worked hard in the harvest field the previous day and it had been a long and stressful night. She was asleep almost as soon as her head touched the pillow. She didn't hear Steven creep up the stairs and peep into the bedroom.

The next time he opened the bedroom door Megan was still asleep, but as he closed it she stirred and called sleepily, 'Is that you, Steven?'

'It is. I'm sorry, sweetheart, I didna mean to waken you.'

'That's all right. Have you had your breakfast yet?'

Steven came right into the bedroom at that and closed the door. 'I've had my breakfast and my dinner,' he said with a smile.

'What?' Megan sat up and looked at the clock. 'It's after

one o' clock! Oh Steven, I'm so sorry. I didn't expect to sleep at all. I c–can't believe . . . Has the hospital phoned? Is there any news?'

'No, and no news has to be good news, Meggie.' In spite of his working trousers, Steven sat on the bed and held her tenderly. His sleeves were rolled up and the front of his shirt was open almost to the waist, showing the springy dark hair on his chest. Megan laid her cheek against it and rubbed gently, relishing his strength and the manly scent of him.

'I feel so guilty,' she said softly. 'We were supposed to be harvesting the second field today, and I promised to go back to keep Dad company and I–I feel torn in two.'

'You have no need to feel guilty, Megan. Nobody can be in two places at once.' He held her closer, enjoying the softness of her as she curried against him like a small animal needing protection. 'I do love you, Meggie,' he said huskily. 'I hate to see you so anxious. Mother told me how things are at the hospital so I thought I would go with you this afternoon, and maybe I can drive your father back home if we can persuade him to let you take his place tonight.'

'But Steven, I can't do that . . .'

'Yes you can, my love. Mother will stay here overnight when Ruth brings Samuel back, and she has offered to look after him again tomorrow. It's the last weekend of the summer holidays, so you must make the most of the opportunity when she has offered to help.'

'But the harvest . . .?'

'Jimmy Kerr has promised to help us tomorrow, even though it is Sunday, so he and Joe should manage the stooking if we work on late. Everyone wants to help, sweetheart . . .'

'They're all so kind.' Megan's eyes filled with tears.

'You deserve it, Meggie.' Steven held her close and stroked her hair.

She clung to him. 'Love me, Steven. Hold me close and love me,' she pleaded. 'I need you so much.'

'We need each other,' Steven said huskily, pressing her against his heart. Moments later he was pushing off his working clothes and lying beside her, with no other thought than to love her tenderly to help her forget her troubles for a little while.

# Six

An hour later Megan felt strengthened by Steven's tender loving. In spite of the anxiety she felt for her mother, a small smile hovered around her mouth as she bathed and dressed. Hannah had kept a meal ready for her and she ate it with genuine enjoyment. Only when she was ready to return to the hospital did the doubts return. She felt consumed with guilt at leaving the responsibilities of home and family.

'Are you sure you will be able to manage Samuel?' she asked anxiously.

'Yes, he'll be fine,' Hannah assured her, 'and if he isn't I shall call on Steven to put his wee son to bed.'

'Yes, you must do that,' Megan agreed. 'He loves his daddy to read him a story. I don't know how to thank you.'

'There's no need to thank me, lassie.' The two women smiled at each other.

'We'd better go now if Steven is to be back for the milking.'

Steven was dismayed at the sight of John Oliphant's drawn face and sunken, dark-ringed eyes, but he was even more shocked as he stood at Megan's side and looked into the small room where her mother lay. He would not have recognized the still, white figure as the kindly, energetic woman he had always known.

'They let me hold her hand for a few minutes,' John said with pathetic gratitude.

'That's a good sign then, Dad,' Megan said, but her mouth trembled with emotion. Her father had always been so strong and in control, but the shock of her mother's illness had shaken him to the core. 'Mum is going to need you when she begins to improve. It will be your company she wants then, not mine, and we don't want her to think she's got a ghost for a husband, do we?'

'I don't look like a ghost. Do I?'

'You do at the moment. That's why Steven has come with me

to drive you home. Our van is still at Martinwold, so he can collect it. You'll have your own car to come back here in the morning.'

'In the morning! I can't leave Chrissie for so long . . .'

'Yes you can because I shall be here and I promise I shall telephone you if there's the slightest change. You really must go home, Dad. You need a proper sleep. You'll feel so much better. I do.'

'What about your work, lassie, and wee Samuel?'

'Ruth is proving a real friend. She has taken Samuel for the day and promised to help over the weekend. Steven's mother is helping with everything else so that I can stay with Mum tonight. Oh, and Mr and Mrs McGuire send their thoughts and good wishes to you both.'

'That's nice of them.' He looked at Steven. 'I confess I need a shave and a change of clothes and I do feel weary now I think about it. I'm glad you're here, lad. I don't think I've the energy to drive the car home right now.'

'Right, we'd better get moving then before you sleep on your feet.' Steven moved to Megan's side and kissed her tenderly. 'Remember how much I love you, sweetheart. If you need me I shall come, whatever hour of the day or night. Right?'

'Right,' Megan whispered over the lump in her throat. 'I love you, Steven.'

John Oliphant was surprised and bewildered when they arrived back at Martinwold and he found his own door locked.

'We never lock the door,' he muttered dazedly.

'Sit in the car while I see who has the key,' Steven urged. His father-in-law was so unlike the brisk and breezy man he knew and he was concerned at the stunned look in his eyes. Before he could go across to the big house to consult Mr Turner, Mrs Richards came hurrying up from one of the Martinwold cottages holding out the large iron key.

'We thought we'd better lock up when we didna ken what was happening, or when somebody would be back,' she said. She came close to the car and peered down at John Oliphant. Steven didn't miss her indrawn breath at the sight of his pale face and sunken eyes.

'Chrissie has had an operation,' he said dully. 'She didna recognize me . . .'

'She is still sedated. Megan is staying tonight,' Steven informed her. 'This man needs a decent sleep and a proper meal before he returns.'

'Aah, I thought he'd need feeding. I have a casserole waiting for ye, John, and dinna worry about your student laddie. Billy has moved his things to our place for now. It was Mr Turner's idea. He said he'd pay for his board and lodging.'

'Thanks, Ida,' John said wearily.

'I'll wait to see you're in bed,' Steven told him with a frown. 'I want to be sure you've the energy left to get up the stairs.'

'I'll be fine, lad.'

'Megan would never forgive me if you went to sleep in a chair and you look fit to do that right now. Mrs Richards, maybe you could bring the food over tomorrow? I think sleep is what he needs most at the moment.'

'Bossy young bugger you've got for a son-in-law,' Mrs Richards remarked cheerfully, giving Steven a good-natured wink and a nod to say she agreed with him.


Back at Schoirhead, Steven realized how much he missed Megan's help. Joe attempted the milking, but when Hannah volunteered to help instead he was relieved.

'You better than I ever be in my life,' Joe said, 'but I strong. I carry the milk to the dairy, yes?'

'Yes, that will be fine, Johan. I shall enjoy keeping in practice,' she assured Steven when he began to protest, 'especially if you leave me the cows ye brought frae Willowburn. Do ye see now what a boon it is knowing Samuel is in safe hands with Ruth? It means I'm free to help you.'

'Ye—es, I suppose so,' he admitted reluctantly. 'I expect Megan will be home tomorrow evening.'

'The schools go back on Tuesday so Ruth will be unable to help then. I suggested to Megan we should accept her help while she is free. It will allow Megan to spend crucial time with her parents during the next couple of days. Why are you so wary of Ruth?'

'I'm not wary. I don't like favours when I can't repay them.'

'There's lots of ways of repaying favours apart from pounds, shillings and pence,' Hannah said sharply. 'Being a friend to the friendless is one way. Anyway, Ruth loves country life. She's not looking for money. Megan likes her, doesn't she? The two of them seem to get on well together.'

'Yes, the feeling is mutual, I think.'

'I don't think Ruth has found it easy to make friends since her experience with Fred. People don't know, or don't understand, that having an illegitimate child does not necessarily make the mother a wicked woman, you know. She really appreciates Megan's friendship. Maybe this is her way of repaying it.'

'I hadn't considered that angle, but I can't be held accountable for Fred's sins, however much I detest what he did, and I always get the feeling she judges us both the same.'

'I think her experience has made her wary of all men, not just you,' Hannah said.

'Maybe,' Steven conceded.

The following day Steven was astonished when Ruth and Avril arrived early at Schoirhead for the day.

'We got up ever so early, Granny C,' Avril sang as she bounded into the kitchen. 'We've fed Sally and Alice and their wee pigs, and Mummy let me help her feed the hens and open up the wee doors into their houses so they can come out into the sunshine when they've laid their eggs.'

'That's splendid. Thank you, Avril. Have you had breakfast?'

'Yes, but I could eat some more. Please?' Without waiting she bounded on to a chair next to Samuel's highchair and smiled widely across at Steven. He couldn't help but smile back at her and there was no doubt his small son was delighted to have her beside him.

Later, Steven was surprised again when Ruth and the two children appeared in the harvest field. Joe had declared he preferred to set up the sheaves rather than ride the binder when he realized Jimmy Kerr was there to help. Ruth followed his example and began to set the sheaves into stooks, while the children played nearby where she could make sure they kept well away from the tractor and binder.

On the next circuit of the field Steven noticed she was having difficulty making the sheaves stand up. If she was going to help she may as well do it right, he decided. He stopped the tractor and sprang lightly to the ground. A few swift strides and he was standing behind her.

'This is the way we do it,' he said, taking one sheaf from her and reaching round her to take the other. He was oblivious to the fact that his brawny arms almost encircled her slender figure.

'Don't do that! Let me go!' she screamed, and flailed at him with her arms and feet, spinning to face him. He was stunned. Instinct made him grab her wrists before she could claw at his eyes. He shook her, none too gently, but he could see the terror in her eyes as she stared back at him. She was shaking. He released her wrists and grasped her upper arms, shaking her again but more gently this time.

'What sort of creature do you think I am, for God's sake?' he snapped. 'Do you react like that with all men? Or is it just me?' She stared back at him, mute, her mouth trembling. As he glared down at her, her eyes filled with tears.

'Dear Lord, that's all I need,' Steven muttered and shook her again. 'Calm yourself. You're in the middle of a field with the children watching and two grown men only yards away. What possible harm could I do you?'

'I . . . F–Fred,' she stammered. 'Y–you reminded me of Fred.'

'I'm not Fred!' Steven spat furiously. 'I'd rather be dead than be like him. Do you think you're the only one who suffered at his hands? He was a merciless bully when we were young.' He frowned and his tone was quieter as he added, 'It would be worse for you, of course, being a girl, and an attractive one at that. I suppose it would be like a red rag to a bull if you ignored him. He never could stand being overlooked.'

'Th–that was exactly how it was. It's even what he said. B–but you remind me of him. A little. Sometimes.' She broke off when she saw his indignant expression. 'Only a little,' she said hurriedly. 'A look, an expression now and then, but . . .' She shuddered. 'It's enough to remind me. When I felt your arms I felt I was a prisoner again.' Her voice sank to a hoarse whisper and the fear in her eyes was plain to see.

'Listen to me. I shouldn't think there's a man in a thousand, in ten thousand even, who would act as Fred did, and I'm certainly not one of them. Apart from anything else I'm married and I love my wife. Do you honestly think I'd betray Megan?'

'I–I suppose n–not. No.' She lowered her head in shame.

'If you panic like that around all men I think you need help. If it's only me I'm surprised you even came near Schoirhead.'

'Y–your mother thought I would enjoy helping. She knows I love being outdoors and – and I thought I could repay her, and Megan, a little if I helped with the harvest.'

'Fair enough then. I'll show you how to set up sheaves to make a good firm stook – which is what I came to do in the first place until you reacted like a wild woman. Look at the base of the sheaf. See how the stems are at an angle?'

'I hadn't noticed. Are – are they all like that?'

'Yes, it's the way they're tied and dropped from the binder. You set them down so that the short sides are to the inside of the stook so they lean towards each other, like this.' He took care to step away from her and set up two sheaves and then another two close against them. 'And don't be afraid to give them a firm push together. They need to withstand the wind and we don't want them falling down and getting sodden if it rains,' he added brusquely.

'Y–yes, I see.' She was chewing hard on her lower lip, but she lifted her head and looked him in the face. He saw how dark her eyes were, how wide and anxious. 'I–I'm sorry I reacted as I did . . .'

'Forget it, but don't ever confuse me with Fred again. It's the worst insult you could offer.' He turned to stride back to the tractor, then he turned towards her again. 'While we're doing some straight talking I may as well tell you that I doubted your story about Fred being Avril's father. She bears no resemblance to him.'

'You doubted?' She gasped and stared at him incredulously. 'You can't think I–I went with other men? Or that I . . .'

'I thought you might be playing on Mother's sympathy, at least since your father died and you are alone in the world apparently.'

'Never! Your mother was very kind to me when I first arrived at Willowburn and I loved being there – at least I did at first. We got on well from the beginning. After she left Willowburn and asked me to visit and to bring Avril I was filled with doubts. I–I still am sometimes.' She shuddered. 'I never want to see Fred again and sometimes I have nightmares about him returning. Surely you can't imagine I would choose a father like that for my child if I could have stopped him?'

'I suppose not, when you put it like that,' Steven acknow-ledged with a wry grimace. 'Anyway, for the record, and in an effort to clear the air between us, I confess I do see odd glimpses of my father in Avril now that I'm getting to know her better. Take this morning, for instance, the way she smiled and the twinkle in her eyes. It was so like the way he used to smile when I was young. There are other things too, the way she twirls a piece of hair around her finger when she's thinking. My mother says the first time she saw Avril she reminded her of her cousin Eleanor, who would have been her real grandmother. So I apolo-gize for doubting you. All right?'

'Apology accepted,' Ruth said gravely. She hesitated a moment then held her hand out to him. 'Perhaps we may become friends?'

'Of course,' he said, taking her hand in his work-roughened palm. A grin transformed his features. 'At least my mother and Megan will be pleased, and maybe I shall be too if I've taught you to set up some good stooks. Now we'd better get to work.'

Twice Lindsey Gray came down to the hospital to see his patient. The first evening he arrived Megan was there on her own.

'Hello, Megan.' His face lit up and he smiled warmly. 'I'm glad to see your father has agreed to let you relieve him for a little while. Mr Higgins was concerned about him. But how are you managing to divide yourself between here and your other duties?'

'I'm lucky to have a wonderful mother-in-law and an extremely thoughtful friend. Ruth is looking after Samuel during the day and bringing him back to Schoirhead at night to sleep. That allows Steven's mother freedom to do a lot of my work, including helping with the milking. Everyone has been so very good. Our next-door neighbours are elderly and Mr McGuire is crippled with arthritis, but Mrs McGuire still made Steven a pot of broth. They were always good to him when he was living there on his own.'

'That's probably because you're both good to them, and to your friend Ruth,' Lint said.

'Samuel loves having Avril to entertain him. I doubt if he's even missing me, except perhaps at bedtime.'

'Avril? Is that another friend?'

'No, no.' Megan smiled, but her smile faded as she realized he was waiting for an explanation. 'Avril is Ruth's wee girl. You met them both at Martinwold if you remember?'

'Yes, I do remember. Your friend has a face which would be hard to forget, but her manner surprised and intrigued me. You say the child is hers?'

'Yes, Avril is seven. She's such a bright, happy wee thing. Samuel worships her.'

'I see. And Ruth's husband doesn't mind her helping out then?' he enquired, though he had noticed Ruth wore no rings.

'Er, no . . .' Megan looked up at him and chewed her lip. He grinned at her.

'Sorry. Am I asking too many questions? I was not intending to pry. Her reaction to me was unexpected and I wondered why. I'm afraid I'm always interested in people and their affairs and families. It helps to get the rounded picture, especially when people are ill or in trouble.'

'As they usually are when they come to you, I suppose.' Megan smiled back at him. 'If I seemed reluctant to talk about Ruth it's because she's very reticent about her experiences too, and it's not my story to tell. Avril is illegitimate.'

'Aah, I see. Well, it does happen. In fact it has happened a lot during the war. Was the father killed?' he asked sympathetically.

'N–no.' Megan frowned and colour stained her face. She felt ashamed and oddly responsible because they were connected to Fred. She swallowed hard. 'I don't suppose you're likely to meet Ruth again so I suppose there's no reason why I shouldn't tell you, but she doesn't talk about it herself and I don't blame her,' she added grimly. 'She came to Scotland as a land girl during the war. She – she worked for Steven's family.' Megan's colour deepened. 'Steven's half-brother was working the farm while Steven was in the army. He – he raped Ruth . . .'

'Surely not!' Lint stared at her.

'Fred is completely different to Steven,' she said in swift defence.

'I'm sure he must be. Where is Fred now?'

'He's gone to Canada. He doesn't know he has a child and Ruth doesn't want him to know, not ever. She never wants to set eyes on him again. Neither do we if I'm honest.' A thought occurred to her and her eyes widened. She grasped his arm. 'You'll not breathe a word of this to Natalie, will you? It's just the sort of thing she'd pass on, and who knows . . .' She put a hand over her mouth and shook her head. 'I should never have mentioned it.'

'Don't worry, Megan. I'm not the sort of person who discusses other people's misfortunes, but even if I was I'm not likely to be discussing anything with Natalie. I told you it's all over between us. I meant it. I shall probably see her when I am working, but I heard on the grapevine that she has handed in her notice so she will be leaving the hospital in about a month.' He gave a wry grimace. 'No doubt I shall be the wicked party. It's unlikely Natalie will want anyone here to know how outrageously she behaved, or how spoiled and selfish she can be.'

'Will you mind? Taking the blame, I mean?'

'I'm sure most people will form their own opinions.' He shrugged, then smiled. 'I'm very pleased your mother is making good progress, Megan, although it may not seem so to you at the moment.'

John Oliphant felt it had been the longest week of his life, but by the end of it the doctors gave him every hope that Chrissie would survive, unless some unforeseen problem should develop. They warned him it would be weeks, maybe months, before she regained a fraction of her former health and vitality. She certainly tired very quickly, but it was an immense relief to be able to talk to her, however briefly.

It was Chrissie herself who broached the subject of their work at Martinwold at the end of her second week in hospital.

'The doctor says it will be at least a year before I am fit to lift the milk churns and the buckets,' she said anxiously. 'What shall we do, John? I've let you down terribly.'

'No you havena, lass.' John Oliphant took her hand in both of his and held it as gently as though it was a tiny bird. 'I've had plenty o' time to think while you were lying there with your life hanging in the balance. What a fright you gave us, Chrissie. I never want to live through that again. I vowed I'd give you an easier life in future if only you were spared. I told Mr Turner we'd be leaving Martinwold at the November term.'

'Leaving Martinwold? At the end of November? But that's only two and a half months away, John. What did Mr Turner say?'

'He was expecting it. He knows you're half the team, love. In fact you're more than half when I think of all the boys you've had to keep over the years, as well as helping with the milking and doing the dairy. I've made up my mind. We've saved a tidy sum. I'd like to buy a wee cottage of our own so that we never have to move again whatever kind of work I take on. We've been in tied houses long enough. I'll take whatever work I can get. I thought I might get some relief milking, maybe a bit of gardening and I'm pretty good at fencing. The more I think about it the more I think I shall enjoy a bit of variety and being able to choose when I work and when I spend time with you, lass. The main thing is for you to get well enough to help me find a cottage where we could be happy for the rest of our days. Aah, Chrissie . . .' he laid his cheek gently against hers, 'don't look so worried, love.'

'It would be lovely to have a house of our own, but I can't imagine you being happy working with anything else but cows, John, and I'd hate you to be miserable because o' me.'

'I'd be a damned sight more miserable without you, Chrissie. Anyway, I've made up my mind. I told Megan what I planned to do and she seemed to think it was a good idea to buy a cottage of our own. There's only the two of us to think about now, and if I'm self-employed we can spend more time together doing what we want to do. Maybe we'll have a wee holiday by the sea next summer, eh?'

'Oh John . . . ' Chrissie was still very weak and her eyes filled with tears. 'You're so good to me. I'm sure you'll miss the cows, though.'

'If I do, I'll visit Steven's. We'll have time to see a bit more of our grandson, too. You'd like that, wouldn't you?'

'Oh yes, I'd love to see more of wee Samuel. That was my one regret about being so tied to the milking seven days a week every day o' the year.'

'Aye, we've done it long enough,' John said decisively. 'It's time to make a change.'

# Seven

As soon as Chrissie began to feel better she longed to get home.

'You've had a very serious illness, Mrs Oliphant,' Mr Higgins said. 'We don't want to take any chances and undo all Mr Gray's good work.'

'I am truly grateful to both of you,' Chrissie agreed meekly.

Megan knew her mother would need her help when she first returned home, but she also wanted to help Steven with the harvest, so it was a relief when all the corn was safely in the stacks. Steven and Joe thatched them to keep them weatherproof until the thrashing machine came round during the winter, and by the time they had finished Chrissie was able to return home to Martinwold.

'I canna believe how tired I get,' she admitted on one of Megan's frequent visits. 'We're really grateful for your help, Meggie, but I feel guilty at taking you away from Steven and wee Samuel.'

'Don't worry, Mum, they're not being neglected. I wouldn't be able to come up so often if Steven's mother didn't help us. Ruth and Avril come with her most Saturdays too. They've all been wonderful while you've been ill.'

'I don't seem to have any energy.'

'Mum, don't you realize how lucky you are to be here at all?' Megan hugged her. 'Dad and I are only too glad to do things so long as we still have you.'

'I suppose so,' Chrissie said with a wan smile. 'Did I tell you Mr Gray telephoned? He says we should call him Lint, as you do, but I'm not used to being so familiar with a man in his position.'

'I know what you mean.' Megan smiled. 'Did he phone to see if you were obeying instructions?'

'No. He said he was telephoning as a friend. We chatted one evening while I was still in the hospital. I told him about your dad giving up the dairying and wanting to buy a wee house of our own. He remembered what I'd said. The friends he stays with near Lockerbie are looking for a man to help with the grounds at Langton Tower. They want someone who knows a bit about gardening, fencing, drains – you know the sort of thing.'

'It sounds right up Dad's street,' Megan said. 'What did he say?'

'He thought that too, but there's a tied cottage and he's determined we should have our own house in case he doesn't like the work. The thought of moving out of here eight weeks from now overwhelms me, but I'd feel easier if I knew where we were going to live.'

'I'll help you pack, and so will Dad. Ruth offered to come and pack kitchen things and bedding if you wouldn't mind?'

'How kind of her. I'm relieved to know there'll be someone to help. You and Sam were still at school when we moved here. We had a few moves before that until your father came to Martinwold. It was the big dairy and the responsibility he'd always wanted. Mr Turner has advertised our job so we shall have people coming to see over the house. He says he'll only send those he is seriously considering for the job.'

'That's considerate of him. Did Dad tell Lint he didn't want the job as a groundsman then?'

'He had to telephone Mr and Mrs Palmer-Farr. They were disappointed because Lint had told them he would be ideal for the job.'

'I don't think Mr Palmer-Farr will be a very practical man. I believe he speaks several languages, though. Did Lint tell you he's married to his half-cousin?'

'No. John said they seemed to understand about him not wanting a tied cottage. He has sent for some particulars so we must start looking at houses. If only I knew how it will all turn out.'

'You mustn't worry, Mum.'

'I know, but if I had measurements I could sew some new curtains ready to hang. I'd be sitting down. I wouldn't feel so useless.'

'I'll chivvy Dad along next time I'm up. He's preoccupied with keeping everything spotless, and all the cows groomed, for prospective applicants looking round.'

'I know. He can't concentrate on anything else until Mr Turner has chosen his successor.'

'Even the McGuires want to help. Mrs McGuire baked the fruit loaf and the gingerbread I brought you today,' Megan said, changing the subject. 'She has her hands full already. Mr McGuire is terribly crippled with the arthritis now. Steven's mother says I should accept whatever she offers because it's their way of repaying us for making it possible for them to stay in their house.'

'Hannah and Annie McGuire do seem to get on well so I think you should take her advice. Most people like to repay a kindness.'

'But we're not being kind, Mum. Renting the McGuires' land is the best thing that could have happened for us,' Megan protested. 'We've almost paid off our loan from the bank with having extra cows and more milk to sell. Steven has heard we're to get a new land agent, though. Mr Wilson is retiring. I hope the new man is not too diligent in his inspections.'

'I should hope not too,' Chrissie said anxiously. 'It would be terrible if they put you and the McGuires out of your farms for breaking the tenancy rules.'

As she drove home to Schoirhead Megan thought about the land agent. She knew Steven would feel easier when he had made his first inspection. He had warned Joe to keep the door between the two byres camouflaged with a pile of hay after each milking. This was easy enough to remember in winter when they were feeding hay to the cows everyday, but in summer the man might think it strange to have a pile of hay lying around. Perhaps it was fortunate they were almost into October. The cows would probably be in for the winter before he came.

They had had enough anxiety with her mother's illness, and Megan had a niggling suspicion they would have another small problem to face before long. She had needed Steven's comfort and loving, but they had not been so careful as they might have been. She was determined to keep her suspicions to herself for now and avoid any fuss. She glanced through the van window at the fields of pale stubble now shorn of the crop. As she passed one of the larger farms she saw potato boxes stacked beside the hedge in preparation for the potato gathering; in another ten days the children would start their school holiday and the older ones would help. There was an autumnal nip in the air in the mornings and in the evenings. The last few swallows had already left and two evenings ago she had heard the call of the geese and seen them flying in their vee formation as they headed for their

winter home on the nearby Solway Firth. Megan gave a contented
sigh. She enjoyed the changing seasons and the different routines
each one brought.

The following evening John Oliphant telephoned.

'Could you and Megan come with us to look at a house?' he
asked. 'It's an opportunity I'd like to seize, but I'm in a dilemma
with Chrissie still being so weak. Whatever happens we have to
be out of here on the morning of the thirtieth of November
to let the new man in.'

'So what's the problem?'

'The Palmer-Farrs have come up with another offer. There's
a pair of small cottages on the edge of their grounds, nearer the
village, completely separate from the big house. The situation
would be ideal but they've been empty for a while and they've
never been modernized so the price they're asking is too good
to miss for a man like me. But there's a condition . . .'

'Isn't there always?' Steven said on a wry note.

'Aye, I suppose so,' John Oliphant agreed, 'but it's only what I
should want to do anyway eventually. They're a bit of an eyesore
to people approaching Langton Tower from the direction of the
village, and the Palmer-Farrs are aiming to open a country house
hotel some day. They want a guarantee that we would repair them
and paint the outsides, make "an attractive front garden", that sort
of thing, but I'm frightened Chrissie might have a relapse doing
things she shouldn't if we're living in a hovel. The Palmer-Farrs
were going to demolish them because they have more cottages
than they need and no capital to renovate these two.'

'I can understand they will want guests to get a good first
impression,' Steven agreed, 'but surely they'll allow you a year to
do up the cottages? They'll not be opening a hotel before then?'

'No, probably not. I don't want to take any chances with
Chrissie and there'll be a lot of work to do before they're habitable. It's not long to the November term and I shall have no
time to do much myself until I finish working for Mr Turner.
One of them hasn't been occupied for three years. The other was
occupied by an elderly couple who had worked for Mr Palmer-
Farr's family. The wife died last year and the old man went to
stay with his daughter. I've only had a quick look from the outside
but I can see why the Palmer-Farrs are ashamed to have them

as part of their property. The gardens are overgrown and a mass of weeds. I could tackle them easily enough. There's two rooms in each dwelling, no hot water system and no inside toilet or bathroom.'

'Aah, I see,' Steven said slowly. 'It would cost a bit to modernize them then?'

'It's not so much the money. The roof looks sound enough and the walls are in good condition, but the woodwork needs some repairs and it all needs painting. I know what Chrissie is like for wanting to get things done. Megan will understand. I'd like you both to see the place and tell us what you think.'

On Saturday Ruth and Avril arrived as usual.

'I'm happy to look after both children here at Schoirhead until you return,' Ruth said with a smile, and Megan realized she smiled more often these days. She was very attractive when that anxious look didn't cloud her lovely dark eyes.

'That would be a big help,' she said. 'You know what Samuel is like for getting into everything and I can't tell whether the buildings are even safe from Dad's description.'

'Well, if your parents do consider buying the houses they could always ask Mr Paterson for his advice.'

'Is he the man who helped Mother convert the shop into living accommodation?' Steven asked. 'He made a good job there. I wonder what sort of fees he charges.'

'I don't think he does charge fees exactly,' Ruth said. 'I'm sure he said drawing plans to improve old properties had become his hobby since he retired. He knows about planning regulations and permits for building materials.'

'Thanks, Ruth. That's worth knowing. We'll suggest that to my parents if they decide to go ahead,' Megan said, 'but I think it's a daft idea when Mum is still so frail.'

'It might give your father an interest,' Steven said. 'I can't imagine what he's going to do with himself after working seven days a week every day of the year. Mr Palmer-Farr only wants him five days at most.'

'He's already talking about taking on relief milking one weekend a month at Bengairney,' Megan reminded him. 'It's near Martinwold.'

It was Chrissie herself who made the decision. Privately she agreed with Steven. She feared John was going to be lost. She still needed his help with many of her own tasks, but she would hate him to be miserable and moping around her feet all day. Doing up a home of their own would give him satisfaction.

'I shall be relieved to know where we're going to live, even if it does mean using an outside closet for a while,' she said firmly. 'We've survived that before. Ruth's suggestion to consult Mr Paterson is a good idea. Your mother was full of praise for him, Steven. He might save us making expensive mistakes.'

'He might save us time too, if he knows his way around the planning people,' John Oliphant said. 'But I shall only consider it if you promise not to go against the surgeon's instructions, Chrissie?'

'I can promise you that.' She smiled. 'There's no way I want to end up back in that hospital, however kind everyone has been to me.'

'Ruth said she would come up and help me do the painting at the weekends if you get to that stage,' Megan said. 'It would be better for Mum if she had a decent living room and kitchen before you move in. I must say it seems to be in better condition than I expected, even though it does still have a box bed in each of the living rooms and a wee hoose at the bottom of each garden.'

Hannah asked Angus Paterson if he would advise the Oliphants.

'It's away from my usual haunts,' he said, 'but if you or Ruth would drive me there I could take a look on Saturday.'

When Megan phoned to tell her mother Chrissie sounded excited.

'That was quick. Your father willna be able to go because there's a man coming to have another look round the dairy and he and his wife want to see the house this time. To tell the truth, Megan, I'd be glad of an excuse to be out when they come. I don't like showing strangers round my home.'

'I can understand that, Mum. Will Dad mind us taking Mr Paterson when he's not there?'

'I don't think so if I tell him everything he has to say.'

'I'll make some notes of his suggestions,' Megan promised.

'I suppose we couldn't take a picnic if this good weather lasts?' Chrissie asked wistfully. 'I love autumn and I'm beginning to feel restless.'

'That's a splendid idea, but I'll make it up.'

'All right. Hannah will be there with Mr Paterson so maybe Ruth and Avril would like to come too and then the children can play while we look around. All children enjoy a picnic and I noticed there was plenty of grass beneath the apple trees at the bottom of the gardens.'

'Mum, I do believe you're beginning to sound like your old self again,' Megan said with delight.

'Yes, I think I am. I was too tired to feel restless before. Although part of me dreads moving to somewhere new, it will be exciting to have a house of our own.'

So on a fine October morning they all arrived at the cottages on the outskirts of Langton Village. Mr Paterson was silent and non-committal and Megan grew anxious as she followed him around the empty, echoing cottages. He poked and tapped and peered into every cranny. Eventually he turned to look at her.

'This place is structurally sound. The walls and the roof are in good condition as far as I can tell without a ladder. There's no sign of damp coming in as there would be if slates had been missing. Of course most of the windows and the doors will need replacing, but with some careful planning and a lot of work your parents could have a good house.'

Megan heaved a sigh of relief. She knew her father had set his heart on buying the cottages with their long double garden. Although he had wanted her opinion, she knew he had hoped for approval, and she hadn't realized until now how much she liked the situation and the possibilities herself. The big problem was her mother's health and the lack of time before her parents must move out of their home.

'My father would have been bitterly disappointed if you had condemned the whole idea,' she said. 'I brought my notebook so that we could pass on everything you suggested,' she said.

He gave her a genial smile. 'And so far I've not suggested anything, have I? We'll join the others and I'll make a few notes and sketches and then we can talk about it and consult your mother.'

'They're all at the bottom of the garden spreading out rugs for a picnic. Did Mrs Caraford warn you? I hope you don't mind.'

'I am delighted to join you. I never missed not having a family while my wife was alive and when I was busy working. Since I met your mother-in-law and Ruth and young Avril I realize what I've missed. I'm very grateful when they invite me to join them.'

When they reached the bottom of the garden they saw Lindsey Gray leaning over the fence, chatting.

'Hello, Megan,' he greeted her. 'I was just saying Katherine has several folding chairs in one of her sheds. I'm trying to persuade Ruth and Avril to accompany me across the paddock to carry some back for your mother and Mrs Caraford.'

'I'd appreciate a chair, too,' Mr Paterson said. 'My old joints don't bend as easily as they used to do.'

'All right, we could bring two each,' Lindsey said, ignoring Ruth's obvious reluctance. 'Of course I'm really angling for an invitation to join the picnic.' He grinned. Megan looked from him to Ruth and back again. How wary Ruth looked. Lint was one of the nicest men imaginable, he would never do her any harm, especially now he knew her circumstances, but he was not used to young women resisting his obvious charm and she guessed he found Ruth a challenge.

'That would be a good idea,' she said. 'I'll lift Avril over the railings.' Ruth opened her mouth to protest but Megan went on, 'I'm waiting for Mr Paterson to make some notes and sketches so I'll be here to chase after Samuel until you come back.'

'We shall not be long.' Lint reached for Avril and set her on her feet then turned to help Ruth. In her nervousness she missed the bottom rail and would have fallen head first, but Lint caught her easily enough and set her on her feet.

'You're light as a feather – not much heavier than Avril.' He grinned down at the little girl and she took his hand and danced along beside him.

'I don't think Ruth was too happy about that,' Hannah said. 'She had been trying to refuse politely.'

'She will be safe enough with Lint,' Megan said, 'and I'm sure it must be good for her to mix a little with the opposite sex. Aren't there male teachers at her school?'

'Yes, two at least. One of them pestered her to go out with him. She got terribly tense and upset when he wouldn't take no for an answer. He was so persistent he arrived at her door un-expectedly one day. Avril answered. He has not asked her out again now he knows she has a child. I suspect he may have been a bit unpleasant in the staffroom, too.'

'Oh that's a shame,' Megan said angrily.

'Ruth was not interested in him anyway, but it made me aware how some men feel about a woman on her own with a child.'

It was not long before Ruth and Lint came back carrying two chairs each. Hannah, Chrissie and Mr Paterson accepted them gratefully.

'Much appreciated,' Angus Paterson said, drawing up the spare chair beside his own. 'If you sit here, Megan, you can see I've made a few sketches.'

Megan took the chair, leaving Ruth and Lint chuckling because they were the two left without after making the effort to bring them. They sprawled on the rugs with Avril and Samuel tumbling around them, and Megan was relieved to see Ruth more at ease. 'I can suggest three alternatives,' Mr Paterson went on. 'If your parents want to spend a lot of money they could raise the roof, have two storeys and a splendid four-bedroomed house.'

'No, no,' Chrissie protested, overhearing. 'We don't want stairs in our old age. John thinks two bedrooms would be enough, but I'd like three if it's possible. I'm hoping Samuel will want to come and stay for his holidays with us when he's a bit older and maybe one day I shall have a wee granddaughter as well.' She glanced at Megan and was surprised to see the colour mounting in her cheeks. She made no comment but Megan was aware of her mother's speculative look.

'Right, then we'll stick to one floor,' Mr Paterson nodded. 'I think we can make you three bedrooms, though one might be a bit small. Presumably you will be the legal owners of the property so you should qualify for a grant of three hundred pounds to help with the modernization. If the landlords were doing it they would be restricted to two hundred and fifty pounds.'

'You mean we can get money to help pay for the bathroom?' Chrissie asked.

'That will be a nice surprise for Dad,' Megan said, scribbling notes.

'I can help him apply as soon as he has made up his mind about the plans. Since time is short, and I know you have been seriously ill, Mrs Oliphant, I'd like to suggest you decide what should be done when the house is complete, but perhaps concentrate on the kitchen, the bathroom and one bedroom initially. You could be comfortable when you move in and do the rest at your leisure.'

'I think that's an excellent suggestion,' Lint interrupted. He smiled. 'I'm thinking of the welfare of my patient. I don't want Chrissie being tempted to do too much yet.'

'I understand,' Mr Paterson nodded. 'I'll draw up one or two rough plans to give your father some ideas, Megan. When he has decided what he wants to do I'd be happy to meet him and draw up proper plans if he wishes me to help.'

'I'm sure he will,' Chrissie said. 'You know so much more about these things than we do.'

Out of the corner of her eye Megan saw Lint make several attempts to draw Ruth into conversation. She responded politely but displayed none of the animation she had shown when she was with the children.

Samuel and Avril filled the empty picnic basket with apples which had fallen from the two trees.

'I hope your cousin will not mind,' Chrissie said. 'We havena bought the house yet.'

'Take as many as you like,' Lint said. 'They'll only go to waste. This will be a nice place to have a swing when the children come to visit.'

'Yes it will. I do hope you will come and bring Avril when we get settled in, Ruth?' Chrissie said. 'I've always liked children, but I was usually too busy to enjoy my own,' she said wistfully. 'I mean to enjoy my grandchildren, though.'

'Katherine said we should leave the chairs here for now,' Lint said. 'She thought you might need them when you come up to see how the work is progressing. Is your father going to take the job on too, Megan?' He grinned. 'He'll have his work cut out explaining what needs to be done if I know Douglas. I believe Katherine may be more practical. Tell your father not to let his moans about money worry him. Douglas counts in hundreds where most people think in shillings.'

When they returned to Schoirhead Megan and Ruth were alone in the kitchen.

'Do you like Lint, Ruth? He's one of the most genuine men I know, always excepting Steven, of course,' she said with a laugh.

'He seems very pleasant,' Ruth said cautiously.

'But you don't feel comfortable with him?'

'I don't think I shall ever feel comfortable in the company of men my own age,' Ruth said unhappily. 'I do like your Mister Gray. He seems a nice person. It's just me. I can't help it. Something seems to curl up inside whenever a man comes near enough to touch me, and I want to run away and hide.'

'But you've got used to Steven now?'

'More or less.' Ruth grimaced. 'We did have a bit of a quarrel when you were at the hospital, but it cleared the air between us. He admitted he'd had as many doubts about me as I had about him. That was a surprise. It made me realize I only think about my own point of view. I do try to be natural with your friend Lindsey Gray, really I do,' she said unhappily.

'I'm glad, because I'd stake my life on you being completely safe with him,' Megan said.

Mr Paterson had worked fast to get the plans approved. He knew two brothers who worked together as builders and joiners and the Palmer-Farrs recommended their own plumber. All they needed was an electrician. The man who kept the cooperative shop in Langton village suggested they should give his son-in-law a try.

'He'll not let ye down,' he said. 'If he makes a good job for you he might get work with the Palmer-Farrs. They're always making alterations up at the Tower.'

So the first stage of the work went ahead faster than Megan had dared to hope. John Oliphant was relieved when Mr Paterson agreed to keep an eye on the work while he was kept busy at Martinwold. All the cows were housed for the winter so there was extra work feeding and cleaning out two or three times each day. He was determined to keep everything running smoothly and looking its best until the minute he handed over to his successor. He missed Chrissie's help badly. Mr Turner had reduced his wages to pay for one of the other farm men until term day, but the man needed constant supervision, whereas Chrissie had known what to do as well as he did himself.

'I do miss you outside, Chrissie love,' he said as he held her tenderly in his arms one cold night in mid-November. 'I've hardly had time to go near Honeysuckle Cottage. Are you sure that's what you want to call our new home, by the way?'

'Yes, I'm sure, and when all the alterations are finished I shall ask you to build me an archway over the garden gate where I can plant some honeysuckle. I've always loved the scent of it in the early mornings and in the evenings.'

'Well it sounds better than number eight and nine Langton Tower cottages,' John agreed. 'It will not be long now before we move.'

Steven worried about Megan. He understood how much she wanted to do the painting at the cottage to save her mother, but he was afraid she might do too much and lose the baby. Although it would not be due until next May, he knew miscarriages often occurred in the early stages and they would both be upset if anything like that happened.

'Please don't worry, Steven. I wouldn't like anything to go wrong either. Ruth has been a tremendous help and I couldn't have done so much if your mother hadn't looked after Samuel and Avril. We've only the bedroom to finish and the bathroom to paint. That might be a bit tricky reaching over the bath and the washbasin, but it's not very big and it does look lovely.'

'Does it make you feel envious, sweetheart?' Steven asked.

'No, I'm happy here. Mother has waited years for this and she deserves it.'

'I agree, she does. I asked Tom Green if he would have his cattle lorry cleaned out ready to move the surplus furniture down here on the Thursday night. He promised to get organized in good time. Earlier on Thursday he's moving the pig and crating your mother's hens to move them to Langton Tower.' He grinned. 'I hear it's Mrs Palmer-Farr who wants to learn about keeping pigs and poultry?'

'Yes, it is. They are providing the houses and the food and Dad or Mum will look after them. The arrangement is they will share the pig and Mum can get as many eggs as she wants. I think Dad is quite pleased. He plans to lay out the garden with vegetables at the bottom and a greenhouse and Mum can have a lawn and flowers nearer the house.'

'I hope it all works out as well as he hopes,' Steven said. 'Things would have been so different if Sammy had been here.'

'Yes, Mum was saying the same thing the other day. I think she's more worried about Dad settling down to the new routine than he is himself. Did Tom Green say he would be at Mum's by eight o'clock on Friday morning?'

'Yes, he understands the new people are due to move in at midday. I'll take Joe to help with the lifting, and with Tom and your father that makes four of us. It shouldn't take long to load up.'

'That's splendid. I promised to go up and help Mum have a last sweep out. She wants to leave the house clean for the new dairy family. They will be doing the afternoon milking so they'll not have much time to sort their new home.'

'I reckon your parents will be too busy to have time for regrets,' Steven said.

'It was a good idea of Mr Paterson's to leave the rest of the house until they move in. According to Lint there's loads to do at the Tower gardens before spring.'

'I'm glad this will be your last weekend for decorating up at the cottage,' Steven said. He drew her into his arms. 'I miss you when you're away all day.' He nuzzled her neck and kissed her ear lobe. 'You will make sure you don't overdo things this weekend, won't you, Meggie?' He slid his hands down to her stomach. 'I worry about you, sweetheart.'

'I know.' She turned into the circle of his arms and kissed him. 'But there's no need. I wouldn't do anything to harm our wee one. I haven't told Ruth that Lint will be staying at the Tower this weekend. He's coming to lend a hand. I think he might reach the bathroom ceiling easier than Ruth would have done.'

'It's very decent of him. I didn't think a doctor would want to get his hands dirty.'

'I don't think Lint is one of those kind. He seems to like to get stuck in. But I do wonder sometimes if he finds Ruth's reserve something of a challenge.'

'Do you think he's attracted to her?' Steven asked.

'I don't know. I wouldn't want him to make her like him and then drop out of her life once she was no longer a challenge.'

'He seems a caring sort of fellow. I don't think he'd do that intentionally, but I do think he'll be lucky if he can penetrate Ruth's resistance to men.'

'It will take a lot of time and patience,' Megan agreed. 'I'll take extra sandwiches anyway. It was a splendid idea of Mr Paterson's to make the original living room into a large kitchen with room for Mum's big kitchen table, and I'm glad Dad agreed to install a Rayburn cooker for her. It makes the kitchen lovely and warm and we can make hot drinks while we're there.'

'I think it was an even better idea of his to knock down the two wee lean-to washhouses and build on the extension for a proper bathroom and a scullery,' Steven said.

'I don't think Dad would have agreed to that if he hadn't been getting the grant to help. That was a pleasant surprise.'

'Your father realizes how fortunate they are to have each other. He says he intends to make the most of the rest of their lives together.'

Megan and Ruth were just unloading the paint and stepladder from the van on Saturday morning when Lindsey Gray walked in. Dressed in a serviceable boiler suit which emphasized his broad shoulders and long legs, he had come prepared to work.

'Good morning, girls,' he grinned. 'I am your slave for the weekend. Your wish is my command.'

'Are you sure about that?' Megan teased, her green eyes sparkling.

'Oh yes. Katherine tells me you need to finish here by Sunday evening. Your parents will be living here by next Friday, Megan?'

'That's right. They have to move out by then whether they like it or not. Steven has offered to move some of the small stuff in the van during the week to make it less for Friday.'

'Everyone must have worked very hard to make such a transformation. I know the sitting room and the three bedrooms still need a lot of renovation, but the place is comfortable now.'

'Yes, I couldn't have managed all the decorating without Ruth,' Megan admitted.

'No, you could not, and should not, from what I hear,' Lint said emphatically. 'I believe congratulations are in order.' He grinned when Megan blushed.

'Aren't I supposed to mention delicate conditions?' He grinned. 'I'm a doctor, remember, so there's not much embarrasses us.'

'I suppose not,' Megan agreed. 'I didn't think many people knew yet, that's all.'

'Steven told me the other night when I phoned.'

'Oh he did, did he? I thought the two of you were having a long chat.'

'He worries about you. Stretching high above your head is not supposed to be good for you at this stage, is it?'

'Well you're the doctor,' Megan quipped. 'Anyway, Ruth has been wonderful. She doesn't let me do anything that might be risky.'

'I know Ruth is wonderful,' Lint said with an enigmatic smile which brought the colour to Ruth's cheeks as he met and held her gaze.

'I – er, I haven't done anything special,' Ruth stammered, and seized a pot of paint and a brush as though they might protect her.

Lint smiled. 'It's always a delight when people don't realize how wonderful they are. Have you heard the latest news about Natalie, by the way?'

'News? What sort of news?' Megan asked. 'She's left her work at the hospital, hasn't she?'

'Oh yes. She started working for one of the other doctors a while ago. She works from his home as his private secretary cum PA cum general everything.'

'What does that mean?' Megan asked, seeing his wry smile.

'It means she's going to be the next Mrs Wright-Manton if the rumours are true, and most of her ex-colleagues seem to think they are.'

'Oh Lint, I'm so sorry,' Megan said in dismay. 'Surely she can't be serious about anyone else so soon.'

'Dear Megan, don't be sorry! At least not for me. I was a fool to allow myself to drift into an engagement with Natalie and I meant it when I said I'd had a lucky escape.' He turned and looked directly at Ruth for a moment. 'I'm glad I'm free to pursue my own desires.' Megan saw the glance, but it was so fleeting she was not sure whether Lint had meant anything by it. She did know that he was intrigued by Ruth's reluctance to be friends with him.

'Is there any reason why this – this Natalie shouldn't marry another doctor?' Ruth asked.

'No, no reason at all. He's done well in his profession,' Lindsey said. 'He lives life to the full and he's a perfect charmer where the ladies are concerned. As soon as he knew I was seeing Natalie he made a beeline for her. The thing is, he has three children aged eleven to fifteen.'

'Goodness me!' Megan exclaimed. 'Natalie is only twenty-three herself. She's the same age as me. So how old is he then?'

'Forty-one.' Lint shrugged. 'He never made any secret of the fact he'd like a young wife, but he doesn't want any more children. That will suit Natalie. She didn't mention the small fact that she had no intention of having any brats until after I bought her an engagement ring, of course. You could say that was the beginning of the end. We should have parted company even without her tantrum the night your mother was ill.'

'Is he a widower?'

'Divorced. The children are at boarding school, but they stay with him during the holidays. His wife married again. She lives abroad, apparently. Nevin lives life as though he's a wealthy man. I suspect that's more wishful thinking on his part, but Natalie seems impressed. Anyway, girls, that's the talking time over if we're to finish decorating by tomorrow afternoon. I'm back to work on Monday.'

'So am I,' Ruth said.

'And I've neglected Steven and Samuel often enough these past few weeks,' Megan said with remorse.

'I'm sure he'll forgive you when you look at him with those big green eyes.' Lint smiled. 'Don't you think so, Ruth?'

'Megan knows he will,' Ruth said stiffly.

'He'll not forgive us if we allow you to tire yourself out. Are you keeping well?'

'Of course I am. Don't you start fussing too, Lint, or I shall be wishing I'd never agreed to you coming to help us.'

'You knew?' Ruth said almost accusingly.

'I telephoned and asked Steven if it would be all right,' Lint said quickly. 'Isn't it all right?' he asked, widening his eyes innocently as he looked down at her. 'Would you have forbidden me to help?

'N–no, I suppose not,' Ruth said reluctantly. 'I'll make a start on painting the bathroom window to save you reaching over the basin, Megan.'

'Can you wait until I've painted the ceiling?' Lint asked. 'I'd hate to splash that beautiful glossy hair.' He grinned and reached out to stroke the swathe of Ruth's hair, but she stepped quickly out of reach and he raised his eyebrows and gave Megan a philosophical smile.

# Eight

The three of them passed a satisfying day and Lint made no further effort to flirt with Ruth, but as they finished work for the day he said, 'How about me taking the two of you for a meal somewhere?'

'I'm afraid I can't,' Megan said. 'I need to get back and relieve Steven's mother from the demands of my wee rascal.'

'What about you, Ruth? Will you take pity on a lonely bachelor?'

'Sorry.' Ruth shook her head. 'I have a child to claim, too. Anyway, I'm sure you're not lonely, except by your own choosing.'

'But I am,' Lint protested. 'I would enjoy your company and getting to know you better.' He sounded earnest and sincere and his grey eyes were serious as they rested on her face.

'There's nothing very interesting about me that you would want to hear. Anyway, Avril is always my first priority and she needs to go home.'

'Maybe another evening then and Avril can come too?'

Ruth's dark brows arched in surprise. She didn't know any man who would welcome a seven-year-old child on an evening out. Come to that, she didn't know many men, certainly none like Lindsey Gray, an up-and-coming young surgeon who appeared to have the world at his feet; yet he had spent his Saturday doing something as mundane as decorating.

She was quiet as Megan drove them back to Schoirhead. When she thought about it, she admitted how kind and patient Lindsey Gray was with Avril and how readily her daughter responded to him. A tiny corner of her frozen heart thawed a little towards him. She loved Avril more than anything in the world.

'We've made good progress today with Lint's help,' Megan said, breaking the silence. 'With luck, and his help tomorrow morning, we should be finished by two o'clock. Steven and Dad are coming up on Monday night to lay the bedroom carpet and they're going to have a go at laying new linoleum in the kitchen.'

'Great-Aunt Ruth used to say it was easier to lay linoleum if it was warm, so maybe they should leave it beside the Rayburn the night before.'

'I'll tell them that. Thanks, Ruth. I don't know how we shall ever repay you for all your help.'

'Oh Megan. You don't owe me anything. I appreciate your friendship, probably more than you realize. Your parents make me so welcome, too. I'm astonished that a man like Lindsey Gray should spend his weekend painting, though.'

'Are you, Ruth?' Megan's green eyes twinkled, but it was obvious that it didn't occur to Ruth she might be the attraction. Deep down she was a little worried that Lint might win Ruth's confidence enough to make her blossom like a flower to the sun, and then leave her fragile petals to wither and die when she was no longer a challenge. She sighed.

'That's a big sigh, Megan. Are you very tired?'

'No, not really, but I shall be glad to have more time with Steven and Samuel when all this is finished. It's only a month until Christmas. I hope you and Avril will join us at Schoirhead? Mother is talking about making Christmas dinner at Honeysuckle Cottage and combining it as a house-warming. They're both so thrilled to be owning a house of their own after years of living in tied cottages. I'm afraid it might be too much for Mother, but Dad seems quite keen. He's intending to decorate the sitting room himself before Christmas if the joiner turns up next week to put the new window in and renew the skirting boards. He's planning to buy Mum a wall-to-wall carpet.'

'I'm sure they'll both have reason to be proud of their new home,' Ruth said with a smile. 'If they've set their heart on it, please don't feel you have to include me. I do understand.'

'Mum wouldn't think of leaving you and Avril out any more than I would,' Megan assured her. 'If they really insist on having a house-warming cum Christmas, maybe I could prepare some of the food and take it up there.'

'That's a good idea,' Ruth said enthusiastically. 'I love cooking, so I wouldn't mind making the pudding and the soup, or some other kind of first course if you prefer. I have a good recipe for pâté. In fact I'd feel better about joining you all if I'm allowed to contribute'

'Thanks, Ruth. You're a gem. We'll play it by ear and see how things go and how they settle in, shall we?'

'All right, but your mother is not the only one who shouldn't be overdoing things,' Ruth said firmly. 'Even if we come to Schoirhead, I'd still like to make the pudding and the mince pies, and maybe something else as well.'

'You're a good friend,' Megan said with gratitude.

'I'm amazed how well you seem to keep. I was so sick and dreadfully tired in the early months when I was expecting Avril,' Ruth said. 'I wanted to die, I felt so awful.' Megan reached forward and patted her clenched hands.

'That was different. You must have been worried sick, and tense too which wouldn't help. Fred really does have a lot to answer for,' she said through gritted teeth. 'I hope he pays for his sins one day.'

Megan had a big washing day on Monday and she was deadly tired by night. She still felt lethargic the following morning, so she could have done without the shock of finding the new land agent on the step when she opened the door in response to a brisk knock.

'I am Fenton McMann from the Department.' He was a middle-aged man with a ruddy face and a pleasant smile. 'You must be . . .' he glanced at a clipboard, 'Mrs Caraford?'

'Yes, that's right. Please come in. Would you like a cup of coffee, then I will look for my husband?'

'I would appreciate a cup of coffee. It's a very cold morning but I don't want to trouble you. No doubt I shall find Mr Caraford around the buildings?'

'Yes, he's probably cleaning out the byre. If he's not there he will have gone to the field for a load of turnips. If he sees your car he will probably come to the house anyway,' Megan said, smiling.

'Do you get many callers?'

'The other smallholders often pop in if they're passing, especially recently while Mr McGuire has not been so well. They're all very friendly. Then there's always the sales representatives selling feed or fertilizer or machinery.'

'Not an easy task. Thank you, Mrs Caraford. These look delicious,' he said as Megan set down a plate of scones and another with her home-made ginger biscuits. She longed to run outside and warn Steven and make sure Joe had covered over the door into the McGuires' byre. She would have liked to warn Mrs McGuire he was here too, but at least he didn't look like the sharp-featured Mr Wilson. She had always thought he resembled a rat, but looks could be deceptive.

'I believe Mr Wilson has retired?' she remarked politely.

'Yes. He has not been keeping too well. Stomach ulcers, I believe.'

'Daddy here! Daddy here,' Samuel called excitedly from the scullery. 'Daddy, there's a man in there . . .' Steven grinned down at his small son and lifted him in his arms as he strode through to the kitchen, a smile still crinkling his blue eyes.

'Oh, good morning,' he said in surprise. 'I thought it must be Ned Jacobs from the feed merchants. I . . .'

'This is Mr McMann from the Department, Steven,' Megan said quickly. 'Do you want a cup of coffee?'

'Yes, why not?' Steven said easily. 'Thanks.' He was relaxed. Everything was in order as far as it was possible. He was proud of his small dairy herd these days and he ran his farm to the very best of his ability. The only concern was if the agent discovered he was also renting the McGuires' holding from them.

Fenton McMann enjoyed his job. He liked travelling around the countryside and he enjoyed meeting people. He was inspecting the rest of the Schoirhead smallholdings that day too, so it was the next day before he had a meeting with his boss, Mr Burrows. There were a few repairs to discuss for which some of the tenants had requested help, two alterations to buildings requiring written permission, and a comment about one of the holdings being untidy, with weeds growing around the stack-yard and the buildings not limewashed.

'There was an odd thing about the Schoirhead holding,' Fenton McMann mused when the rest had been discussed. 'It's by far the best farmed wee place – well, it and the one next door belonging to an elderly couple named McGuire. I didn't see Mr McGuire. His wife said he was ill. She was eager to show me her pigs and poultry, but she seemed a bit uneasy when we went to look around the buildings. I can't think why because they were all clean and tidy, but I did notice there was a door in their byre which appeared to open into the next-door byre. I hadn't noticed it from the Schoirhead side but there was a lot of hay piled in the corner.'

'I see.' Mr Burrows frowned thoughtfully. 'It was probably a double-sided byre which was divided down the middle when the original farm was converted to smallholdings after the Great War. Maybe they left a door?'

'Maybe. I did notice there were milking machine taps on the Carafords' side but not on the McGuires', and yet the cows all looked as though they belonged to the same herd – really good Ayrshires, all well groomed. Mind you, Mrs McGuire did say she had very good neighbours and they had helped a lot during her husband's illness. How much and what sort of help they give I don't know. The McGuires' dairy was dry and it didn't look to be in regular use, and yet all the stalls in their byre were filled with milking cows.'

'What about the fields? Are both holdings growing their quota of cereals?'

'Oh yes. They each had a ploughed field. A nice job too, with straight, well-turned furrows. Mrs McGuire told me Mr Caraford had a tractor and plough now so he had ploughed the field for her husband.'

'So you couldn't fault the running of either place?'

'Oh no, definitely not.'

'Well, that's the main thing, and the rent is paid on time. It will be some time before they're due another inspection and by then McGuire will either have recovered or retired, wouldn't you say?'

'Probably . . .'

'Meanwhile, we'll leave well alone. If Steven Caraford is farming the McGuire holding as well as his own, he must be happy to do it. The McGuires probably pay him for his help.'

'I doubt if they can afford to do that indefinitely on thirty acres. To tell the truth, I wondered whether there was a bit of subletting going on, but all the other smallholders had a good word of the Carafords. They're a pleasant young couple with a toddler and another on the way, I reckon.'

'I'll make a note of your comments and if things are still the same the next time you make an inspection you can enquire more deeply. Meanwhile, we shouldn't discourage young Caraford if he's making a good job of things. The country still needs as much home-produced food as we can manage.'

Christmas dinner was one of the happiest Megan could remember. She wouldn't have left Joe on his own, so she was pleased when Jimmy invited him to join the Kerr family.

'My cousin, Evelyn, is coming down for the day and Joe is sweet on her.' He grinned, winking at Steven.

Joe blushed, but he knew Jimmy well enough now to tease in return. 'And her friend Fiona?' he asked innocently. 'She stay at home, yes? So Jimmy very sad?'

'Oh, I expect Fiona will be coming with her,' Jimmy admitted.

'Of course she come.' Joe grinned. 'Jimmy makes good plans for Fiona.'

Megan, Hannah and Ruth had all contributed towards the food so that Chrissie only had to cook the goose and the trimmings. Chrissie had insisted on inviting Angus Paterson so that he could see how well his plans were working out, but Megan was surprised to find Lint had been invited too.

'Katherine wanted to spend Christmas with her parents, but she didn't want to leave the Tower unoccupied in case we get a hard frost,' he explained. 'I volunteered to stay for three nights while I'm off duty. Your father invited me to join the family party.'

'Well, laddie, you saved Chrissie's life. That's a Christmas present no amount o' money could buy,' John Oliphant said simply.

'We lead a simple life, Lindsey, but you'll always find a welcome here,' Chrissie said sincerely.

After dinner the men went through to the newly decorated sitting room where John added more logs to the fire until they were in danger of falling asleep as a result of warmth and too much good food. As soon as Lint heard the women approaching he gave a wicked smile and grasped a piece of mistletoe which he had discovered growing on an old apple tree in the Langton Tower orchard. Amidst a great deal of laughter he stood outside the door, refusing to let them by without a kiss.

'I think I'm a bit past being kissed by eligible young men.' Hannah laughed.

'Mmm, me too,' Chrissie said. 'All those young nurses would be fair jealous.'

Megan guessed his real target was Ruth, and she glanced at her friend clinging tightly to her small daughter's hand and hanging back.

Ruth knew her face had paled a little and she could feel her heart thumping. It's all in fun, don't be so ridiculous, she admonished herself, but it was no use. Avril giggled as she lifted her cherubic face to be kissed and Ruth would have slipped by.

'Oh no you don't!' Lint chuckled. He had kissed all the rest on the cheek, but he tilted her chin with his forefinger and brushed his lips lightly but slowly over her mouth. 'I shall look forward even more to the next time,' he said in a low voice. Admiration flared in his grey eyes as he watched the delicate pink which coloured her pale skin and the agitated rise and fall of her breasts beneath the red jersey dress which she had made especially for this occasion, never dreaming Lindsey Gray would be one of the guests. 'Red really suits you, Ruth, with your shining dark hair and creamy skin. You should wear it more often.'

Lint had already presented Chrissie with a beautiful bouquet of flowers and John with a bottle of malt whisky, but now he produced a gift for the two children. Avril's was a beautifully made rag doll with a complete set of exquisitely knitted garments, even to shoes and socks and a cloak and hat. The little girl threw her arms around his neck and hugged him exuberantly.

'I asked Santa if I could have a daddy like Samuel's for Christmas,' she said, 'but you're even better.' Lint glanced up and saw the horror in Ruth's eyes and the way the colour drained from her cheeks, but Samuel wanted to hug him too as he clutched his hand-made horse and cart.

'They're lovely gifts, Lint,' Megan said. 'Where did you find them?'

'My favourite lady friend got them for me.' He grinned. 'She's an old lady in her seventies but she's always busy. She and her friends make toys to raise funds for one of the charities at the hospital.'

Steven and Megan needed to be back in time for milking, so they were preparing to leave about half past three.

'The daylight is beginning to fade already,' Chrissie sighed, 'but at least we've passed the shortest day now.'

'Aye,' John Oliphant agreed as he gave his wee grandson another

hug before passing him into Steven's arms to carry to the van.
'I'm glad I've no cows to milk tonight.'

'We'll give you a couple of weeks, Dad, and I'll bet you'll be
longing for them again.' Megan chuckled at her mother's expression of dismay.

'Oh I do hope he'll not miss them so soon,' she said seriously.

'No, no.' John grinned down at her and pulled her close to drop
a kiss on her cheek. 'I've other things demanding my attention
these days. I mean to make the most of it. Drive carefully and safe
home, you two.'

As they drove along the narrow roads, Samuel suddenly sat up
straighter on Megan's knee. 'Man,' he said, ''nother funny man.'

'It's a tramp,' Megan said. 'Since we've been coming up to
Honeysuckle Cottage I've seen him walking on this road several
times. He must keep to a certain area, I think, but isn't it awful
to think he's out there and all alone on Christmas Day.'

'Shall we offer him a lift in the back of the van?' Steven asked.
'He must have places where he finds shelter.' He drew to a halt
beside the shuffling man in his long coat and battered hat. It was
hard to tell how old he was, but he had a long grey beard and
straggly grey hair peeping from beneath his old trilby.

'If you'd like to hop in the back we'll give you a lift,' Steven
said. 'I think it's coming on wet.'

'No thank ye, sir. Not going far tonight.'

'All right, if you're sure.' Steven felt in his pocket and held out
half a crown. He tossed it to the man. 'It's Christmas.'

'I thank ye kindly, young sir.' The tramp tucked the money
into one of his deep pockets.

'Mum made us a parcel of food to bring home. Wait a minute,
Steven. I'll give him the goose's leg and a couple of mince pies.'
Megan gathered the food from the basket at her feet and Steven
passed them through his window. The man took them gratefully
and Megan wondered whether she had glimpsed tears in his eyes
or whether they were naturally bright and watery.

'Blessings on you and yours,' the man said gruffly. 'May good
fortune go with ye all.' He stepped back on to the grass verge
to allow Steven to drive on.

Joe arrived back at Schoirhead as they drove into the yard.

'Hello, Joe, just in time for the milking,' Steven greeted him.

'That's a good fellow. I thought that lady friend o' yours might keep you late.' He grinned.

'Oh no. She know the cows are first of my work. Must be done.'

'Would you like a drink of tea and a mince pie before we start the milking then, Joe?' Megan asked.

'No thank you, Mrs Megan.' Joe blushed. 'I do work and then go back. Mrs Kerr says I go for tea tonight.'

'Ah.' Steven grinned. 'Does that mean the lovely Evelyn is still there?'

'Yes, she wait for me to take her to home. I buy motorbike yesterday. Jimmy get it for me.' He beamed at Steven, obviously well pleased with life.

Megan had felt rather guilty at leaving the McGuires on their own on Christmas Day. As a compromise she had suggested the previous day that she would keep Samuel up later and go round there for Christmas tea. Mrs McGuire was delighted at the idea.

'I'll bring a trifle and some cold chicken,' she said.

'That will be grand, lassie. McGuire will be pleased to see you and have a chat with Steven and see the wee fellow open his present. I've made a cake and iced it and he'll like to see my wee robin and the snowmen. I've some roast ham and we'll have some pickles and . . .'

'You don't need to make anything, Mrs M,' Megan admonished. 'We shall probably still be full of Christmas dinner anyway and I don't want you to go to any trouble.'

'It'll be a pleasure, lassie, a real pleasure.'

After tea it was obvious that Samuel was getting tired after his exciting day. 'We'll get you into your pyjamas,' Megan said, 'then you can show Mr McGuire your new slippers and your lovely long dressing gown.' Samuel agreed readily as the new dressing gown was a novelty. When he had it on he paraded around for everyone to see.

'Look like man,' he said, 'the funny man.'

'Oh, he means the tramp in his long coat,' Megan explained. 'We passed him on the way home. I've seen him a few times lately.'

'Have you?' Mrs McGuire said. 'I wonder if he's the same one that we used to see. He came quite regularly along this road.

I suppose he knew he'd find a place to sleep in some of the buildings, and some folk said he slept outside on the shore in the summertime. He slept in the McKies' loft more than once. McKie didna mind, he was a kindly man. That was before your time, of course, Steven. After he died Mrs McKie was nervous about staying in the house on her own, and one morning when she got up she found the tramp asleep in one o' the stalls in the byre. She went hysterical. After that she couldna wait to move out. We've never seen the tramp round here since then.'

Samuel fell asleep on Megan's knee, and a little while later Steven carried him home to bed. Neither they, nor the McGuires, could have guessed the chain of events that their next sight of the tramp would set in motion.

# Nine

John Oliphant enjoyed the challenges of renovating Honeysuckle Cottage and his work at Langton Tower. Getting the Tower grounds into order would be an ongoing task, but the large walled garden and the glasshouse were the first priority as far as Katherine was concerned. She hoped to open her hotel restaurant in a year's time and she wanted as much fresh produce as possible. Apart from thirty acres of neglected woodland, there were still several acres of parkland which had escaped the plough during the war due to some ancient oak trees dotted here and there, and two small paddocks, plus the fruit orchard leading off the walled garden.

'I'm not surprised Lindsey Gray spends most of his time up here when he can get away from the hospital,' John Oliphant said. 'It's a beautiful place to work. The Palmer-Farrs think they're almost paupers because the farms were sold off by the last generation.' He shook his head wryly. 'There's a lot more ground than they realize. I've no fear of running out of work.'

Apart from his work at the Tower, he looked forward to changing his own garden from the two long strips with a dividing path to broad sections with curves and borders. He still kept in touch with his beloved cows by doing relief milking once a month for an elderly farmer called Geordie Samson whom he had known since he was a boy. One of Geordie's fields shared a boundary with one of the Martinwold fields. Once it became known in the district that he did relief milking, he could have had work every weekend, and more, but he had resolved that he and Chrissie should spend more time together.

The only cloud in their sky was the memory of their only son, Sammy, and nothing could change the past or bring him back. Otherwise they were happier than they had ever dared to hope a few months earlier, when Chrissie lay unconscious in hospital.

At Schoirhead Megan was feeling cumbersome as the time drew near for the birth of her second baby.

'It's ridiculous having a milking machine in one byre and still milking by hand in the McGuires' byre,' Steven said irritably one evening. 'Joe and I will miss you when you're having the baby, Megan.'

'I know. It seems strange that Joe is able to milk with the machine and yet he's never managed the hand-milking. I'm afraid you'll have to milk those yourself, Steven.'

'I've been thinking about that. We shall probably be at the turnip hoeing, too. I've decided to continue the vacuum line through to the McGuires' byre and have the vacuum pump operating both. Jimmy Kerr said he would help me fix up the line.'

'Does he know our arrangement with the McGuires then?'

'We've never talked about it, but he must guess the cows are ours. Jimmy willna gossip, though.'

'What if the land agent notices the milking machine pipes?' Megan asked anxiously.

'We'll have to risk it. There's no reason why the McGuires shouldn't have a milking machine anyway. Nearly everybody has one these days and we're not doing any harm putting the pipes through the wall and installing the line and taps.'

'I suppose not,' Megan said slowly.

'Think how much quicker and easier it will be, especially when you have the baby. I hope it's not going to be too much for you, Meggie? All the work you do outside as well as two infants to look after.'

'Of course not. My mother managed when Sam and I were little. It's only the land agent that bothers me. He seemed a nice man, but he does have a job to do and we all know we're breaking the terms of the tenancy.'

It was a sad day for the nation when news came over the radio that King George VI had died in his sleep. Princess Elizabeth was summoned home from her visit to Africa and proclaimed Queen Elizabeth II. Although she felt saddened by the news and deeply sorry for the young Princess and her husband, Megan was dismayed at the depressing effect the news seemed to have on Annie McGuire.

'Such a brave, good man he was, stepping into his brother's shoes, and then the war coming and him staying in London,' she mourned. 'And his poor lassie. She's too young to shoulder such a heavy burden.'

Megan murmured what comforting words she could, but she was relieved when Steven's mother came to lunch the following day and the two older women were able to commiserate and reminisce together.

In May 1952 both Chrissie and John Oliphant were overjoyed when Samuel came to stay with them for two whole weeks while Megan gave birth to a baby daughter. They had considered all sorts of names, but in the end it was Steven who suggested Christianna – a combination of the names of both her grandmothers.

'We don't want to offend either of them,' he said, 'especially when they have both been so good at helping us. Even if we have more children there's no guarantee we shall have another wee girl, is there?'

'No,' Megan said solemnly, hiding a smile, 'no guarantee at all.'

Samuel was unable to pronounce Christianna when his Granny Oliphant tried to explain about his baby sister and her name. 'Tania, Tania,' he chanted.

Avril was thrilled when Ruth brought her to Schoirhead to see the new baby for the first time.

'What shall we call her?' she asked, wide eyed, as the baby's tiny fingers curled round one of hers.

'We shall christen her Christianna,' Megan explained, 'but Samuel can't say that yet. He is calling her Tania. I wouldn't be surprised if that's what she becomes.'

'That's the name of the fairy queen, isn't it, Mummy?' Avril asked excitedly.

'She was Titania in the story I told you.' Ruth smiled. 'She was the wife of Oberon.'

'But there is a Tania in one of Shakespeare's plays, I think, now you mention it,' Megan said slowly. 'I hadn't thought of that. Wasn't she a Russian fairy queen or something.'

'I believe you're right. In Midsummer Night's Dream.'

'I shall think of our new baby as the queen of the fairies,' Avril announced, clapping her hands gleefully. Over her head Megan and Ruth smiled at each other, but Ruth raised her eyebrows and mouthed 'our' new baby?

Megan nodded, smiling. 'I'm glad this wee one is being accepted so happily. Samuel will follow Avril's example. Incidentally, has Lint asked you to go with him to the Theatre Royal next weekend?'

'He did ask.' Ruth's colour rose.

'And?' Megan prompted.

'I, er . . . I said I couldn't go.'

'Oh Ruth,' Megan said, her tone full of disappointment. 'I'm sure you would have enjoyed it and I'm certain Lint would be a perfect gentleman in your company.'

'I–I know. He's very pleasant company, b–but I'm just not ready for any sort of commitment or relationship, or – or anything. I don't think I shall ever be at ease with any man,' she said unhappily, and Megan knew there was nothing she could say.

When Chrissie brought Samuel home to Schoirhead he poked curiously at the tiny bundle lying in her crib, but otherwise he didn't show much interest in acquiring a baby sister. Then she began to cry and his lower lip trembled; he was on the verge of tears himself. Megan tried to explain it was only a baby's way of letting them know she was hungry or wet, or had a wee pain, but he demanded she must have immediate attention. It was to set the pattern for the rest of their lives, with Samuel the protective older brother whenever he thought Tania needed anything, and sometimes when she didn't.

The remainder of the year seemed to pass at lightning speed. Joe had purchased a larger motorbike and he and Jimmy Kerr spent most Saturday nights taking out Jimmy's cousin and her friend.

'You seem to be getting serious about Evelyn, Joe?' Steven remarked as the young man polished his shoes until they mirrored his face.

'Yes.' Joe hesitated, although he spoke quite well since Ruth had undertaken to teach him to read and write in English. 'I would like her to be my wife,' he said at last. 'We are saving money.' He looked unhappily at Steven. 'I do not want to leave my work here with you, but . . .' he shrugged, 'Evelyn says I shall have to try for new work so we can get a house from a council.'

'Aah, Joe. We should be sorry to see you go,' Steven said sincerely. 'I don't know much about getting council houses. I think you put your name on a waiting list.'

'We agree we wait eighteen months more and keep saving money.' He shrugged again. 'I want Evelyn very much for my wife, but I do not like to work in a factory.'

'What do Evelyn's parents think about it?'

'I believe her mother think I am not . . .' He frowned. 'Not good, not rich enough. Her father works on a farm. He is good with me. He says we should get a job on another farm with a cottage for us to live.'

'I see . . .' Steven said slowly. He sighed. 'Well, nothing stays the same forever, Joe. I'm sorry I can't help you, though.'

'I know. Mr Smith says you cannot get a cottage for me.'

'Evelyn's father?'

'Yes. He says this farm is too small for you to have a cottage. He understands I like to be here.'

'Eighteen months is quite a while, Joe. Something will turn up,' Steven assured him.

When Tania was a year old Steven's mother came for the day and Megan's parents joined them for her birthday tea. Ruth had promised to bring Avril after school and look after the children while Megan was helping with the milking. Amazingly, Mr McGuire had also agreed to come if Steven would lift him round in the van. His doctor had retired and the new doctor had prescribed different pills. Although he would never be free from pain, he was able to hobble around the house again. Annie McGuire loved company, but she had never liked leaving him alone so she was delighted they could both join the birthday party. It was more a gathering for the adults since Tania was too young to understand, but Annie McGuire spoiled the children at every opportunity. She was continually knitting jumpers for Samuel or tiny cardigans for Tania. She also insisted on saving her sweet ration to buy them treats.

'It's such a shame things are still on ration, even if they are a bit easier,' she lamented. 'I wonder if they'll ever see selection boxes like we used to get before the war, or the big boxes of chocolates tied up with ribbon. I remember when we were courting Ted used to buy me a big box of chocolates for my birthday.'

Megan was always relieved when Hannah was there to hear these reminiscences, as she had so little time to sit and listen with two children to watch over and her work to do. Tania had learned to walk at ten months and she was a lively child, never content to sit in the pram for long, as Samuel had done. It had been Chrissie's idea to celebrate Tania's first birthday. She had regained her strength and much of her old vitality. Megan was thankful she had made a full recovery, but she was short of time and energy herself these days. She didn't want to disappoint either of Tania's grandparents, but it was a big effort to prepare for a family gathering. Years later when she looked back she was glad she had summoned the energy and made everyone welcome. It had been such a happy day, and none of them could have guessed at the changes that lay ahead.

John Oliphant was also pleased by his wife's return to health and her enthusiasm for her new garden. She had taken over the care of the poultry and the few pigs which were now at Langton Tower. She got on well with Katherine Palmer-Farr, who constantly asked questions in her eagerness to learn more about country life and the care of the animals.

Megan was surprised when her father arrived at Schoirhead only a few days after the birthday party.

'I passed that tramp fellow on the road today,' he remarked. 'I haven't seen him around for ages. He wasn't all that far from here.'

'I haven't seen him much either,' Megan said, 'but you didn't come to talk about the tramp. Is Mum all right?'

'Yes, she's fine. Good as new, she says. Did you hear Hannah saying she has ordered a television so that she can watch the Queen's Coronation?' he asked.

'Yes, I thought Mrs McGuire looked quite wistful, but she said they couldn't afford one. She's a great royalist, you know.'

'So is your mother. I've been thinking I might buy her a television for an early birthday present. If I could get it now she could watch the Coronation too. What do you think, Meggie?'

'Gosh, can you afford one, Dad? I–I mean after buying the house and everything . . .'

'Aye, I wouldna think of it if I didna have the money, and your mother would be the first to say we've spent enough after buying the house. It didn't cost as much as I'd expected, thanks to

Mr Paterson. Anyway, I want it to be a surprise. I'll not tell her until it's delivered.' He grinned like a small boy, reminding Megan of Samuel, and of how her brother Sammy used to look.

'Well you'll have to hurry up then. It said on the radio that thousands of new televisions have been sold ready for the Coronation. Jimmy Kerr says his firm have sold ever so many in Annan. If you really want one you should mention it to him. He said they were expecting another consignment, but it would be the last for a while. Mind you, it's not his department. He's in charge of the mechanics but he knows the manager of the shop. I'm sure he'd put in a word.'

'That's a good idea, lassie. I suppose you wouldn't ask him for me? You'll see him before I do.'

'All right. Steven's mother has asked me to go down there for the day to watch. Avril will have a day off school so she will help keep my two rascals occupied. Steven says he can't afford to spend the day watching crowds of people on a wee screen.' She pulled a face. 'We shall be back in time for milking.'

'Aye, there's always another job waiting to be done and he works hard. Your mother will be disappointed you can't come up to us, though. Lindsey is on call that day too, but he said he didn't mind. The Palmer-Farrs have got a TV and he thought he might come up in the evening and watch the newsreels.'

'He does spend a lot of time with them, doesn't he? Do you think he has any regrets about splitting up with Natalie Turner?'

'He knows he's had a lucky escape, I reckon. The Palmer-Farrs have given him his own room and a bathroom and they leave it ready for him now, but he does a lot of odd jobs for them. He seems to like pottering about and mending things. He's a clever fellow.'

'I'm sure he is, but he must be lonely sometimes.'

'Well he's better off with no wife than the wrong one. He says Natalie has fixed the wedding date to that other doctor. Mr Turner willna be pleased about that. You know I do the relief milking for old Mr Samson? He was—'

'I certainly do.' Megan laughed. 'Mum says you're there three weekends out of four lately.'

'He hasna been keeping so fit recently. His wife died last year and he misses her. He was telling me Mr Turner had called in to see him and he's furious with Natalie for wanting to marry a divorced man, especially when he already has a teenage family.'

'I gather Lint doesn't have much of an opinion of him either,' Megan said slowly, 'but I suppose Natalie knows what she's doing.'

'Well, if she makes her bed she'll have to lie in it. She always did like her own way. I doubt if she knows how to love anybody but herself.'

The day of the Coronation was bitterly cold, but Hannah had made a large pot of soup and plenty of sandwiches and Ruth had baked sausage rolls. Megan took buttered scones and a ginger-bread for afternoon tea. Angus Paterson joined them, but Megan suspected it was as much for the company as for the television. After lunch he seemed as pleased as the children to get out into the fresh air. He pushed Tania in her pram while Avril and Samuel skipped along beside him. This was a great relief as two other elderly neighbours had also come to see the Coronation and they kept telling the children to hush.

After that the summer and autumn seemed to fly by for Megan and Steven. They tried to visit one or other of the grandparents on Sundays, but sometimes it was easier to invite them all to Schoirhead, especially as the days grew shorter. It meant they didn't need to rush home to milk and feed their animals. Ruth and Avril always joined the family gatherings and Steven welcomed them as part of the family now. Sometimes Lindsey Gray came with Megan's parents if he happened to be staying at the Tower for the weekend. Megan knew he had asked Ruth out several times to various functions, but she always managed to find an excuse, and yet the two of them seemed to get on so well in company.

'They look so at ease together,' Megan said to Hannah as they watched them chatting together in the farmyard.

'Yes.' Hannah sighed heavily. 'Ruth is a lovely person. She deserves happiness, but she doesn't seem able to feel at ease alone with any man, even Lindsey. He's so good with Avril, too.'

'Yes, and they have a lot in common. They enjoy the same kind of books and music. They both like living in the country.'

'Yes, but there's nothing we can do about it. Ruth will have to work things out for herself. She appreciates your friendship very much, Megan. You've been very kind to her.'

'I like Ruth and she's helped me a lot when I've needed her, when Mum was in hospital and when Christianna was born.'

'I know. She's like one of the family. If only Fred had been more like Steven. I shall always wonder where I went wrong with him; why he became so jealous and so spiteful.'

'I don't think there's anything anyone could have done if that's the way nature made him,' Megan said gently. 'Do you ever hear from him? Does he keep in touch with anyone round here?'

'I don't think so. When I look back he never seemed to have many friends, even at school. It's a terrible thing to say, I know, but for Ruth's sake I hope he never returns.'

The Christmas celebrations were more lavish than usual that year because rationing had ended for everything except meat, and that didn't affect Megan and Steven much with their own poultry and ham.

Joe celebrated by buying Evelyn a neat little engagement ring with a single diamond. 'We'd like to get married at the end of May,' he told them shyly. 'I must look for a new job on a farm with a cottage and that makes me not happy.'

'You'll not be sad for long, Joe.' Megan smiled. 'We wish you both every happiness and if we hear of anyone wanting a general worker, we'll tell you, won't we, Steven?'

'Of course we will.' Steven clapped him on the back. 'But we shall miss you.'

It was a cold, wet morning in January, but Annie McGuire had been an early riser and a hard worker all her life and she liked to get her outdoor jobs done before McGuire got up. The weather had made his aches and pains worse and he needed help again. The doctor had told her to let him sleep whenever he could. He had warned her his heart was not so good and that made him more tired. Hard work had never worried Annie, but she hated to see Ted in pain and in low spirits. She pulled on her old coat and tied a scarf around her head against the biting wind and rain.

Even the hens were reluctant to venture out of their huts on such a day. Annie decided to bed their nests with fresh straw. Since they no longer had their own horse, Steven had used the stalls in the stable for rearing his young heifer calves, and he always kept a pile of hay and straw beneath the stairs into the loft. He had told her to use whatever she needed for her nest boxes. She made her way across the yard, head down against the buffeting wind. She paused as she passed the wee calves in their pens and stopped to stroke one who had poked her head through the temporary gates which Steven had erected. She loved all animals. She sighed and moved to the end of the stable and reached down to clutch a bundle of straw. As she lifted it she uncovered a face. She screamed in shock. It was the elderly tramp, stiff and cold in death.

She jerked back, gasping, and turned to run for help. If she had been thinking clearly she would have realized there was no hurry; the man was long past aid. But she was still in shock and in her haste her foot slipped on one of the smooth granite sets which made up the stable floor. She fell heavily. Her hip cracked as she hit the unyielding stone and the excruciating pain almost made her faint. She lay motionless, fighting down nausea.

# Ten

Annie McGuire called feebly for help, but the noise of the wind drowned her cries. Steven and Megan had finished milking and gone in for breakfast, and she lay there fighting the threatening nausea. Moving was impossible. Even breathing seemed to make the pain worse. She was aware of the dead body of the tramp lying a few feet away. She had never been afraid of him when he was alive, so why should she feel so troubled now? The poor man had probably been too weak to climb the ladder to the hayloft above. Maybe he had died of cold on the hard stable floor, burrowing beneath the small pile of hay for warmth. I could do with some of it myself, she thought, or that's what will happen to me if I don't get help soon. She made an effort to call out again, and again, but her head slumped back as faintness overwhelmed her. She was floating and the beams above her seemed to be swaying. Would Ted be awake now? Would he miss her? Would he alert someone? Gradually, the pain seemed to recede, as did the stable and the calves and everything around her.

Ted McGuire had slept late. He glanced at the clock for the fourth time then struggled into his trousers. The effort and the pain exhausted him. Had Annie forgotten he'd had no breakfast? She liked him to stay in bed until she'd got some of her work done, but this was ridiculous. Where could she be? The clock ticked away the minutes . . . the quarter-hour, the half-hour. Irritably he grasped his two sticks and hauled himself on to his feet. He hobbled towards the hall and the phone and sank on to the chair. Fumbling awkwardly he telephoned Megan. She answered almost at once.

'No, I haven't seen Mrs McGuire this morning,' she said. 'It's terribly wet and cold outside. Are you sure she's not upstairs?' Megan knew they had made their sitting room into a bedroom since Mr McGuire found it impossible to climb the stairs, but his wife still stored her clothes and bedding upstairs.

'No, I've shouted for her. I havena had any breakfast and the fire has gone out.'

'I'll go and look for her. Don't you worry.' But Megan felt alarmed. Annie McGuire never neglected her husband. She bundled the children into coats and boots and hats, knowing they would hold her back, but knowing she dare not leave them alone in the house. She grabbed her own coat and scarf, tying it as she went. She searched the next door's hen houses and the pigsties, but there was no sign of Annie McGuire. Tania was perched on her hip and Samuel whined about the cold as he followed them. She was making her way back to their own yard to shout for Steven when she met him and Shandy coming through the orchard.

It was Shandy who found Annie McGuire lying on the stable floor. She was unconscious and he stood at the door barking furiously for attention.

'Keep the children in the house, Megan. Telephone for the doctor,' Steven called. She knew by his urgent tone that something was very wrong. 'Tell him Mrs McGuire has had a fall. She's unconscious. Ask Joe to bring a blanket.'

Shandy sniffed around the pile of hay, scratching it away. His short, sharp barks caught Steven's attention. He gasped in astonishment when he recognized the body of the tramp.

The doctor arrived quicker than Megan had dared to hope. She hadn't telephoned Mr McGuire. She didn't know what to tell him until they knew how badly Annie McGuire was hurt. His heart was not so good and she didn't want to alarm him. The doctor came to telephone for an ambulance.

'I'll go round and explain to Mr McGuire myself,' he said. 'He's not fit to be left on his own. I will try to arrange a bed for him too until we see how things go with Mrs McGuire. I'm fairly certain she has broken her hip and she is severely chilled. Perhaps you would telephone the police? They need to be notified about the tramp's body.'

'The tramp?' Megan echoed incredulously.

'Yes, he's lying in the hay. I'd say he's been dead some hours. Possibly the discovery gave Mrs McGuire a shock. She must have fallen in her haste to get outside.'

Megan thought the new doctor might be clever, but she felt his manner was cold and abrupt. She called Joe to keep an eye on the children while she went to pack some things for Mrs McGuire to take to hospital. She followed the doctor round to the house and was in time to hear him explaining that Mrs McGuire had had a fall.

'A fall? Annie? Help her inside then, man!'

'I have sent for an ambulance. She's unconscious and severely chilled. She's probably broken her hip. We shall be lucky if she doesn't get pneumonia.'

'The doctor didn't seem to notice how white Mr McGuire had gone,' Megan told Steven later. 'He didn't even pay attention when the poor man clutched his chest. He made the strangest noise, like a wail and a sob. "Oh Annie! My Annie . . . " he gasped. Then he slumped against the wall. The doctor said it was a heart attack and he would never have realized what was wrong. He was so cold about it. B–but it – it w–was awful.'

'You're in shock yourself, Meggie,' Steven said with concern. 'I'm glad my mother has volunteered to go to the hospital instead of you.'

'Yes, so am I. I knew we couldn't leave Annie all alone, especially now. She'll be terribly upset.'

'My mother is older and they'd become good friends. She'll know how to break the news of Mr McGuire's death. Come on, I'll make you a cup of sweet tea and lace it with brandy. It's supposed to be good for shock. The police are still in the stable with the tramp's body, poor old fellow.'

Ten days later, Megan took the children to stay with her mother. John Oliphant accompanied her and Steven to the double funeral of Annie and Ted McGuire. It was held in their home. All the other smallholders were there, and Tom Green, the young haulier who was their only living relative.

'The sister at the hospital said she didn't think Aunt Annie had really taken in what had happened to Uncle Ted,' he said. 'She was on medication for the pain and then the pneumonia set in.'

'It's hard, but perhaps it's for the best,' Hannah Caraford said comfortingly.

Megan had helped Tom Green's wife remove the bed from the McGuires' living room and tidy the house ready for the mourners, as Annie McGuire would have wanted. They had made plates of sandwiches for when the men returned from following the coffin to the cemetery, and Hannah had brought two fruit loaves and some scones.

'I believe it is how they would have wanted it,' she said, 'a simple service in their own home. Annie told me what a nice funeral Mr McKie had had with all the neighbours present.'

'Well I'm sure you would know better than we do,' Tom Green said. 'We didn't see much of them. You always think folk will go on forever. I knew Great-Uncle Ted was not well, of course, but I never dreamt of anything like this. I don't know how to thank Steven and Megan for all they've done.'

'No thanks needed,' Steven said. 'They were kind to me from the day I came here and they've been grand neighbours.'

Megan and Steven had always been aware of the consequences if anything happened to Mr McGuire, but it took some time for things to sink in. Tom Green came down a week after the funerals.

'I shall need to empty their house,' he said dully. 'If there's anything you want, help yourselves. My wife doesn't want anything at all. She doesna like old-fashioned furniture and we've no room anyway. They made a will years ago, long before you two came to Schoirhead – not that they'd anything much to leave, but I was the only younger relative they had. If Aunt Annie had guessed this might happen she'd have left everything to you two. Whenever I saw her she told me you were like a son and a daughter to her.'

'We only did what neighbours do,' Steven said.

'Samuel can't understand why they're not here any more,' Megan said. 'They were so good to him and Tania, and Shandy is almost as lost.'

'The poultry and the pigs are no use to me, so I'd be glad if you'd take them over, and anything else there is about the farm you can use. I've notified the Department of Agriculture what has happened.'

'Yes, of course,' Steven said.

'The man I saw was called McMann. He said his boss was in hospital having a gall bladder operation, but he would come down to see you himself to ask you to keep an eye on things until they find a new tenant. I've to let them know when the house and the buildings are cleared.'

Steven nodded. He felt sick at heart. He had had a bad start at Schoirhead due to Fred spitefully sending him diseased cattle, but he had weathered the storm and built up a small herd of cows from his father's Willowburn stock. Now half of them would have to be sold. They had as many pigs and poultry as they had room for once they were reduced to their own holding again, but Steven thanked Tom Green and said he would sort out everything next door. Megan knew how despondent he felt. She cradled him tenderly in her arms when they went to bed each night, seeking and finding comfort together in their love for each other.

'I think I'll go up and see Mr Griffiths before I start selling off the cows,' Steven said a few mornings after Tom Green's visit. 'He was the land agent for Willowburn when my father was alive. I could ask him whether he has any farms coming to let on the estate.'

'That would be a good idea,' Megan said, relieved to hear Steven sounding more positive, but they both knew they had to prepare for changes and it was hard to be optimistic.

Chrissie and John Oliphant worried too. They loved Steven like a son. They knew how hard he worked, how proud he was of his cattle. They understood that selling half their milking cows would mean they had only half the income coming in from milk, and they had two children to keep now.

'I suppose Megan could always go back to teaching when Samuel starts school, if things get too bad,' Chrissie said slowly, 'but she would need someone to look after Tania, and I don't think she will want to do that.'

'No love, but there's no use you worrying,' John said. 'They're young and they love each other. They'll pull through. Life's full of ups and downs. Even the Turners of this world don't get things all their own way. Natalie has married that doctor fellow and according to Geordie Samson, Mr Turner detests him. He thinks he's married Natalie for her money.'

'I know you're trying to take my mind off Megan.' Chrissie smiled wryly. 'I didn't realize Mr Turner was such good friends with his neighbour.'

'He calls in to chat with Geordie regularly since the old man lost his wife. He and the Samsons always got on all right as neighbours, even though Bengairney is an estate farm. Geordie was telling me he was born at Bengairney and he remembers the Turners buying Martinwold when they got married.'

Mr McMann, the land agent, came to see Steven on a cold day at the beginning of February. Megan invited him in for a cup of coffee and Steven joined them a few minutes later.

'I have been next door and I see the house is empty and everything is clean and tidy as usual.'

'Yes, and I've drained the water in case of frost,' Steven said. He sighed heavily. He and Megan had had endless discussions. Mr Griffiths had no word of any farms coming up to let on the estate, but he had promised to ask the two land agents he knew well. He had suggested Steven should try to rent some summer grazing rather than sell off his cows, but they both knew that was only putting off the evil hour until the grazing ended in November, unless there were prospects of another farm.

'I may as well tell you, Mr McMann,' Steven said reluctantly, 'Mr McGuire has not been well enough to farm for some time, but he didn't want to leave his holding.'

'They both told me what good neighbours you two were.'

'No.' Steven shook his head. 'We benefited as much as they did, but we both knew we were contravening the terms of the tenancy. I farmed most of the land and used the buildings and I paid the rent to the McGuires. They paid their rent to the Department as usual. We both took a risk.'

'Yes.' Mr McMann nodded, but there was a twinkle in his eye. 'I suspected something like that, but you seem to have made a good impression on my boss, Mr Caraford. He said we should leave things as they are so long as the McGuires paid the rent and the holding was being well farmed. Mr Burrows is still off work, but he's out of hospital and getting on fine. I went up to see him before I came today. He suggests you continue as you are until the May term, the twenty-eighth.'

Steven looked troubled. 'I shall need to reduce my milking cows then,' he said. 'If they have to go I'd be better to sell the older cows as they calve, rather than wait until they're looking stale and be forced to sell them at any price.'

'We hadn't considered that. Mr Burrows thought you might bid for some seasonal grazing to keep them a bit longer in case something else came up, although we're not expecting any larger holdings to fall vacant.'

'That's more or less what my father's land agent advised, but there's no prospects there either. The estate are letting the Home Farm for summer grazing this year for the first time. When the new tenant moves in next door I shall only have stalls for eight cows. We have been using the McGuires' byre, you see.'

'I noticed it was still full of cows. You installed the milking machine line?'

'Yes.' Steven flushed guiltily. 'I'm sorry we didn't get permission.'

Mr McMann nodded. 'At least you've shown some initiative, and that was the original reason for creating these holdings, to give young men a start in farming. I'm afraid I must leave the decisions to you. If we leave Number Two Holding in your care until the end of May, will you guarantee to farm it as you have been doing? The incoming tenant will pay you full valuation for seeds, fertilizer and cultivations. Please keep a record and invoices. Any remaining stocks of hay and straw will be paid for by the incoming tenant, of course.'

'Yes, I can do that,' Steven agreed. It was what he had done for the past three years, except now there was no future for the freshly sown crops, and no benefit from the pasture he had ploughed and reseeded. He wondered how he would get on with the new tenant, whoever he turned out to be.

The year of 1954 had begun badly, and both Megan and Steven felt it was only getting worse as time went on. Joe had got the chance of work on a farm near Lockerbie, but he needed to start at the end of March instead of waiting until May. It had a tied cottage, and Evelyn was eager to get married and set up house, but Joe knew Steven had been expecting him to stay until the new tenant moved in next door.

'You'd better take it while you get the chance, Joe,' Steven said wearily. 'It seems workers move at any time of year these days. They don't stick to the term days any more.'

'But you will have much work until the cows go to grass,' Joe said anxiously, 'and then all the buildings to clean and limewash.'

'You have to seize the opportunity when it comes, Joe. Remember we have a milking machine now. We'll manage.

After the end of May I shall only have eight cows again so I shall not be able to afford to pay a man anyway when I have a wife and two wee bairns.'

So Joe and Evelyn arranged a small wedding at the end of March. They planned to have two nights away and then return to their own cottage. Megan and Steven were invited so Chrissie looked after the children and John Oliphant offered to do the milking so they needn't hurry home.

As things turned out they were pleased to come home early. Evelyn's mother was clearly displeased at her daughter marrying Joe. She kept referring to him as 'that German'. Megan had to bite her tongue several times when she heard her disparaging tone, but she was not feeling well and she had to concentrate on forcing down a few mouthfuls of the cold meat and salad which had been provided for the guests. Joe and Evelyn were oblivious to the undercurrents and Megan was thankful for that.

It was Steven who was provoked into defending Joe. 'He's a kind and thoughtful young man and a grand worker. He's honest and thrifty. What more could you ask?'

'Nothing, lad. He's a fine young fellow,' Evelyn's father boomed, cutting short his wife's indignant reply. 'I'm sure they'll get on all right when they settle in to their own wee hoose.'

'Let's go home,' Megan said wearily.

'You don't look well, Meggie,' Steven said, looking at her keenly on the drive home. 'You haven't looked so good for a couple of weeks. I hope you're not worrying about things? We shall still have thirty acres and that's all we had when we began. We'll manage so long as we have each other.' They were using John Oliphant's car, and he pulled into the side of the road and drew her into his arms, kissing her tenderly, and then with increasing passion as he felt her response. Suddenly she jerked away and scrambled out of the car. He stared after her in dismay, then he realized she was being violently sick. He got out and held her gently.

'Is that the effect my love making has on you these days, Meggie Caraford?' he teased.

'Yes, I'm afraid it is,' Megan said with a wobbly smile, then she laughed aloud at his startled expression. 'I think I'm expecting another baby, Steven,' she said softly. 'I was never sick with Sammy or Tania, but I've been feeling rotten in the mornings lately.'

'Oh my God! Why didn't you tell me, Meggie? We've just let Joe go off to another job.'

'Well for one thing I didn't know when we told him he could go, and for another we can't afford to keep him.'

'But I don't want you to be ill, Meggie. Do you think it's the tension of all the upheavals?'

'I don't think so. I expect it will pass. Ruth told me she was very sick when she was having Avril so I'm not the only one. Don't you start worrying, Steven. And another thing, we'll not tell the family until we have to. They're worried enough about us already.'

This was true. Although John Oliphant had forbidden Chrissie to worry, he couldn't help being concerned himself. Even Geordie Samson had thirty milking cows at Bengairney. How would they make ends meet with only eight cows?

# Eleven

Steven and John Oliphant attended three different auctions, but the summer grazing lots were all making more money than Steven dare offer considering the uncertainty which lay ahead.

'It would have been worth bidding more if I knew I could keep my animals after November when the seasonal grazing ends,' Steven said on a note of despondency, 'but if I've to sell them anyway it's pointless paying all that money.'

'Aye, I understand that, lad,' John said. 'But there's still the paddocks on the Dornielea Estate. Mr Griffiths mentioned they were being let this year, didn't he?'

'Yes, they might be a bit cheaper when it's the first time they've been let. We'll go to see them auctioned, but they're the last I can consider.'

The Dornielea Estate grazings made even more money per acre than the other grazing had done.

'Mr Griffiths has made sure they're fresh,' Steven said to his father-in-law as they watched the prices rise. 'He's retiring from the estate next year so I expect he wants to go with everything in top condition. There's nothing for it but to start reducing my cows. I'll take our oldest Jessie cow to market on Friday. She's newly calved but it's her fourth calf and I've another Jessie coming on. This will be as good a time to sell as any if she's got to go.'

John Oliphant knew he was reluctant to part with the cow, but there was nothing else to do.

On Thursday afternoon Megan stood the children in a small pen to watch while she helped Steven groom the cow and shampoo her.

'Doesn't she mind having her hair washed?' Samuel asked, watching intently. 'Will she cry if the soap gets in her eyes?'

'No she will not.' Megan laughed. 'She closes her eyes and the shampoo never goes in. See how smart and clean she looks now she's finished. You two can help me bring some clean straw for her to lie on and then she will get dry and stay clean ready for the market tomorrow.'

'I like her fluffy white tail now Daddy has combed out the tangles,' Samuel said admiringly. 'Won't she mind going to live at another farm? I wouldn't like to live anywhere else.'

'Jessie won't mind if she gets a nice home and plenty to eat,' Megan reassured him, and hoped she was right. They had grown fond of all their animals. Samuel knew most of them by name now and he was already taking an interest in everything that was done.

The cow made a better price than Steven had expected, considering her age.

'I think it helped when Mr Fraser, the auctioneer, announced I was selling because I needed to reduce numbers. The buyers knew I wasn't getting rid of her due to faults. He told them she was bred from the Willowburn stock, too. He did his best for us.'

'Well it's better for him, too. He gets his shilling commission from every guinea,' Megan said.

The following weekend John Oliphant was relief milking for the third weekend in a row for Geordie Samson at Bengairney. He always looked into the house to tell the elderly farmer everything was in order for the night when he was ready to leave. He was surprised to see Murdo Turner sitting on the opposite side of the fire with a glass of beer in his hand.

'Hello, John. It's good to see you again,' Mr Turner greeted him almost eagerly, and his expression brightened at sight of his ex-dairyman. 'How is Chrissie keeping?'

'Very well, thanks. She's made a good recovery, thanks to Mr Gray.'

'Aye, Lindsey is a fine man and dedicated to his profession.' Mr Turner sighed. 'God knows why Natalie couldn't see that. You'll have heard she's married?'

'Yes, we heard.'

'Aye, well, I don't mind telling you I'd have been a lot happier with Lindsey, or young Steven, for a son-in-law. You're a lucky man, John.'

'Yes, we know that. Steven is a grand laddie.'

'Speaking of Steven, I read in the paper that he'd got a good price for one of his cows at the market last week. Somebody said he's having to reduce his numbers?'

'Yes, that's right.' John explained about the deaths of the McGuires. 'He bid for some of the seasonal grazings but they all made too much money.'

'Lor', I could let the laddie graze my two top fields now I've got rid o' the sheep,' Geordie said. 'I've more grass than I know what to do with.' He drew on his pipe and frowned. 'I don't know whether the estate would approve o' that, though. If they let one tenant do it they'd have to let the rest, then they'd never know whose stock they were going to have on their farms.'

'Oh I don't know, Geordie,' Mr Turner said slowly. 'Griffiths seems a reasonable man and he knows you're cutting back on your stock. You could always ask him. He can only say no. Steven is a good stockman, isn't he, John? I expect you'd be willing to herd his animals if he brought them up to Bengairney?'

'Of course I would. I'd do anything I could to help him,' John Oliphant said.

'I'll have a word with Griffiths then, but I doubt if he'll agree. It's against the tenancy agreement, I think, so dinna get the laddie's hopes up,' Geordie warned.

'If you do let some of your grass fields, the money will help pay your rent,' Murdo Turner said, and winked at John Oliphant.

The following Monday Geordie Samson rang the estate office but Mr Griffiths was not available.

Mr Griffiths didn't return his call, but the following day he drove into the Bengairney farmyard in person. This suited Geordie much better, as he was not good at talking on the telephone. He explained the situation.

'Mmm, it's not a policy I'd favour. I should need to discuss it with the laird himself,' Griffiths said doubtfully.

'I didna think ye'd approve.' Geordie nodded. 'It's a pity, though. I don't know the young fellow myself, but I knew his father when he was at Willowburn and John Oliphant is his father-in-law. He does my relief milking. I don't think I could keep going without his help.'

'What would you have done, Geordie? Sold off your cows? Or retired altogether?'

'I dinna ken. I did think about retiring after the wife died, but I dinna ken what I'd do with myself all day.'

'It's not a good time to take such a decision when you've just lost someone close,' Mr Griffiths said. 'How long have you been on your own now?'

'Two years, but it seems longer, especially in the winter. In the summer it's not so bad. I can take a walk round the fields and see the cattle. I can't imagine living in the town, but I confess it worries me sometimes, being on my own, specially when I get the bronchitis. Old Ben McClymont has been with me most of his life, but he's too old to do much work now and I canna bring myself to ask him to leave. The young fellow in the other cottage isna reliable. He told me he'd worked with cattle, but I reckon he'll be lucky if he'd ever been close to a cow before he came here. He'll be moving on at the term. Ye'll take a wee cup o' tea, Mr Griffiths? Mrs Oliphant sent me down a tin o' shortbread. They're a grand couple, the Oliphants.'

'A cup of tea would be very welcome, Geordie.' He sat back in his chair and waited quietly while the old man boiled the kettle and found cups and saucers. He was considering a proposition and wondering how to put it across to Geordie Samson. He and his father had been good tenants long before his own time, but things were beginning to deteriorate and they would get worse as time went on.

He accepted the cup of tea with milk and sugar and waited until Geordie was settled by the fire again.

'I shall be retiring myself in a year's time,' he said. 'We're moving to Berwickshire to live nearer our daughter. You'll be having a new land agent then.'

'Aye, he'll likely be a new broom, making changes and telling us what to do,' Geordie grumbled.

'He'll be a lot younger than me.' Mr Griffiths smiled. 'I've been thinking, Geordie, I'd like to see you settled for your retirement before I move. I've a suggestion I'd like you to consider.'

'Oh aye?' Geordie muttered suspiciously.

'You know the estate has started letting the Home Farm paddocks for seasonal grazing this year?'

'Aye, I heard.'

'We need a man to keep an eye on the cattle while they are in our care, May to November. It would suit a good stockman like yourself, walking round the fields each day in the summer, notifying the owner if there's a sick or injured animal. It's up to

him to treat it or remove it. You'd be free to sit by your own
fireside in the winter when the animals go back to their farms.
You could move into the foreman's house. It's a good cottage
with a wee bit o' garden and it's not far from Jock White's, the
estate joiner. You'd have your privacy, but you wouldn't be far
away from company if you wanted it.'

'You mean I'd be another estate worker in a tied cottage?'

'Not exactly. The new agent will not know the older tenants
as I do, so before he takes over I'd draw up a lease to give you
security for your lifetime. You would need to pay a reasonable
rent, of course. You can be the herd for the summer grazing as
long as you feel up to it and you'd be paid for doing that.'

'Paid? Just for looking round the fields and keeping an eye on
the animals? I count that sort o' thing as a pleasure.' Geordie
grinned.

'Yes, I imagine you do.' Griffiths smiled. 'All the same, you'd
be paid. When you stop herding you will still have your rented
cottage. Nobody will be able to put you out. I'll mention it to
the laird, of course, but I know he'll agree. You've been at
Bengairney all your life and you've been a good tenant. We don't
need all the cottages at Home Farm now that we're not farming
it ourselves.'

'Mmm, I see . . .'

'As I said, take time and think it over. Discuss it with your
neighbour, Mr Turner, if you like. I'll come back and see you in
a few days.'

'And what would ye do with this place if I moved out? Would
you be letting it? D'ye have a tenant in mind?'

'We'll have to see about that. I might consider Steven Caraford,
Mr Oliphant's son-in-law. I've a mind to see the lad have his
chance before I move away, but this place is more than twice as
big as the place he's been farming. He may consider a hundred
and eighty acres is too big an undertaking.'

Megan was feeling wretched every morning. It was an effort to
get up, and even more of a struggle to tackle her morning chores
outside and attend to the children. By evening she felt exhausted.

'You're the only one I know who seems to understand,' she
said to Ruth. 'Steven's mother and my own parents would only

worry if they knew, especially with everything else going on. Steven was really upset when he found one of the Clydesdales lying dead last week. Daisy was such a canny mare. He learned to plough with her when he was a boy.'

'Yes, Hannah was sad about Daisy too, but she said she was a fair age and it was better for her to die naturally.'

'Yes, you're right, it would have been hard to have her put to sleep. Horses need quite a bit of grass to keep them fed and we shall have none to spare soon. I hope Steven will look at it that way eventually. He loved the horses, even more than the cows, but we don't use them as much now we have the tractor. We still have Ben when we need a horse and cart.'

'It's strange how things all seem to go wrong together,' Ruth mused. 'You wonder how you will cope, and yet life does go on and things do get better. When I knew I was expecting a baby I wanted to die, but then Avril was born and she looked so innocent and so perfect I couldn't help but love her. Then when my father died my world seemed to turn upside down again, especially knowing I had to move out of the only home I'd ever known. Out of the blue Hannah invited me to visit.' Ruth smiled. 'I was filled with doubts. I never dreamed things could turn out so well.'

'I'm pleased for you, Ruth. You deserve to be happy. And how about Lint? Have you seen him recently,' she asked with a grin.

Ruth's cheeks grew pink. 'We haven't been out on our own, if that's what you mean, but he has been down for a meal a couple of times, and he took Hannah and Avril and me for dinner at a hotel near the shore. It was lovely.'

'Lint's a lovely man, and very genuine.'

'I know. I keep thinking he'll get tired of me soon. I admit I would miss his friendship now, but I – I can't . . .' She shuddered. 'I can't ever visualize being married to anyone.'

Her colour deepened. The last time he had called to see her he had stayed later than usual after Avril had gone to bed. They had sat side by side watching a film on television and afterwards she had made coffee before he had to drive back to the hospital. He had taken her by surprise when he turned back in the tiny hallway. She had been close behind him. She didn't have time to think, or to move away. He drew her into his arms, gently but with insistence, and she knew he was going to kiss her. It was a slow, lingering kiss, and it had awakened feelings she didn't know she possessed. Apart from the brief episode under the mistletoe, it was the first time he had held her close or kissed her.

Megan watched Ruth curiously as the colour washed over her clear skin. Mention of Lint had obviously awakened some memory or other and she guessed it was not an unpleasant one judging by Ruth's blush.

Jimmy Kerr called in one evening on his way home from work. The children were already in bed.

'Have you heard who your new neighbour is going to be?' he asked.

'No, not yet,' Steven said. 'But I can guess you have, and judging by your expression you know him already. Am I right?'

'Yes. It's a fellow called Adam Fortescue.'

'Never heard of him,' Steven said flatly. He didn't really care who came. In another six weeks the holding would be nothing to do with him. He had done as Mr McMann had asked and ploughed and drilled the field for cereals as usual. He planned to graze some of the fields and then remove his stock to allow the fields to freshen up before term day. All the land had had manure in rotation with his own holding; he had done the best he could and he hoped the new tenant would appreciate his efforts.

'He's the youngest of three sons,' Jimmy said glumly, 'and they're all as cocky as hell and as tight-fisted as they come. Their father farms at Windyedge. The eldest son works at home; the second one got married last year and he rents a small farm nearby. This is the youngest and he's as bad as his father and brothers. You'll need to watch him over the valuation,' he warned grimly.

'How's that?' Steven frowned, but he sat up and paid attention. Jimmy dealt with most of the farmers in the area and he rarely criticized any of them.

'They're the worst buggers I've ever had to deal with . . .' He glanced at Megan. 'Sorry, I . . .'

'That's all right, Jimmy, don't mind me. They must be bad if that's how you feel, though.'

'They're as miserable as sin. They want everything for nothing and they always try to get the prices knocked down. If it's a repair they complain something's not been done right. If it's a new machine they want a bigger discount than anybody else. I'm not the only one who dreads them coming in either.' He grinned suddenly. 'Mr Anderson is in charge of the electrical side at Bradshaws. He knows what they're like. Mr Fortescue wanted to buy a television for his wife before the Coronation, so Anderson added twenty pounds to the normal price. As usual Fortescue started his bargaining and arguing. Mr Anderson said he'd knock ten pounds off.

'"No, no," says Fortescue. "We deserve more than that. We're good customers. We always pay our bills."

'"Aye, a month late," says Mr Anderson.

'"I'll pay this television at the end o' the month, but I want a discount."

'"All right," says Mr A. "Fifteen pounds off or you can go somewhere else if you're not satisfied."

'Well, the TVs were scarce before the Coronation if you remember, and they had left it a bit late. He took it and thought he had a bargain. The boss says if they come to me for a new machine I've to do the same. We're all fed up with 'em. I'm just telling you so you'll be forewarned. They're tricky customers and liable to do a dirty deal if they think they can get away with it.'

'Thanks for the warning, Jimmy. I hate that sort of haggling. I ask a fair price and I expect to pay a fair price.'

'Aye, well, the Fortescues are the next thing to dishonest when it comes to bargaining. Spite and sharp practice seems to be their motto.'

The following weekend Chrissie eyed Megan with concern. 'I've never seen you look so drawn and haggard, lassie. You've rings under your eyes. I know it must be a worrying time for you and Steven, but you must look after your health.'

'I'm fine, Mum. Don't worry about me. Steven has sold two of the cows and got good prices, but we shall have to sell all our in-calf heifers and more of the older cows when they calve.'

'It's sickening for both of you, after all your hard work and when you were making such progress, but think about the children. You must keep well for their sake.'

'Mum, I do!' Megan snapped. She screwed up her face, almost bursting into tears. She was so tired. 'I'm sorry. I know you mean well.' She hesitated, wondering whether she should tell her mother she was expecting another baby, but she changed her mind. Everyone would know in another month or six weeks if the baby was due in October, as she thought.

'I wish there was something we could do to help.'

'Nobody can help, and we shall be fine once things get sorted out. Jimmy Kerr doesn't think our new neighbour is a very likeable fellow, though. Steven says he sounds a bit like Fred.'

'Geordie Samson told your father he had asked Mr Griffiths if he could rent two of his fields to Steven, but the factor wouldn't give permission.'

'I know. Dad told us, but Steven understands. He says it would cause trouble with the other tenants if one got away with it.'

Geordie Samson had not told anyone of the proposition Mr Griffiths had made him. He took his time mulling things over in his mind. A cosy cottage was tempting. Bengairney farmhouse had five bedrooms and three rooms downstairs, as well as a big kitchen and all sorts of back places and a cellar. It had always been far too big for him and his wife. They'd had a single man living in at one time, then they got a milking machine and there had been a father and son in one of the cottages and old McClymont and his wife in the other. Mrs McClymont had been as good as a man for working with cattle. Mrs Temple from the village came in to clean and do his washing, but she only did the kitchen and the downstairs room which he used as a bedroom.

He wondered if he would get anybody to help him if he moved up to the cottage at Home Farm. It was a big decision to leave the place he had known all his life, and Mr Griffiths hadn't given him much time to think about it if he had to be out by term day. His heart quailed at the thought of arranging a farm sale. He wondered whether John Oliphant would be free to help him get the animals groomed and ready. Then there was his three horses and the machinery. If only he'd had a son to follow in his footsteps. He wondered what the new agent would be like if he kept the farm on. He knew things didn't look as good as they used to do; he was getting too old.

He could understand why Murdo Turner was so bitter about his daughter's marriage to a man who already had children and didn't want any more. Although Murdo was a wealthy man now, he had worked hard when they were both young men and he had done well for himself. Neither of them would have children or grandchildren to carry on their work. Geordie wondered whether his neighbour really would make a new will and carry out his threat to prevent his son-in-law, and his offspring, getting their hands on his money. He sighed. That was none of his business. He had his own life to think about, what remained of it.

It was the prospect of a new land agent who might want him out of Bengairney, plus the thought of being settled for the rest of his life in a cottage with no stairs to climb every time he wanted a pee, which finally made up his mind.

# Twelve

Steven stared at Mr Griffiths. He was speechless. He had been surprised to see the land agent drawing into the farmyard at Schoirhead, but the news he had brought left him stunned into silence.

'You mean Mr Samson is giving up the tenancy? My father-in-law never mentioned anything and he sees him regularly.'

'I know. Your father-in-law's help has probably kept Geordie Samson going longer than he might have done. There are two problems to consider, though.'

'There had to be something,' Steven said. 'Will you come in and meet my wife? Megan will make us a cup of tea.'

'I never say no to that,' Mr Griffiths said with a smile. Steven introduced Megan and they settled round the kitchen table.

'So after offering such an opportunity when we need it badly, what are these problems?' Steven asked.

'Well, I'm offering you the tenancy of Bengairney, but it is a hundred and eighty acres – more than twice the acreage you've been farming here, even with the next-door holding. That means you'll need more stock, which means more capital, and of course a considerably bigger rent to find. One thing about Bengairney, though, Mr Samson has been winding down for the past five years or more, even before his wife died. There will not be a lot of valuation to pay. On the other hand, most of the fields need lime as soon as possible, and a lot of the pasture would benefit from reseeding. As far as money is concerned, it probably amounts to the same as a high valuation, except it could be done gradually.'

'That's a challenge rather than a problem,' Steven said. 'What about the second problem?'

'Entry is at the end of May.'

'The end of May!' Steven and Megan echoed in unison.

'Yes, I'm afraid so. I've arranged for Mr Samson to have life rent of a cottage at Home Farm. He is going to herd the cattle coming to the summer grazing. It will break him gently into retirement, but I need him to start as soon as possible and I want a new tenant for Bengairney by the term. I know six months is the usual notice, but I shall have no difficulty finding a tenant for Bengairney. The question is, how would you stand with the Department? Would they insist you stay here until November?'

'We would definitely be interested in Bengairney, wouldn't we, Megan?'

'We–ell, yes. We've built up a bit of capital, but we should need to take out a bank loan again to buy extra stock.'

'We repaid the last loan quicker than Mr Masters expected. He's the new bank manager,' Steven added, looking at Mr Griffiths. 'He said I could come to him again if I saw an opportunity to expand. We would need extra cows, but we have six in-calf heifers of our own coming forward and another five for next year. We kept as many cows as we had stalls for, but we have been rearing all the heifer calves while we had the McGuires' land.'

'I see. So what about the termination of the tenancy? Presumably the terms are six months' notice?'

'Yes.' Steven sighed and looked down at the table. 'That is a problem.'

'We can only ask,' Megan said encouragingly, reaching out a hand and laying it on Steven's arm in silent support.

'Exactly,' Mr Griffiths said. 'Let me know as soon as you can, by the end of the week if possible.'

When he had gone Steven whistled aloud and hugged Megan, then waltzed her around the kitchen. Samuel and Tania had been making mud pies outside and they stood in the doorway watching with round eyes.

'Daddy, why are you doing that to Mummy?' Samuel asked.

'Because we're happy, darling.' Megan laughed, forgetting for a little while the recurring cramp and the constant feeling of nausea which threatened to sap her strength and spirit.

'Everything depends on whether the Department will waive the period of notice,' Steven said, sobering. 'I'll telephone Mr McMann and make an appointment to see him. It's easier to talk face to face.'

It was two days before Steven got an appointment, two days in which he was exuberantly optimistic one minute and sunk in gloom the next. If only they'd had more time. His spirits sank when he saw Mr McMann's blank expression as he listened to Steven's explanation. At last he nodded, but he still kept his expression remarkably neutral and Steven wondered if he had understood what he had been saying.

'As it happens,' he said at last, 'I have had two telephone calls concerning you, Mr Caraford . . .' Steven's spirits plummeted even further. He had already had a dispute with Adam Fortescue, their new neighbour, but to his surprise Mr McMann continued, 'Yes, one was from a land agent named Griffiths. The other was from a Mr Turner. They both speak highly of you and feel you should be given this opportunity. So, knowing the reason for your appointment I telephoned Mr Burrows to get his views on the matter. When we advertised the smallholding next to you it was difficult to decide which of three applicants should get it. One of them has since moved east to rent a small farm in Roxburghshire. The other young couple are still looking for a place. I think they will jump at the opportunity to take over Schoirhead, even at such short notice. If they do, Mr Burrows suggests we allow you to move on.' At last his face relaxed and he looked up at Steven, his eyes twinkling as a broad grin spread across his face.

'You mean . . .? You really mean you will w-waive the period of n-notice?' Steven stammered in his excitement.

'If you'll take a seat in the outer office I will make a telephone call, and then I can tell you for certain what can be done.'

Half an hour later Fenton McMann called Steven back into his office.

'You're in luck. The young couple I mentioned are going to bring forward their wedding. They are desperate to move in to Schoirhead as soon as you move out.'

'So I can tell Mr Griffiths we're free to sign a lease on Bengairney at the end of May?'

'You can, but he's half expecting you will anyway. He and Mr Turner pleaded your case very eloquently, if I may say so.'

'Thank you, sir. I hardly know what to say, but I'm delighted you've managed to arrange things so well for us.' Steven beamed.

'And what about the other tenant, Mr Fortescue? Have you discussed the valuation yet?' Steven's smile disappeared. He chewed his lower lip.

'We did discuss it.'

'But you haven't reached an agreement?'

'No, we haven't.'

'Being difficult, is he?'

'Unreasonable in my opinion. He doesna think he should pay any valuation at all. He says it was not my holding so he doesn't consider me the outgoing tenant. I showed him all the invoices and an estimate for the tractor fuel and labour.'

'I see.' McMann nodded. 'Some of the staff in the offices here have found the Fortescues difficult to deal with regarding grants which are available. Incidentally, you will get five pounds per acre for ploughing up pasture when you move to the bigger farm, as well as a subsidy for lime. Presumably you will grow more cereals for a year or two?'

'Yes, probably. I haven't had time to think about it yet.'

'No, of course not. My advice would be to get the valuations for both holdings agreed now. It would be worth asking Mr Fraser, the auctioneer, to value the growing cereal crops and the grass leys. It will be a similar valuation for both holdings and the Fortescues can't argue with an independent opinion. It will be worth paying Fraser's fee to have peace of mind. If you have further problems come back to us. Mr Burrows will deal with young Fortescue.'

Steven couldn't wait to get home and break the news to Megan. If her enthusiasm was less than he had expected he was too full of plans to notice. Megan knew this was an opportunity beyond their dreams, but the prospect of packing up everything in the house, moving the cattle, the pigs, her hens and the henhouses, overwhelmed her. How would she summon up the energy? It was Steven who telephoned to tell his mother and her parents their news. He and her father talked for ages, discussing Mr Samson's cows and which ones would be worth bidding for at the sale.

'Your father knows the cows well by now so I shall take his advice. He says there's only five or six older cows he wouldn't recommend. We'd need extra cows anyway and it's customary to bid at the sale of the outgoing tenant. The neighbours usually do the same to give him a good sale. We know Mr Samson's cattle are healthy. They're familiar with their stalls too, and no hauling them about and risking injury. I can't believe things are coming right for us after the past few months when everything has been so bleak. Tomorrow I must telephone for an appointment with Mr Masters to arrange a bank loan.'

Megan sighed. She wished she could summon up more energy and enthusiasm, but Steven was still too excited to notice.

Ruth telephoned the following evening. 'I'm so pleased to hear your good news, Megan,' she said. 'I wish Avril and I were on holiday from school to help you move. It's all so exciting. You'll be a bit nearer your parents, too.'

'Yes. We shall be further away from you and Steven's mother, though.'

'Not much further. Hannah says we're like three sides of a triangle, and if we cut across country on this side it will not take us any longer to get to Bengairney. She's really pleased for you. She's always regretted Steven not getting a chance to farm Willowburn, but she says Bengairney is bigger so maybe it was worth waiting.'

'I hope so,' Megan said fervently.

'Megan? You don't sound very happy about it. Are you worried about the money, or are you still feeling as tired and sickly?'

'I don't seem to have any energy to do anything. It's as though I have a heavy weight pressing me down. I don't know how I'm going to cope with all the packing and the organization it will take to move everything.'

'Don't you think you ought to tell your parents and Hannah about the baby?' Ruth urged anxiously. 'I'm sure they'll understand and want to help.'

'They would only worry and fuss and I can't seem to cope with that sort of thing. Once or twice I've snapped at the children and at Steven and then I want to cry my eyes out with remorse. I've never felt like this before. I thought the hormones were supposed to make you feel on top of the world.'

'They don't always,' Ruth said with a faint note of cynicism. 'You know I'll come up at weekends to help you pack, don't you? I could help with cleaning the other house whenever you can get in, too. Hannah said the tenant will be moving out as soon as he has had his farm sale.'

'Yes he is. The sale is arranged for the third week in May, so that gives us a week before we need to be out of here. If Steven buys any milking cows, Dad has agreed to go over to Bengairney to milk them until we get moved in. He's discussed it with the Palmer-Farrs and they're agreeable. Of course they pay him by the hour, so it will be Dad who is losing out, but he knows we can't afford to pay him to make up.'

'I'm sure he is as pleased to help you as we are.'

'You're a good friend, Ruth. At least you cheer me up a bit.'

Ruth laughed. 'I'm glad to hear it.'

Megan had always been methodical, and in spite of her exhaustion she set about the packing with her usual efficiency. Steven helped her lift the carpet in the sitting room and push the furniture to one side, then they piled the boxes in there as she packed and labelled them.

'I don't know what I'd do without you, Meggie,' Steven sighed. 'You will be careful not to overdo things, won't you, sweetheart.'

'My energy levels don't extend to overdoing anything,' Megan sighed. 'I feel like a car with the brakes on. As soon as we get the keys I plan to move some of these boxes in the van, and Ruth has promised to help me clean the bedrooms before we move the furniture. When the house has been occupied by a solitary man it's unlikely to be very clean.' She twinkled up at him and he was pleased to see the mischievous glint in her green eyes.

'Is that what you think of the male species?'

'Indoors yes, though I admit you're a very tidy worker outside. How shall we move all the poultry?'

'Tom Green said he would bring us some wire crates and Jimmy Kerr has promised to help us catch them. I think you'd better stay away from that job; bending and chasing flighty hens isn't good for someone in your condition.'

'That's a relief. I think we should sell the poultry next door. They're not laying well considering it's the time of year when they should be in full production. Maybe they're older than Mrs McGuire realized.'

'Whatever you say, Megan. There's no use feeding them if they're not producing. The young couple who are moving in would like to buy our henhouses, by the way. Your father is mending up the two that are at Bengairney. Mr Samson said we could have them for nothing. We shall just need to buy one new one. Will you order it or shall I?'

'I'll leave it to you,' Megan said wearily. Steven gnawed his lip and looked at her keenly.

'Come on, my love, let's go to bed. You're tired out and we've both done enough for today.' He knew Megan was not feeling herself when she complied so readily. He felt they ought to tell their parents about the baby, but she was adamant they would guess soon enough. She didn't seem to be putting on much weight, though, but then she had no appetite.

Steven was surprised to get a telephone call from a telephone kiosk.

'I am sorry to be a trouble to you, Mr Steven,' Joe said in his careful English. 'Jimmy told us you will move to another farm soon?'

'Yes, we shall be a bit nearer to you, Joe. We're moving to Bengairney on the Dornielea Estate.'

'It has cottages, Jimmy says. When you need worker will you have me, please?'

'You want to move already, Joe?'

'I not like here as much as with you. They—they call me Finkel, the German toad, and make fun.'

'I'm sorry to hear that, Joe. To tell the truth we don't know what we shall need yet. Both the cottages are occupied, but Mr Samson has asked one of the men to move out. The other is an elderly man. Mr Samson has asked me to leave him there if I can spare the cottage. He will not be working for me; I can only afford to employ one man. Give me your address, Joe, and I will write to you if I have a cottage and work for you.'

'Oh, Steven, I'd love to have Joe back working for us,' Megan said as soon as he told her about the telephone call. 'At least we know he is reliable, which is more than Mr Samson had to say about the man who works for him.'

'I know, Meggie, but we don't want Joe to hand in his notice and then find the man has not moved out of his cottage at Bengairney. We'd have nowhere for Joe and his wife to live. We shall not know for sure until the term day. Mr Samson has given him notice to leave, but there's no guarantee he will move out of his cottage unless we force him to vacate it.'

'Oh I hope he's not a troublemaker,' Megan groaned. 'I couldn't face solicitors' letters and the things it would need to force him to move.'

'We'll hope it doesn't come to that, but Mr Samson says he could be an awkward so and so.'

When Chrissie heard Ruth had volunteered to come up to Bengairney for the weekend to help Megan clean out the house she immediately offered to have Samuel and Tania so Megan would be free.

'That would be a big help, Mum. I'll bring them up fairly early on Friday morning. It would give me all day to clean, then Ruth and I will stay Friday and Saturday nights at Bengairney. Steven says he will manage on his own. I've ordered two new beds for the children to be delivered; we'll use them. Mr Samson couldn't get everything into his two-bedroomed cottage so he's left lots of stuff. He told Steven to burn everything we can't use. The house is a bit of a mess, but no worse than I expected and it will be a lovely place to live once we've had time to sort things out. Everything has to be out of Schoirhead by next Friday morning. Tom Green is moving all the animals here on the Thursday, and he's asked another man who has a lorry to help. It will take a few loads to move them all. The big furniture will come on the Friday morning.'

'You're going to have a hectic week,' Chrissie said anxiously. 'It was bad enough moving house without having to move animals and machines.'

'I know, but I expect we'll manage, and Dad is a tremendous help milking the cows Steven bought at the sale.'

'He's enjoying it, but if we have Samuel and Tania for the weekend he'll come home quicker. He enjoys them even more than the cows.'

'I should think so too!' Megan teased.

'Lindsey will be staying at the Tower this weekend and he's always very good with them. It's a pity he doesn't get married and have children of his own.'

'I suppose he's waiting for the right woman,' Megan said non-committally.

'Yes, and we can both guess who that is. I only wish we could help.'

'Well we can't, Mum! Please don't interfere.'

'I wouldn't dream of it,' Chrissie said innocently, but Megan knew she would if she could think of a foolproof scheme.

There was no such thing where love was concerned, and especially not with Ruth. She might never be able to conquer her fear and distrust.

Megan dropped the children off at her parents' house on Friday morning and arrived at Bengairney in time to take delivery of two new beds and a carpet.

'If you will carry them up to the landing and leave them there, please? I want to scrub out the room before I put in any furniture.' The men did as she asked and Megan set about sweeping away cobwebs and dust. Mr Samson had left all the curtains and some of them would be useful, but she had washed and ironed the curtains from home for the children. She wanted some things to look familiar for them. Samuel insisted he didn't want to live in another house and she hoped he wouldn't be difficult. She set about scrubbing the floor and opened the windows wide to let it dry; at least one room smelled fresh and clean enough to sleep in. She knew Ruth would help her screw together the two beds when she arrived. Tania still slept in her cot, but Megan was preparing to move her into a bed before the baby arrived in October.

She had brought a large box of food and a primus stove to boil the kettle, but Mr Samson had left a pile of sticks and logs and a small heap of coal in one of the sheds so she cleaned and blackleaded the kitchen range and kindled the fire. The big kitchen seemed cosier and less echoing and forlorn with the fire. Amongst the many items of furniture he had left there was a Berkeley armchair to one side of the kitchen range. It would have to go as it would take up too much room once they all moved in. It was grubby from constant use, but Megan was sorely tempted to curl up in it and have a rest as the fire began to blaze. The flicker of the flames gleamed on the brass fender and the polished hinges on the oven door, making her efforts seem worthwhile. She sighed and pushed the kettle on to boil while she chewed on one of the sandwiches she had packed for her lunch.

After her short break she set about the large front bedroom where she and Steven would sleep. She guessed it was years since it had been used and it badly needed decorating, but she had neither the time nor the energy to do that before they moved in. The view made up for the cobwebs and faded walls. She looked down the glen at the freshening fields which she and Steven would soon be farming. May was a lovely time of year. In the garden she could hear a chaffinch singing his heart out. There was a little wood and a burn a short distance from the side of the house, and she wondered if there would be bluebells there like the woods at Martinwold. The day was bright and a few fluffy white clouds floated lazily across the clear blue of the sky. She gazed into the distance and saw the glitter of the Solway Firth. The tide must be coming in. Once this baby was born and they were settled in she must take Samuel and Tania down to the shore. The Cumberland hills rose in peaks beyond the Solway, and to the west the Galloway hills rolled gently across the skyline. She breathed in deeply. It was all so lovely and they were so lucky to be given this opportunity. If only she felt more energetic.

Ruth arrived after school. 'Hannah insisted on sending a bacon and egg pie for our evening meal,' she said with a laugh. 'I see you've lit the range so we'll put it in the oven. She said it would taste better if it was hot.'

'She's so thoughtful,' Megan said. 'I've just finished cleaning the bathroom. It's not very posh but it will have to do for a while. I hope you'll not mind roughing it, Ruth.'

'Of course not. I'm pleased to be able to help. I hope you've not been working too hard today?'

'There's still plenty left to do,' Megan said with a sigh. 'I've laid the carpet square in the children's room. Perhaps we'd better put the beds up in there before we eat. I have a feeling that once I sit down I may never rise again and it's the only clean place for us to sleep.'

'That's fine with me. Oh, and Hannah said you're not to worry about Steven. She has promised to take Avril down to Schoirhead tomorrow morning so they will look after the hens and feed the pigs, and she will cook his dinner.'

'Oh that's wonderful,' Megan said with relief. 'I have been wondering how he would get everything done on his own. The cows are out at grass during the day, but they're still sleeping in the byres at night so he will have all the mucking out to do as well as the milking, and he'll need to wash the dairy things. He's not used to that.'

'I'm sure he'll not mind and it will be a lot better if we can get things sorted out here before the big furniture has to be moved in – although it looks full of big furniture already,' she said, opening one of the doors off the hallway. 'Doesn't Mr Samson want his dining-room suite?'

'He hasn't room at the cottage. He told Steven to burn what we couldn't use. Actually, I think it will wash and polish up beautifully if I ever get around to it, but I'm shutting the door on the rooms we don't need immediately. He's left chairs and a cabinet in the sitting room but some of them will have to go. There's a smaller sitting room too, but it's empty, thank goodness. I think they used it as a bedroom.'

'It will be a lovely family home once you're all settled in,' Ruth said, and Megan wondered if there was a wistful note in her voice.

They ate their meal and washed up, but Megan pleaded exhaustion and climbed wearily upstairs to bed.

'I'll clean out some of the kitchen cupboards before I join you, if that's all right,' Ruth said. 'I'll try not to disturb you when I come up.'

'I doubt if anything will disturb me,' Megan said, trying to stifle a yawn.

She was wrong about that, but she certainly didn't hear Ruth come to bed around ten o'clock. She was wakened some time later by a terrible cramp in her stomach. It was dark but she could see the luminous hands of her big alarm clock said ten to two. She tried to relax but the pain grew worse; she knew this was no ordinary stomach ache. She got up to creep to the bathroom and it was then the first bleeding began.

# Thirteen

Megan found the towels she had unpacked earlier and swathed one around herself, but the room was spinning and she was thankful to reach the bed.

'Megan?' Ruth whispered. 'Are you all right?'

'Sorry. I didn't mean to disturb you. I . . .' She couldn't stifle a groan as the cramps gripped her. She felt an alarming flow of blood. Ruth got out of bed and switched on the light. She was dismayed at Megan's pallor and the tension around her mouth.

'Is it the baby? Is something wrong?' she asked anxiously.

'I–I'm bleeding a bit,' Megan admitted reluctantly. 'Could you get me another towel from the bathroom please? I think it's better if I stay still. Maybe it will stop.'

'Don't you think I should call the doctor?'

'No! N–no . . . Anyway, we don't have a doctor here yet.'

Ruth brought the towel, but she was shocked as she removed the one Megan had already used. 'I think I should call an ambulance. It's a threatened miscarriage, isn't it?'

'I–I just want to lie still and quiet,' Megan said on a moan.

'I'll go and rake up the fire and see if I can boil the kettle.' Ruth was frowning. 'We ought to let Steven know . . .'

'No! Please, Ruth. You mustn't. It's the middle of the night and he has so much work to do. If – if I can lie still, perhaps it will be all right . . .' In her heart she knew it would not, and so did Ruth. She pulled a cardigan over her nightdress and shoved her bare feet into her shoes. Her footsteps sounded loud and echoing down the bare wooden stairs. She shuddered. The house seemed big and creepy at night. She hoped Megan would forgive her for what she was about to do, but she was desperately worried. She closed the doors behind her and lifted the telephone, asking for Langton Tower.

Katherine Palmer-Farr answered eventually, sounding sleepy and irritable.

'Is Lindsey there, please? Lindsey Gray?'

'Is that the hospital? He's supposed to be off . . .'

'N–no. Please, it's urgent. Tell him it's Ruth and it's about Megan. We're at Bengairney.'

'Yes I know. I'll get him.'

'Ruth?' Lindsey knew it must be urgent for Ruth to phone him at all, especially during the night. He barely waited to pull on his trousers before he was running down the stairs to the hall.

'Ruth? What is it?'

'Oh Lint, thank goodness. It's Megan. I think she's having a miscarriage. She's losing a lot of blood but she doesn't want me to call an ambulance. They don't have a doctor yet. I don't know what to do. I'm terribly worried.'

'Of course you are. I'd no idea she was—'

'No, none of their parents know. Please help me . . .'

'I'll telephone an ambulance right away. I'll be with you before it arrives. I'm no expert in such things, but try to keep her still and calm. Don't tell her about the ambulance until I get there. And Ruth . . . thanks for trusting me.' He put the phone down and dialled for an ambulance.

Ruth stirred the embers of the fire and added sticks gradually until it was well alight then she carefully added some coal. She put water in the kettle and shoved it on to boil almost automatically, but she couldn't believe it when Lindsey strode into the kitchen so soon. She moved to the stairs, but as she went to go in front of him she remembered she was still in her nightgown and the thin cotton was almost see-through against the naked light bulbs. She gasped and tried to hide herself, her face flaming with embarrassment.

'J–just go up. I'll follow you. I–I must get dressed.'

Lindsey had noticed the outline of her slender figure and long legs and he bit back a smile. This was no time to think of such things, unfortunately. He was dismayed at the sight of Megan's chalky face and he went straight to her side and took her wrist in one hand while he smoothed her brow with the other.

Ruth seized her clothes and scurried to the bathroom to pull them on. She didn't waste any time. Even in the short time she had been downstairs Megan's condition had deteriorated. She was really frightened now. People could bleed to death. 'Please God let Meggie be all right,' she whispered.

Lint was speaking to Megan in a low voice but she didn't seem to recognize him. 'It's moving round,' she muttered.

'I think she means the room,' he said quietly. 'Her pulse is weak. She must have lost a lot of blood.'

'Will they let me go with her in the ambulance?' Ruth asked.

'I'll see that they do. Keep talking to her. Keep her with us. I'll telephone the hospital. I'm certain she will need a blood transfusion. I wish I knew what blood group she is.'

'She's the same as me.'

'Good girl! You're sure?'

'Yes.'

'They'll not take our word for it but they'll be prepared. I'll tell the ambulance to take her straight to the Infirmary instead of the maternity hospital. I'll follow in the car to bring you back.'

'Don't you think I should telephone Steven? She said I must not, b—but she looks so ill . . .'

'I'd certainly want to know if it was my wife,' Lint said grimly. 'We'll wait until we see what they say at the hospital. We can contact him from there, and it will give him a little longer to sleep before his day begins. I imagine he will want to be in two places at once – with Megan and milking his cows.'

The nurses and doctors were calm and reassuring, but Ruth knew by the way they were hurrying that Megan's condition was serious. She felt so useless. When Lindsey arrived he explained they were friends of the family and Megan had been away from home. When he mentioned he was a surgeon from over the Border they were more deferential, but Ruth was embarrassed because the nurse in charge assumed they were a married couple. Ruth opened her mouth to contradict her, but Lindsey simply shook his head and gave a small smile. It was after four in the morning before the doctor could give them any definite news, and it was Steven to whom he wished to speak.

'We shall telephone now,' Lindsey said, and he went on to explain about moving from one farm to another and how Steven was tied up with essential work. 'I know he will want to see Megan as soon as possible. Shall I ask him to come immediately, before he starts the morning milking?'

'No. We are giving Mrs Caraford blood right now. She has lost the baby, as you probably realized. We shall give her something to help her sleep for the next four or five hours. Ask Mr Caraford to come in about eight thirty to nine o'clock. I would like to speak to him before he sees his wife. Will you be sure to tell him that?'

'Very well, Doctor Sugden.' They watched him stride away.

'Poor Megan,' Ruth sighed. 'She will be so upset.'

'So will Steven, I imagine,' Lindsey said. 'Let's get back to Bengairney and we'll telephone him from there. By then it will be nearly time for him to start his morning chores anyway. He will feel better if he can get them done before he visits the hospital, then he will have time to spend with Megan.'

It was Ruth who spoke to Steven and tried to explain, but Steven's first reaction was to go immediately to the hospital.

'He's very upset,' she whispered to Lint. 'Will you speak to him?' Lint took the receiver from her.

'We were not allowed to see Megan, Steven.' He explained about her losing the baby and the blood transfusion. 'You are the only one who will be allowed to visit, but Doctor Sugden specifically asked for you not to go until after eight thirty. They want her to sleep. Her condition is stable now but she will be very weak and extremely tired.' They talked a little longer, with Steven clearly shooting questions at Lint, not all of which he could answer.

'I'm afraid it's not my field,' Lint said apologetically. 'Can we tell Megan's father when he comes here to milk the cows? I think it would be better if he explained to Chrissie in person, don't you?'

'Yes,' Steven said wearily. 'I must tell my mother too. I wonder if Megan had some sort of premonition this might happen when she didn't want to tell anyone. Ruth was the only one she confided in.'

'Yes, it's a blessing she was here too. If there's anything we can do, Steven, I'd like to help. Ruth intends to stay here and get on with the house if it's all right for your mother to keep Avril? I'm not returning to the hospital until Sunday night.'

'I don't know how to thank you both for what you've done already. Suddenly the cows and the farm and the move seem unimportant. I shouldn't have agreed to let Megan go up there, scrubbing and cleaning . . .'

'I doubt if it was anything to do with that. She will be all right, Steven, but she will need time to get her strength back.'

While they were talking, Ruth had poked up the fire and put the kettle on to boil.

'I'm afraid we only have one pan but we have plenty of eggs. Would scrambled eggs on toast do for breakfast?' Ruth asked.

'They would be very welcome if you're inviting me to stay?' Lint sounded diffident.

'You've earned more than breakfast. I was so terribly worried, and yet Megan was adamant she didn't want to go to hospital.'

'You did the right thing, Ruth. Sometimes there's no option, whatever the patient thinks they want.'

'I suppose so.' Ruth nodded. She had lit the primus stove and was busy whisking eggs with a fork while a generous chunk of butter melted in the pan. 'Would you like to make the toast with that long fork, please, Lint. Can you slice the bread?' She flushed. 'What a stupid question to ask a surgeon.'

He grinned at her. 'Oh I don't know. The loaf may not be very straight when I've finished.'

They ate in companionable silence, and for the first time Ruth felt it was perfectly natural to be alone with Lint. He went out to greet John Oliphant when he heard the car.

'I expect he'll want to get finished as quickly as possible and get home to tell his wife,' he said to Ruth. 'I thought I might help him carry the milk to the dairy, if he'll have me. Surely there can't be anything too complicated about that, can there?'

'No.' Ruth laughed. 'Especially not when you're so tall for lifting up the buckets to pour over the water cooler, and so long as you don't let the milk churns run over beneath the cooler.'

'Mmm, I see. Perhaps I should telephone Katherine and explain what has happened and warn her not to say anything to Chrissie Oliphant. She goes up to the Tower to feed the hens and the two sows when the children are not there. I don't know whether she will take them with her this morning or leave the feeding to Katherine.'

John Oliphant was dismayed and alarmed when he heard about Megan's miscarriage.

'I don't know for sure, but I think they'll keep her in a week at least, maybe even ten days to a fortnight.'

'She'll be better staying in for a while,' John said gruffly. 'I know Megan, she's like her mother, she'll see all the work needing done here and she'll want to do it. I expect that's what's happened. She'll have been doing too much, or lifting things. I don't know how I'm ever going to repay you, Lindsey. That's both my women you've saved.'

Steven's heart sank when he saw the doctor's grave expression. He badly needed to see Megan to reassure himself that she was going to be all right.

'I have just come from your wife, Mr Caraford. She is naturally upset at losing the baby. She seems to be blaming herself, but I believe this miscarriage would have occurred anyway, as I tried to tell her. By the time she came in things were far advanced and she had already lost a lot of blood, but I believe the placenta may have been lying in the wrong position. A miscarriage is often nature's way of discarding an embryo too. Do you understand?'

'Yes, it is sometimes the way with animals,' Steven agreed. 'But in this case I blame myself for allowing Megan to work so hard and go off to clean the house on her own.'

'Well we can never know for certain, so I think you should both set aside your feelings of guilt and show each other the utmost consideration. In any case, your wife will need to stay in hospital for ten days. She lost a lot of blood, much more than we would normally expect in a miscarriage. I must ask you to make sure she does not become pregnant again for at least a year and preferably eighteen months. Mentally and physically she needs time to recover from this experience.'

'I understand,' Steven said. 'May I see her now?'

'Yes, but you will probably find she is very sleepy. That is partly due to medication. It is nothing to be alarmed about. It would be better if she had no other visitors for a couple of days. They can be very tiring and sometimes tactless.'

'Very well.' Steven was impatient to see Megan for himself. In spite of the doctor's warning he was shocked at the sight of her pale face. Her auburn hair was spread over the pillow, but its vibrant colour seemed to accentuate her pallor. He moved quietly to the bedside and took her hand in his. He had difficulty holding back his tears as he looked down at her, so small and fragile-looking beneath the white sheets. At his touch she opened her eyes. As she focused on him her eyes swam with tears.

'I'm sorry, Steven. I'm so dreadfully sorry I've lost our baby . . .' He wiped away the tears with the pad of his thumbs and cupped her face gently in his hands.

'Don't cry, Meggie. You are all that matters to me.' He bent forward and kissed her gently on her forehead. He stroked back her hair with a soothing hand and she closed her eyes. He saw the blue-veined lids and the dark shadows beneath her eyes. She opened them and looked at him, and again they filled with tears.

'They will blame me. They'll say I shouldn't have been cleaning . . .'

'Who will blame you, sweetheart?'

'My mother, and yours . . .'

'Of course they'll not blame you. No one will. We all want to see you well again, Meggie. That's all that matters. You're all that matters to me in the whole world.'

'How will you manage, Steven? The doctor said I must stay here at least a week. They may give me more blood today. I told him I can't. The children . . . and the flitting . . .' The tears slipped silently down her pale cheeks. 'I've let you down so badly when you really need me.'

'No you haven't, Meggie. Everyone will rally round. I've a bit of good news for you anyway. We have a vacant cottage; Joe is working two more weeks then he is moving in. He has two weeks' holiday due to him so his boss says he can take that in lieu of notice. Does that cheer you up a wee bit?'

Meggie tried to smile. 'Yes,' she whispered, and gave his fingers an answering squeeze, but her grasp was weak. 'I feel so tired,' she said. 'It is such an effort to open my eyes . . .'

'I understand, my love,' Steven said softly, stroking the back of her hand with his thumb.

'I'm so sorry . . .' she repeated.

A nurse stepped forward. 'I think your wife needs to sleep now, Mr Caraford. You can come again for the evening visiting.'

Steven had already telephoned to tell his mother what had happened, and he knew she would be at Schoirhead by the time he returned. Avril would be with her, but at ten years old she was a sensible little girl and there was no doubt his mother enjoyed her company and loved her like a granddaughter.

'She's no bother,' his mother had assured him, 'in fact she's a great help with collecting the eggs and feeding the chickens. She loves to do it.'

He decided to go round by Bengairney and then call on Megan's parents. He owed them that at least. They would be very worried. He'd forgotten Ruth would be at the house, and he was even more surprised to find Lindsey Gray still at Bengairney, carrying the milk for John Oliphant. They were just finishing up in the dairy and the cows had been turned out to grass in a nearby field. His father-in-law was relieved to see him.

'How is she, Steven? How's ma lassie?' His voice was gruff with emotion.

'She's very tired. I can go back at visiting time this evening, but they would prefer she had no other visitors for a couple of days. I'm sorry . . .'

'Aye, I expect Chrissie will be upset when I tell her. She'll not rest until she's seen her.'

'I thought I'd go round that way now. I was forgetting it's still early.' He glanced at Lint and gave a half smile. 'I had an early start to the milking after I got your phone call. As soon as I'd turned the cows out I went to the hospital. I shall have the byres to clean out and the milk units to wash properly when I get back, but I had to see Megan.'

'If you'd like to go with Steven to tell Chrissie now, John, I'll clean the byre here. I know nothing about milking cows but I can wield a brush and shovel,' Lint offered.

'Oh we canna let you do that, Lindsey!' Steven and John spoke almost in unison.

Lint threw back his head and laughed. 'Don't you trust me to fill a wheelbarrow?'

'Of course we trust ye, laddie, but that's no job for a surgeon,' John Oliphant said with something like horror.

'It will be good exercise, and I insist you both go and explain things to Chrissie. I expect you're both ready for some breakfast. Ruth only has eggs and one pan or I'm sure she'd have made you some.'

'Did she make you some?' John asked curiously.

'Yes, scrambled eggs on toast. They were very good, but after being out here I reckon I shall be ready for another.'

'Well there's plenty of milk here. Ask her to put a rice pudding in the oven if you're staying for dinner,' John suggested.

'Mmm, that's not a bad idea, but I doubt if they brought any rice.' Lint grinned. 'They planned to exist on camp rations for the weekend. You get away to Chrissie now.'

'You'll get rice and things at the shop,' John Oliphant suggested. 'It's not far down the road to the village. Since things came off ration that shop can sell you just about anything from buttons and bacon, to shirts and sugar, and even wellingtons.'

'I think I'll need to go back to the Tower for a change of clothes and some money if I intend to stay here the rest of the day.'

Chrissie Oliphant knew there was something wrong as soon as she saw Steven's van drawing up behind John's car.

'What is it? What's wrong? I didn't expect you home so early . . .'

'Calm down, Chrissie,' John said gruffly, but he drew her into his arms, steadying her. 'It seems Megan was expecting another baby. She had a miscarriage during the night.'

'Oh no! I'll need to go over to Bengairney and bring her here . . .'

'No, she's in hospital.'

'Hospital? B–but when was the baby due?'

'October,' Steven said unhappily. 'My mother didn't know either. I don't know why Meggie didn't want anyone to know. Ruth was the only one she confided in. She hasna been keeping well and it made her tired and – well, and a bit irritable.'

'I knew there was something wrong with her!' Chrissie declared. 'I kept telling her she didna look well, but I thought it must be the shock o' the McGuires dying and the worry and upheaval.'

'I shouldn't have agreed she could come to Bengairney to clean on her own this weekend,' Steven said. 'I blame myself, but she said it would be easier if she did it before we moved in with our stuff, especially when most of the house hasna been lived in for a while. She wanted to freshen up the rooms we shall be using, especially for the children.'

'It's no good blaming yourself, Steven,' John Oliphant said. 'Lint agreed with the doctor. He said it was probably nature's way, or something like that.'

'Poor Meggie. I'll need to go and see her.'

'The doctor says she will be in for a week to ten days,' Steven said. 'He wants her to get as much rest as possible. I can see her for a short time this evening and again tomorrow. If things are going all right she will be allowed visitors after that.'

'I see.' Chrissie frowned and drew away from her husband. She looked from one to the other. 'There's something you're not telling me, and why was Lindsey Gray there?'

Her husband and son-in-law looked at each other. John shrugged philosophically. 'There's no hiding anything from Chrissie.'

'We didn't want to worry you. Apparently Meggie lost a lot of blood and they had to give her a blood transfusion.'

'Oh!' Chrissie turned, went into the kitchen and flopped down on the nearest chair. 'Are you sure she's going to be all right?'

'Yes, that is what the doctor said,' Steven assured her.

'So why was Lindsey with her?'

'Ruth telephoned him in the middle of the night. She knew it was serious but we don't have a doctor here yet. Lint took charge of everything. Ruth went with Megan and he went to bring her back. That's when they phoned me. The doctor wouldn't let them see Megan; I couldn't see her either until nine o'clock, so I did the milking then went straight to the hospital. My mother and Avril were going to feed the rest of the animals. I ought to get back there now.'

'Just a minute, Steven.' John Oliphant laid a restraining hand on his arm. 'Does that mean you've had no breakfast?'

'I couldna have eaten anything until I'd seen Megan.'

'Well you must be ready for some now,' Chrissie said, getting to her feet. 'There's plenty of porridge for two. You can be eating that while I cook you both some bacon and eggs.'

'Where's Samuel and Tania?' Steven asked.

'Och, they're playing on the see-saw at the bottom o' the garden. They've been up since the crack o' dawn, the rascals.' Chrissie smiled, her eyes softening. 'Thank God you have two healthy bairns, Steven, not that it will make losing this one any easier for Megan for a while,' she added unhappily.

'If Megan is to be in hospital for at least a week, you'll need to move out of Schoirhead before she gets home,' John Oliphant said as they ate their breakfast.

'Yes. Ruth is being very good. She's offered to stay on at

Bengairney today and tomorrow and do some of the things she and Megan had planned to do ready for moving, but there's still a lot of stuff to pack, and there's the children . . .'

'Don't worry about them,' Chrissie said quickly. 'I'll look after them until Megan gets out of hospital, but I could do with the rest of their clothes and toys here. I expect Hannah will do what she can, but you'll have all the outside work to do on your own. You'll have your hands full, Steven.'

'I know. More importantly, I want to visit Megan as often as I can. She'll hate being in hospital and I can't bear to see her so upset.'

'I've been thinking about that,' John Oliphant said. 'If you could get Tom Green to move your milking cows up to Bengairney this weekend— Yes, love, I know tomorrow is Sunday,' – he nodded when Chrissie opened her mouth to protest – 'but Tom and his lorry are more likely to be free. I'm thinking it's a bit daft Steven milking and mucking out and washing up in the dairy down there, and me doing the same thing up here. If you bring all the milk cows to Bengairney I'll look after them until you can get the rest of your stuff moved, Steven. It's less than a week and I reckon the old man in the cottage would lend a hand with carrying the milk. He's come into the byre in the afternoons for a chat. He can't milk with a machine but he used to carry the milk. He's been working all his life.'

'I'd pay him if you really think you could manage all the cows. It would be a tremendous help, but God knows how Meggie and I will repay you both.'

'Och, Steven,' Chrissie said with a break in her voice, 'listen to those two wee bairns, laughing and healthy and full of fun. We're well blessed, thanks to you.'

'Chrissie's right, we're proud of you, Steven. Trouble always seems to come when we can least cope and we'd like to help.'

'Thank you, both of you,' Steven said.

'So you'll telephone Tom Green when you get home? Better still, why don't you phone from here then we'll all know what's to happen.'

'You're sure about this?'

'I am, laddie. You get into the hall and phone Tom,' John Oliphant said.

# Fourteen

Back at Bengairney, Ruth was surprised when she glanced out of the kitchen window and saw Lint still in the farmyard, wheeling a barrow of manure from the byre to the midden. She thought he had gone back to Langton Tower. Although she didn't want to admit it, she had been disappointed when he had not called in to say goodbye after sharing such a night of trauma.

Shortly afterwards he came in at the back door and Ruth wrinkled her nose at the smell.

'Any chance of a cup of coffee before I go back to change?' he asked with a boyish grin.

'I thought you'd already gone. I can't believe that a surgeon would wheel smelly muck around.'

'I wanted John and Steven to get home and explain to Chrissie about Megan before she runs into Katherine. Anyway, I'm sure you're a very good teacher, Ruth, but I believe you enjoyed working on the land and with the animals once?'

'I . . .' She gave him a wary look and frowned. 'I enjoyed helping Hannah, and still do,' she said ambiguously.

*In other words, I'm not ready to discuss that period of my life*, Lint thought.

'I can understand that. I enjoy physical work when I'm away from the hospital. Since I've been visiting Katherine and Douglas it has made me think I'd like to buy a house in the country myself, with a bit of land to play around with – maybe keep a pony if I had any children. My sister and I were away at boarding school most of the time and my father was never a hands-on countryman. It was my mother who encouraged us to have pets and helped us look after them, although it fell to her when we went back to school.'

'I–I assumed you were a townsperson.'

'Oh no. My maternal grandfather was a farmer in Gloucestershire. The land was sold when he died, but my parents still live there. The house is far too big for them now. They have made one end into an apartment for my sister and her husband, so they can stay nearby but still be independent when they come home.'

'Where does your sister live?'

'Abroad most of the time. Her husband is in international banking. They spend eighteen months in one country or another, then come home on leave.'

Ruth sighed inwardly. Lindsey's family must be very wealthy, although he never gave that impression. 'There you are, one milky coffee coming up.' She pushed the enamel mug across the kitchen table, another piece of furniture left by Mr Samson. 'You'll need to excuse our best china. Megan thought there'd only be the two of us and we don't mind camping out.'

'Neither do I if the company is good.' He looked at her over the rim of the mug and there was a definite twinkle in his eyes. 'Mmm . . . it's good coffee too.'

'Sorry I've no biscuits to offer you.'

'This is all I need, thanks. So what are you planning to do today?'

'I'm going to clean out this big kitchen cupboard and the pantry so that the food and cooking utensils can go straight in there. It's what Megan planned to do. After that I'm going to try to sort out the boxes which are piled in the empty sitting room. Some need to go upstairs and I think some may be for the kitchen. They will need one empty room downstairs to put the furniture in on Friday, especially when Megan will not be here to organize things.'

'I'm going home to change, but I'll help you sort out the boxes and carry the ones for upstairs when I return.'

'Oh no, there's no need for you to do that!'

'I've promised to help John Oliphant with the milking again this afternoon and I had no special plans to do anything else. I often help John up at the Tower anyway.' He drained his coffee mug and rinsed it at the big white sink. 'Which room do we need to empty for Friday? Can I have a look?'

'Of course. Mr Samson has left the dining room almost fully furnished, so Megan planned to shut the door on that for now. I don't know why he didn't sell his furniture at the farm sale. Some of it is good stuff, or it will be when it's been washed and polished. The front sitting room is the most pleasant room. The windows face south and west, but Mr Samson has left an assortment of chairs in there too, as well as a display cabinet.'

'So I see,' Lint said, opening one of the doors. 'If we dispersed some of the boxes from the smaller room we could stack these spare chairs neatly in there and empty this room. I should think it's been rather nice at one time. The carpet is still in good condition.' He turned to look at Ruth. 'I'll tell you what, I'll ask Katherine if we can borrow her electric sweeper. You're not supposed to need to lift the carpets and beat them on the clothes-line if you use one, at least according to the salesman. It sucks the dust into a bag.'

'I've heard about them but I've never used one,' Ruth said doubtfully.

'We could give it a try. I'll take the curtains down when I come back. We'll give them a really good shake outside. I've often helped my mother do her brocade curtains. These are brocade, aren't they?'

'Yes they are, and they're in good condition, except for the dust and a few cobwebs around the curtain poles. Mrs Samson must have had good taste. The linoleum surround should come up well too if I wash it and give it a polish,' Ruth added with growing enthusiasm. 'All right, if you're sure you don't mind wasting your Saturday here?'

'I wouldn't offer if I did,' Lint said with a smile. 'And I shall not be wasting my time.'

'Megan will be grateful for anything we can do to make the moving day easier. Steven, too. He'll have his hands full, though I expect Hannah will do the rest of the packing in the house. Mrs Oliphant will be busy enough looking after Samuel and Tania. She'll want to visit Megan at the hospital, too. Poor Megan, I expect she'll be fretting about being stuck in hospital at such a hectic time.'

'She will, but it's the best place for her. Right,' Lint clapped his hands, 'I'll go home and change then I'll go to the shop for some rice. Did you see the big can of milk John sent in? He suggested we make a rice pudding for lunch. Have you got a suitable dish?'

'Y—yes, I think so. There's three enamel dishes in the pantry and about three creaming pans, and loads of empty jam jars. I don't think Mr Samson ever threw anything away.'

'I'll bring some potatoes out of the barn. They're beginning to sprout a bit but I'll scrub them and put them into the oven to bake. Meat is still on rations, isn't it? But maybe I'll get some bacon or sausages or something at the shop. Would they cook in the oven too?'

'Well, y—yes, but I thought you'd be leaving . . . I mean, I didn't expect you to . . .'

'Don't worry, Ruth, I'm enjoying myself. I almost wish I was preparing my own house, don't you?'

Ruth gave him a strange look, but he went outside, whistling happily, and she shook her head. 'It takes all sorts,' she murmured, but Lint was the first man she had met who seemed happy and handy around a house. She hoped his cousin would let him have the electric sweeper to try out on the carpet. She and Megan had both agreed it could be a lovely room when all the old chairs were removed and it had had a good clean.

Katherine was happy to loan her Hoover for the whole weekend. 'I expect Chrissie will want to visit Megan at the hospital as soon as she's allowed,' she said.

'That will not be before Monday. Only Steven is allowed to see her. I suspect it was no ordinary miscarriage, but I'm not an expert in that field.' Lint frowned. 'She seemed to have lost a lot of blood. Don't worry Chrissie, though.'

'As if I would. If you see her before I do, tell her I'd be happy to look after the children for the afternoon.'

'You would?' Lint raised his eyebrows. 'I thought you were forever declaring you were not maternally inclined.'

'It's a woman's privilege to change her mind, dear Cos. Anyway, they're lovely kids. They come up with Chrissie to see the poultry and the pigs. I swear young Samuel knows more about looking after them than I do.'

'He wouldn't need to know a lot, would he?' Lint's eyes glinted wickedly and Katherine pretended to box his ears.

'I was looking up in the old nursery. There's a lovely rocking horse and all sorts of books and toys. I think they might enjoy exploring.'

'I'll tell Chrissie then. I'm sure she'll be grateful. I know she'll not be happy until she's seen Megan for herself. Are you needing John for anything urgent?'

'No, he's worked really hard since he started. I'm amazed at the difference he's made. He's planted up the vegetable garden and it's coming along beautifully. You tell him to help Steven as much as he wants until they get settled in at Bengairney. I know he'll not neglect us if we need him.'

'Good. I thought you'd find him a good man, and practical too.'

'Shall I assume you'll be taking Ruth out for a meal this evening?' Katherine asked with a glint in her eye.

'You may assume, dear Katherine, but I never assume anything with Ruth. I shall try my best to persuade her. Neither of us will have much in the way of clothes, so it would need to be some-where ordinary.'

'There's a nice wee country pub opened in the next village, the one where Chrissie and John used to live. Dornielea, isn't it?'

'Yes, that's right. What's the name of the pub and does it do meals?'

'It's called the Highland Lad. They have a little room through the back where they serve meals. There's not a lot of choice, but it's good wholesome food. I expect there'll be more choice when the meat comes off ration. They do a good rabbit casserole with lots of vegetables, and they serve a lot of fish. I think some of the customers are fishermen.'

'Mmm, sounds just the job.'

True to his word, Lint returned to help Ruth with the boxes. He'd put four large potatoes in the oven to roast and she spooned in the rice and sugar and a pinch of salt to bake a rice pudding as he had requested.

'They can be cooking while we work,' Lint said with satis-faction. 'I see you've scrubbed out the cupboard.'

'Yes, and I'm almost finished with the pantry, so if any of the boxes need to come this way we'll just bring them through here. Thank goodness Megan has labelled each one. She's so methodical. I feel like weeping for her when I think of her losing the baby and having to lie in hospital.'

'Unfortunately tears will not help in this case,' Lint said gently, 'but I'm certain she'll appreciate all you've done in her place. You're a good friend, Ruth.'

'I'm glad to be able to do something to repay Megan a little. It has made a big difference to my life knowing Hannah and having Megan for a friend.' She spoke emphatically, leaving Lint in no doubt of her sincerity.

It was after one o'clock when Ruth wiped her forehead with the back of her hand and tugged off the bright-red scarf she had used to keep her hair back. They had carried most of the boxes to an empty bedroom and the rest were in the kitchen waiting to be unpacked. They had made room to store the spare chairs and emptied the large sitting room. Ruth was eager to try out the electric Hoover.

'I'm famished,' she said. 'I need to eat before I do anything else.'

'That's the best suggestion I've heard all day.' Lint grinned. 'I brought a hunk of cheese and some more butter from the shop. Would baked potatoes and cheese do instead of waiting for the sausages to cook? We can eat them for breakfast in the morning.'

'Can we?' Ruth's dark brows rose in surprise. 'Are you helping with the milking tomorrow too?' She was getting the hot potatoes from the oven.

'Of course, and on Sunday afternoon. After that I need to get back to the hospital. I like to have a talk with all my patients on Mondays before I operate on Tuesday. You'll be going home tomorrow afternoon too, I suppose?'

'Yes, I must collect Avril and get her ready for school on Monday.' She lifted the dish of rice pudding on to the table. 'The skin looks a bit brown, but I think it's nice and creamy underneath. It will need time to cool while we eat the potatoes. I never knew I could feel so hungry.'

'You've had a busy morning. You ought to have a rest after lunch, you didn't get much sleep last night.'

'Neither did you, but I'd rather get on. I want to wash that linoleum and have a go with the Hoover.' She smiled up at him and Lint was thankful to see her so natural, at least when they had the table between them. He had been aware of the way she tensed whenever he had needed to be very close to her as they worked, especially when she had to squeeze past him coming out of the linen cupboard on the landing. Her hair had tickled his chin and he had been conscious of the soft swell of her breasts against his chest. He had avoided looking into her eyes, but he was sure she must realize how he felt about her.

Later Ruth knelt to scrub the linoleum surround in the big sitting room. Lint had never seen her in slacks until yesterday evening, and as she bent over he couldn't help but admire her neat little rear.

'I've already washed the windows. Are you going to hang the curtains back up before I get round to that side?' she asked without looking round.

Lint found himself colouring guiltily, like a small boy with his hand in the sweetie jar. He sighed and wondered whether he would ever manage to break through Ruth's reserve. He was happy to help anyone when they needed it, but he knew he was more than willing in this case because Ruth was working beside him and he enjoyed being with her.

About three o'clock they were startled by the sound of a lorry drawing into the yard. Ruth went to the window to look out.

'Gosh, there's another lorry following. Steven is driving it. I didn't know he could drive a lorry.'

Lint followed her to the back door as Steven jumped down from the driver's seat. 'I expect he drove lorries in the army, and these are only small cattle lorries. He looks exhausted,' Lint remarked.

'He loves Megan even more than he loves his animals and the farm,' Ruth said quietly. 'I expect it's worry as well as lack of sleep. He said he'd started his day's work when we phoned him at four o' clock.'

'He'll feel better after he's seen Megan again this evening,' Lint said, 'but I expect he's wondering how he's going to manage moving the farm without her.'

Steven strode towards them. 'Megan's father has offered to milk all of the cows here so I can get everything else organized at Schoirhead,' he explained. 'The owner of this lorry couldn't come himself, but he said I could borrow it for the weekend. We've brought eight cows today and we'll bring the other eight after I've milked them tomorrow morning, even though it is Sunday.' He smiled and shrugged. 'Mother doesn't approve of extra work on Sundays, but she admits this is an emergency. I've plenty to do before Friday.'

'It looks as though you've brought some more boxes too?' Ruth remarked.

'Yes, Megan brought stuff up in the van each time she came. These were ready so I filled the passenger seats. Anything to make less work for Friday morning. I don't want to keep my father-in-law away from his own work any longer than I can help.' He looked at Lint.

'You needn't worry about that. Katherine was telling me what a difference he's made already. He's doing a fine job, exactly what Douglas needs.'

'I'm glad, for everybody's sake,' Steven said. 'Mother wondered if you had any empty boxes I could take back, Ruth? Granny Oliphant needs extra clothes and toys for the two rascals now they'll be staying all week. Avril is enjoying helping Mother pack.' He wiped a hand across his brow. 'Everybody is being so good. I don't know how to thank you all.'

'There's no need for thanks,' Ruth said. 'Have you time to look at this cabinet before you unload? We've moved everything else out of the room ready for your own furniture to go in, but it is rather a nice cabinet Mr Samson has left, or it will be once the glass has been washed and polished up.'

'It's lovely inlaid wood,' Lint said.

'If you two both think it's all right I'll not bother looking,' Steven said. 'I'm sure you'll know better than me. Mr Griffiths, the land agent, said Mrs Samson was a woman of taste so I suppose it would be her choice.'

'Right, Steven,' Tom Green shouted. 'I've backed the lorry up to the byre door. Do you think we shall manage or do you want to wait until Mr Oliphant comes?'

'I can help if you like,' Ruth offered diffidently. She threw Steven a challenging look. 'I'm better with animals than I was at setting up the sheaves.'

He grinned at that. 'She's a feisty wee woman, this,' he said to Lint. 'I wouldna like to cross her.'

'No, I'm being careful,' Lint quipped. 'I don't know much about cows, but if you tell me what to do I'll do my best.'

'All right. I don't want to hang about. I need to get back and get the rest milked so that I can get to the hospital for visiting time. They seem to be very strict.' He told them both where to stand as the cows came down the ramp. They went straight into the byre and Tom Green slammed the door shut behind them.

'Now getting them tied in to their new stalls might be a different kettle of fish,' he muttered. And it was. They got the first three into the empty stalls with relative ease, but the fourth went galloping down the byre and tried to shove her way into every stall on the way back up, even though there were already two cows in most of them. Eventually they got her in beside her mate and she stood as quiet as a lamb while Steven tied the chain around her neck. Tom moved his lorry and they did the same with the other cows. This time there were two awkward customers, and Lint had to jump quickly out of the way or get knocked down, but with patience and some persuasion they got them all tied into their places.

'I think they would be better kept tied up for a day or two,' Steven said, 'until they learn which are their stalls. I expect Megan's father will agree, but maybe you'd mention it to him, Lint?'

'Yes, all right. Do they really stand in the same stalls every time? Do they know where to go?'

'Oh yes. They're not long in learning and they don't like being changed around. There's always a boss cow if you watch them going to and from the field. Now we'll unload the boxes and then I'll get away home, if you'll give me the empties, Ruth? Oh, I nearly forgot, Mother sent you a gingerbread and a few scones. Avril said I'd to tell you she'd made one of them specially for you. It's supposed to be a donkey.'

Lint and Ruth stood side by side watching the lorries depart.

'I think I'd better make you a cup of tea and one of Hannah's scones.' Ruth grinned. 'It looks as though you're going to have more milk to carry than you bargained for tonight.'

'It does make sense to have the cows all in one place, and I reckon John enjoys being back at the milking, at least for a little while. If Roger Bannister can run a mile in under four minutes, I'm sure this doctor ought to be able to carry a few pails of milk. Megan or her mother used to do that all the time at Martinwold. If they can do it I'm sure I can.'

'I'm sure you manage anything you put your mind to,' Ruth said, smiling.

'Not quite,' Lint said seriously. 'Not yet anyway, but I don't give up easily.'

Ruth had a feeling his words had a hidden meaning and she was not sure she wanted to know what it was.

He watched her as she set out the tea. 'Mmm, this looks good.'

'Yes, I suppose I shall have to eat the cuddy or Avril will be offended.'

'The cuddy?'

'The donkey. She has made it out of scone dough. Hannah has so much patience with her. I had great doubts about moving to Scotland after my father died, but it's been the best thing I could have done for Avril.'

'Only for Avril? Have you regrets from your own point of view, Ruth?'

'N–no, I suppose not.' It was true most of the time. She couldn't tell Lint of her secret dread that Fred Caraford might return one day and discover Avril was his child. She knew Hannah had never heard from him since the day he left Willowburn, but Fred only considered himself.

Lint watched the shadows in her dark eyes and wished she would confide in him. He longed to protect her from whatever private demons troubled her.

'We'll go out for our meal this evening. We both deserve to be waited on for once.' He was deliberately matter of fact about it but Ruth tensed immediately.

'I–I can't go out for a meal. I mean . . . Anyway, I've nothing to wear.'

'Well that's better than washing your hair as an excuse,' Lint said wryly. 'Come on, Ruth. You came straight from school yesterday, didn't you? Did you wear your slacks to work?'

'No, but . . .'

'No buts. Put on whatever you wore for school. We're only going to a little pub down the road. I don't know about you but I'm nearly ready for bed now. We didn't get much sleep last night either so don't waste your energy making a meal. We'll go, we'll eat, and I'll bring you back for a good night's sleep and another busy day tomorrow. Right?'

'It sounds more like an order than an invitation.'

'It is. Doctor's orders, but they're for the sake of the man himself. If you don't keep me company I shall probably fall asleep over my rabbit stew or fish, whatever it is.' He looked at her with the pleading eyes of a small boy.

'In that case it would be churlish to refuse.'

'It would indeed.' Lint grinned, feeling well pleased that he had achieved this small step forward.

# Fifteen

Ruth was a keen dressmaker and she enjoyed making most of Avril's clothes and her own dresses and blouses for work. The money she saved on these she invested in buying well-made coats or jackets which required more tailoring skill than she possessed. She had begun to use her great-aunt's treadle sewing machine when she was twelve and she valued the old woman's strict training, but she felt less than confident in the red dress she had worn to school on Friday and she had only the minimum of make-up in her handbag. She hadn't expected to be dining out anywhere, least of all with Lindsey Gray. She sighed, wishing she had brought her pearls to adorn the plain square neck.

'I'm ready,' Lint called, 'and I'm hungry!'

'Yes, so am I,' Ruth called back, and ran lightly down the stairs to where he waited with a big grin on his face. He wished he dared catch her in his arms and swing her round, not to mention giving her the sort of kiss he dreamed about. He had never met a woman who challenged him as much as Ruth; in fact he had never met a woman who challenged him at all. Usually they succumbed quite readily to his charm, or more likely to his bank account, he thought wryly.

They found the Highland Lad without difficulty. There were very few cars in the car park; most of the customers were within walking distance, but there was one large Bentley. Lint frowned and drew in his lips when he recognized it, but he made no comment to Ruth.

'I do hope it isn't too posh inside,' she said anxiously, noting the large, polished car. She looked up at him. He was wearing grey flannels and a blue open-necked shirt. His newly washed skin glowed with health, but he hadn't brought his shaving tackle to Bengairney and there was a faint shadow around his lean jaw. It added to his masculine attractiveness in Ruth's opinion. He held her elbow as he guided her through the low, heavy oak door. There was a crowd of customers around the bar and sitting at small tables dotted about the room. At the far side a wood fire burned in the grate and the atmosphere was jovial and friendly. This was spoiled when a couple came through from another room, looking completely out of place in such homely surroundings.

The man was wearing an evening suit and bow tie and the woman looked elegant with her hair piled on top of her head in an elaborate coiffure. Ruth gasped as she recognized Natalie Turner. She couldn't remember her married name. Her evening gown was obviously expensive, but the beige shade, combined with the vee neckline, thickly embroidered with rows of bugle beads, made her look far too mature for her age. Perhaps that was intentional, Ruth thought, remembering Megan had said her husband was much older than her. She raised her eyes and froze. She had seen that calculating look in men's eyes before, the detailed perusal limb by limb, mentally undressing her, assessing her as though she were an animal at auction. Usually a man who gave her that sort of look made Ruth cringe and want to hide away, but the man's insolent expression made her dark eyes spark with anger. Who did he think he was? Her glance moved briefly to the young woman following them from the dining room. She was wringing her hands and chewing desperately at her lower lip, evidently struggling to hold back tears as she looked help-lessly at the man behind the bar. Ruth guessed he was her husband.

'Is there a problem, sir?' he asked politely.

'I'd say you have a big problem, my man.' Wright-Manton answered more loudly than was needed. His lip curled. 'You call yourself an eating establishment and the best you can offer is rabbit or fish. No doubt you poached them from the local landowners anyway and . . .'

'No sir, they're bought and paid for. We only sell fresh whole-some food which my wife cooks herself,' the man said earnestly. 'You must know that beef and lamb are still rationed.'

'I–I did offer them roast ham, or cold ham salad,' the woman began, 'b–but . . .'

'Ham salad!' the man scoffed. 'We can have that at home anytime.'

'Pity ye didna stay there then,' a voice growled from the group near the fire.

'Well we're hungry enough to eat a horse,' Lint intervened.

He smiled warmly at the young woman. 'Mrs Palmer-Farr specially recommended your rabbit pie and your baked trout in butter. May we go through to the dining room if this couple are leaving?'

'Oh sir,' the woman looked pathetically grateful. 'Sir Douglas and his wife were here a couple of weeks ago, but I never thought they would recommend us to their friends.'

'I assure you they did. You said you would like the baked trout, Ruth?'

'Yes please.'

'I'll have the same,' Lint said. 'It will be quicker to cook two the same presumably?'

'It is.' The woman smiled for the first time. 'But if you're so hungry, sir, I have some good chicken soup and home-made bread to start you off.'

'That sounds delicious.' Ruth nodded. 'And can I have a glass of cider please – long and cold.' She ran the tip of her tongue over her upper lip. Both Lint and Doctor Wright-Manton saw and appreciated that unconsciously enticing gesture, but Natalie resented anyone else being the centre of attention. She jerked her husband's arm.

'Aren't you going to tell them their service just isn't good enough if they expect to build up a business in Dornielea?'

'We can't offer you what we haven't got, Miss Turner,' the landlord said patiently.

'Mrs Wright-Manton,' Natalie corrected abruptly, and flashed a large diamond ring in front of his nose.

'Pardon me, I'd forgotten. Yes, Barney, what can I get you?' he asked, looking past her to a waiting customer.

Natalie was furious. She yanked her husband's sleeve impatiently, but his eyes were still on Ruth.

'So is this the reason you messed up the opportunity to go to London and work under Professor Glaister?' he drawled, his glance moving to Lint and back to Ruth.

'I didn't mess up anything,' Lint said coldly. 'I didn't apply for the vacancy because I have never had any intention of returning to London. I understand you'll be leaving us soon yourself?'

'Who told you that?' Wright-Manton demanded with a scowl.

'Doctor Sissons said you were planning to retire and spend more time with your new wife,' Lint said blandly, with a glance at Natalie. She flushed angrily. Having worked at the hospital she knew as well as anyone that the other doctors had teased her husband unmercifully about marrying a rich young wife and needing to preserve his energies.

'I've decided to keep going for a while,' Wright-Manton declared, 'so you'll not be rid of me yet.' He shot a warning look at Natalie. It was true he had intended to retire; he had believed Natalie would have a generous income from her father and he had planned to keep on a few private patients and generally enjoy life. Instead his tight-fisted father-in-law had given them a wedding present of a modest house, adequate for the two of them with a consulting room attached, but scarcely spacious when his children came to stay, which they did regularly. This evening they had been invited to dinner at Martinwold to meet some friends of Murdo Turner, but they had quarrelled even before the other guests arrived. He had been helping himself to a third measure – admittedly a very generous measure – of best malt whisky when Murdo had pointedly removed the decanter. He resented being chastised like a schoolboy and had threatened to walk out.

'You go ahead,' Murdo Turner said smoothly.

Even Natalie's mother had not tried to persuade them to stay, hence their arrival at this local dump. His mouth thinned. He was hungry and he didn't have enough cash on him to go to one of the better hotels in town.

'Maybe the baked trout would do,' he said ungraciously.

'We're not going back in there after the things you said to that woman,' Natalie protested. 'Come on.' She marched towards the door. It was plain that her husband was less than pleased but he followed her.

'Would you come through now, sir,' the landlady called with a smile, and led Ruth and Lint into a smaller room. Two other couples were finishing their meal and they praised her cooking, bringing a flush of pleasure to her homely face.

'I thought for a minute we were going to have to put up with that horrible man,' Ruth said, breathing a sigh of relief.

'I agree he's an obnoxious character. I suspect they had other plans for the evening. They weren't exactly dressed for a country pub. We'll forget about them and enjoy our meal. Those two deserve each other.'

Ruth was glad Lint seemed to have no regrets about parting with Natalie, and she tucked into both the soup and the trout with relish. Afterwards neither could eat dessert, but they enjoyed a leisurely cup of coffee accompanied by miniature crisp biscuits which the landlady had made herself.

When they arrived back at Bengairney, Ruth couldn't help tensing when Lint followed her in. 'Empty houses always seem cold and creepy at night,' she said.

'You'll be snuggled up in bed and fast asleep before you've time to think about it,' Lint said reassuringly. 'I promised John I would look at the cows to make sure none of them have slipped their chains, or are in danger of hanging themselves if they've been struggling in their new surroundings.' He grinned. 'Not that I would know what to do if any of them were in trouble, but John said I should telephone if I was concerned. I'll slip on my wellingtons. You go on up, Ruth. I'll make sure I lock up. Sleep well, and thanks for your company.'

'I should be the one to do the thanking – for everything you've done today, and for a lovely meal. I'm sure I shall sleep the moment my head hits the pillow. Goodnight, Lint.'

Ruth slept dreamlessly until about three o'clock when she had an awful craving for a glass of cold water. She went to the bathroom but there was no glass in there yet. She wished she'd brought her slippers. She padded barefoot down the stairs and was about to switch on the kitchen light when she heard a creak of wood and a movement, like someone stretching or turning over in bed, which was ridiculous, of course. She pushed the door wider so the light from the hall shone into the kitchen. The embers of the fire still glowed faintly in the grate, and stretched out in front of the range was Lint in a sleeping bag and with a pile of cushions for a pillow. One bare arm and shoulder was flung out and he looked young and oddly vulnerable with a lock of brown hair falling over his forehead and his lips slightly parted as though ready to smile. Seeing him like that it was hard to believe he was a capable surgeon. Earlier she had wondered why he had three cushions in the back of his car. He must have intended staying all along. She chewed her lower lip. He hadn't mentioned it. Had he sensed her tension when they arrived back last night? Amazingly she realized she was not afraid, even though they were alone in the house. In fact she felt oddly reassured by his presence. She decided to forgo the water and crept quietly back up the stairs.

When Ruth went down in the morning there was no sign that Lint had spent the night there and she almost wondered if she had dreamt it. She smiled to herself as she raked out the ashes and kindled up the fire. Once it was drawing well she opened the flu to heat the oven, thankful she knew all about dampers and flues from the old range at the vicarage. In one of the boxes Megan had packed she had found various groceries, including unopened packets of flour, salt, sugar and oatmeal. There was more than half a can of milk left from yesterday, so she carefully skimmed off the cream and put water on to boil to make a pan of porridge. Then she put the sausages which Lint had brought yesterday into the oven to cook. John Oliphant would probably enjoy some breakfast too, especially if he intended waiting to unload the rest of the cows. She pulled on her cardigan and went out to the byre to tell him she had made breakfast for all of them.

'Thank you, Ruth,' John Oliphant said gratefully. 'That would suit me very well. I can get cleaned up here until Steven and Tom arrive. Chrissie wasna sure what food you would have left so she sent some soda scones and some eggs and bacon and a bit o' butter. They're in the car.'

'Thanks, I'll get them. We might not have had much left, but Lint treated me to a lovely meal at the pub which has reopened in Dornielea. It was very good.'

'Oh he did, eh?' John gave them a quizzical look and his eyes twinkled. He had noticed Lint coming out of the farmhouse soon after he arrived to begin the milking, and he wondered whether he had stayed there overnight. Well it was none of his business, but Ruth would make him a darned sight better wife than Natalie Turner would have done, or at least she would if he ever managed to win her trust.

Megan was not allowed home until the Monday after the moving. She fretted about the work to be done and she missed the children and worried about her mother looking after them. Worse still was her feeling of guilt over losing their baby. The doctor's reasoning and reassurance could not console her. Tears flowed far too easily and she felt overwhelmingly tired and dispirited.

'Your wife is very low in spirits, Mr Caraford, so I have not burdened her further. I must repeat it is your responsibility to see she does not become pregnant until she has regained full health – possibly in about eighteen months. She needs plenty of nourishing food and fresh air.'

'Thank you, Doctor, I shall see she gets them.' They would be easy to supply, but Steven knew Megan needed his love and reassurance even more. Had the doctor any idea how much they loved each other, or how swiftly the fires of passion had always flared between them? Even with the hateful condoms there was no guarantee he could keep her one hundred per cent safe. He would have to learn to control his desire.

Although there were still boxes to unpack and a great deal of work to do outside, the moving had gone remarkably smoothly.

'We owe our parents and Ruth and Lint a debt we'll never repay,' Steven said ruefully as he followed Megan into the kitchen. 'Do you think you will like the house once you have arranged it the way you want?' he asked anxiously. 'It will make a difference once we have a stair carpet.'

'The house is fine,' Megan answered listlessly. 'Even the children have settled better than I dared to hope after being with Mother for a fortnight. It sounds as though Mrs Palmer-Farr has had them at her house most afternoons. Samuel talks of nothing else but the rocking horse and the electric train and I see Tania has come home with a stuffed panda.'

'I suppose we should be grateful that everyone has done their best to help,' Steven said.

'Oh I am,' Megan said, but she could feel the tears springing to her eyes and she turned away. 'If only I didn't feel so tired,' she said in a muffled voice.

Steven could not help himself. It hurt to see Megan so low in spirits. He crossed the kitchen and drew her to him, stroking her hair and nuzzling the creamy soft skin of her neck. She turned into his arms immediately and clung to him as though she would never let him go. In spite of his best efforts, Steven could feel the desire rising in him at the softness of her body pressed so close to his, even though he knew Megan would not be ready for making love again for quite some time. He broke their embrace and moved away, mumbling an excuse about being needed in the yard.

It set the pattern for many such incidents, and each one left Megan feeling more bereft and inadequate than before, especially as time went on and she began to regain her health and a yearning to be loved. She was filled with a fear that Steven no longer desired her since the horrible miscarriage. She still felt traumatized by the events of that awful night, the strange surroundings of the hospital, the doctors and nurses who treated her body as though it did not belong to her. Some of the memories were vague, but others were a recurring nightmare.

It was good to have Joe back and settled into the cottage next door to old Ben McClymont, who had been at Bengairney most of his life with Mr Samson and his father before him. No one knew his age; Steven wondered whether he knew himself, except that he claimed to have had his three score years and ten and anything extra was a blessing from the good Lord. Whatever happened, he went to the Kirk on Sunday mornings. Although he was retired he appeared at the farm every day, often walking round the cattle or the small flock of breeding ewes which Steven had recently bought and which seemed to give him great pleasure. He did odd jobs, sawing logs or chopping sticks for Megan, and in return she frequently invited him to join them for their midday meal.

'That's a grand wee wife ye have, laddie,' he said repeatedly to Steven.

They had more harvest than they had been used to and Steven was grateful for John Oliphant's help. Even Ben played a part, climbing stiffly up the ladder when the stack grew high so that he could pass the sheaves from the man on the cart to the man building the stack. This saved a lot of time and effort and helped speed up the task. Steven employed two casual workers who lived in Langton village and who had once been employed by Douglas Palmer-Farr's father when he owned the estate. Now they followed the thrashing machine in winter and helped on local farms with hay and harvest, turnip hoeing and any other seasonal work which came their way.

'They're good workers,' Steven remarked one evening. 'I'm glad Ben told me about them. They appreciate the food you send down to the field for them, Megan, so I'm sure they'd come again. They asked me to tell you.'

'It's a good job somebody appreciates me,' Megan muttered.

'Oh, Meggie, we all appreciate you. Old Ben is forever telling me what a lucky man I am to have a wife who is such a grand cook.'

'It seems that's all I'm good for these days, cooking.' Megan uttered these cryptic remarks more and more often these days. Steven frowned. She seemed so changed, so unhappy, and he couldn't seem to find the right thing to say. He hated the brittle retorts. Her green eyes had lost their sparkle.

'Would it help if you had Evelyn to help you in the house?' he asked. 'I'm sure she would be willing, and now that Samuel is at school there's no one to keep an eye on Tania.'

'No! I don't want anybody else in the house. Isn't it clean enough? Is your washing not done on time? Is your food not ready when you sit down?'

'Oh, Meggie . . .' Steven sighed heavily. He never seemed to say the right thing. 'You know that's not what I meant. You do everything, and more, than any man can expect.'

'Do I?' she challenged. 'Do I do everything you want in a wife?'

'Of course you do, my—'

She spun round on her heel and raced upstairs, but not before he had seen the glint of tears in her eyes. He longed to go and take her in his arms and ask her what was really troubling her, but he knew if he did he might not be able to hold his desire in check. Megan no longer had hollow cheeks and dark rings beneath her eyes. She had begun to put on a little weight and the colour had returned to her cheeks; her hair had regained its lustre. He loved her to distraction. That was the trouble, he wanted her desperately. How could he resist making love to her as they had always done whenever either of them had needed comfort or reassurance, and even more often for the sheer pleasure of being in each other's arms? It was hard enough lying by her side in the same bed every night. Should he risk the condoms even after the doctor's stern warning? Then he remembered how white and ill she had looked when he had first seen her in the hospital bed with someone else's blood dripping into her. He had been shocked to the core. Megan's health mattered more to him than anything in the world. Surely he could curb his desires for a few more months.

# Sixteen

Ruth and Avril often came to Bengairney at weekends, and Steven was pleased to see them, if only because Megan seemed more relaxed in Ruth's company. Even with her parents she was edgy and sometimes sharp. It was so out of character and it convinced Steven she had still not recovered from the loss of the baby. Hannah sensed all was not well and she was afraid her presence at Bengairney might add to the tension.

Christmas was drawing near when Steven called on Chrissie.

'Do you know anything about electric sweepers?' he asked. 'When Megan was in hospital Lint borrowed one from the Palmer-Farrs and Ruth said it was wonderful and a lot easier than brushing carpets on your hands and knees. You don't need to lift the carpets and beat them at spring cleaning time, either.'

'I've heard they're very good,' Chrissie said, puzzled. 'Why do you ask?'

'I wondered if you could ask Mrs Palmer-Farr where she got hers and how much they cost. I'm thinking of buying one for Megan for Christmas.'

'I think they'll be fairly expensive,' Chrissie said doubtfully. 'Are you sure that's what she wants?'

'I don't know what she wants,' Steven said, unaware that his own unhappiness was evident to a woman like Chrissie. 'But I thought it might make her work a bit easier.'

'But her health has improved a lot recently, hasn't it, Steven?' Chrissie asked anxiously. 'She's not keeping anything from us, is she?'

'If she is, she's keeping it from me too,' Steven said flatly.

'I'm sure you'd know, Steven. Megan wouldn't keep anything from you.'

'I'm not so sure these days.' He frowned thoughtfully. 'I don't think there's anything physically wrong, but she seems so listless. The doctor was adamant we shouldn't risk having any more children for at least eighteen months, but sometimes I think another baby might be the only thing to assuage her feelings of loss and guilt. I can't convince her that losing the baby was not her fault.'

'I can tell things are not right between you, Steven,' Chrissie said. 'Are you sure it's only the loss of the baby that's bothering her?'

'What else could it be?'

'I don't know, laddie. I wish there was something I could do, but you know Megan never did like me interfering.'

'I'm sorry. I didna mean to worry you. If you can find out about the Hoover I'll think about getting one and see if that helps.'

'I can ask Mrs Palmer-Farr, but surely Jimmy Kerr would be the man to find out for you? They sell electrical goods as well as hardware at Bradleys, don't they? It's all part of the same firm.'

'Of course! I'd forgotten about Bradleys.'

'You should pay Jimmy a visit one evening. It would do you good to have a gossip. You and Megan have both been over-working since you moved to Bengairney, but I know what a lot you've had to do. Now tell me how Samuel is enjoying school.'

'Oh, he likes it most of the time.' Steven smiled. 'But he doesn't see why he should have to go every day when he wants to do other things at home. They're starting rehearsing for a nativity play. He brought a letter home to ask Megan if she would dress him as a shepherd.'

'Tell her I have a wee striped towel if that would do for his headdress. He's a rascal, but he's a bright wee thing. I'm sure he'll get on all right. And Steven . . .'

'Yes?'

'Talk to Megan. Make her talk to you. Whatever the problem is, it's no use sweeping it under the carpet. It'll take more than a fancy machine to cure it.'

'I'll try,' Steven said unhappily, 'but it's easier said than done.'

On Friday evening Steven got washed and changed ready to go out. Megan looked at him in surprise. Neither of them ever went out in the evenings these days, and when they did they'd always been together. They'd always done everything together, Megan thought miserably.

'I'm just going out for an hour or two, but don't wait up if I'm a bit late,' he said.

When he'd gone Megan sat down and burst into tears. It was bad enough Steven no longer wanting to make love to her, but things were even worse than she'd thought if he needed to find other company.

When Ruth came on Saturday Megan was still subdued, and the atmosphere in the house seemed more strained than ever, although the children were lively and eager to go outside with Avril.

'Lint asked me to thank you for your invitation to Christmas dinner, Megan,' Ruth said, 'but he'll be on call so he's not sure whether he could be here on time.'

'Och, tell him we'll just expect him if he's free,' Megan said.

'All right. He has been terribly busy recently. One of the surgeons moved to another hospital so they were a bit short anyway, but then his boss, Mr Higgins, has been off for nearly a month. I don't know what's wrong with him. Lint says there are rumours circulating that he may not be well enough to return to work. Lint takes his responsibilities seriously while he's in charge.'

'I'm sure he does. He's a fine man. Dad said he hadn't been up to Langton Tower so often lately, so that must be the reason.' She looked at Ruth. 'Do I take it he still makes time to see you, Ruth?'

'S—sometimes.' Ruth's cheeks coloured. 'We've been out for a meal a couple of times, and when it was better weather he took Avril and Hannah and me out for a run in the car, and for lunch before he went back to the hospital for evening rounds.'

'So how do you feel about him now?' Megan asked. 'I'm sure he's keen on you or he wouldn't keep coming.'

'I know,' Ruth said unhappily. 'And I feel guilty because I would miss his company if he stopped, b—but . . .'

'But you still keep him at arm's length?'

'Y—yes, I suppose I do. I—I can't help it.'

'Sometimes I think it would be better if Fred hadn't gone off to Canada. If you'd seen him again, face to face, it might have helped you slay your demons.'

'No! I never want to see him again. I would never have come back to Scotland if I'd thought I might run into him. And I never, ever want him to know he is Avril's father,' she added vehemently.

'I'll make some coffee,' Megan said, knowing Ruth hated to think about the past, yet it seemed impossible for her to put it behind her.

Ruth sat at the table deep in thought. Since the weekend they had worked together here at Bengairney, Lint had visited her often. They had become good companions, but even before he declared his intentions Ruth's instincts had told her he wanted more. He needed more, deserved more. He was a young, virile man and he had so much to offer; he was wonderful with children. Their outings had been less frequent since he had had more responsibilities at the hospital, but they had had one extra-special evening when he had asked her to accompany him to a ball as a foursome with Katherine and Douglas Palmer-Farr. She had been nervous but he had persuaded her. She bought herself a lovely evening gown in crimson shot silk, which gleamed with light and shadow as she moved. The colour suited her fair skin and dark hair and the styling gave her confidence. When Hannah had seen her she insisted on lending her a necklace – a pendant set with rubies and a matching bracelet. Ruth had been reluctant to borrow the jewellery in case it got broken or lost.

'I hardly ever have occasion to wear such things these days,' Hannah said. 'These belonged to my grandmother so I suppose the style is out of date.'

'They're beautiful,' Ruth declared. 'I don't think the gold filigree design could ever go out of date, it's so delicate. I should think it's worth rather a lot of money – more than I could afford if I needed to replace it.'

'You won't lose it. I'd like you to wear it, Ruth.'

She had made herself a black velvet evening cape and lined it with satin, and the combination of finery and jewels, combined with Lint's open admiration, had given her a confidence she'd never felt before. It had been a delicious dinner, followed by the dancing. Both Lint and Douglas Palmer-Farr were excellent dancers and Sir Douglas obviously knew most of the people there so neither Katherine nor herself lacked partners.

On the way home Lint had been quieter than usual, apparently deep in thought. They were still a few miles from her home when he drew the car into a secluded lay-by and turned to her.

'Dear Ruth, I can feel the tension mounting in you already.' He sighed. 'Even after all this time, can you still not trust me?'

'I–I . . . Yes I do trust you, Lint. It's just . . . Oh, I don't know. It's been such a wonderful evening. The best I've ever had. Please don't let's spoil it.'

'I enjoyed it too, but you must know how I feel about you? I didn't like to see you dancing in other men's arms, and you looked so relaxed.'

'Yes,' Ruth said in surprise, 'yes I suppose I was. But I knew you were never far away. I knew I was safe.'

'So you do trust me then?'

'I know you'd never hurt me.'

'Ruth, I've fallen in love with you, even though I knew you didn't want anything like that to happen. I knew it was foolish, but there it is. I would like to marry you and make you my wife and adopt Avril and bring her up as my own daughter, but . . . Hush,' he said, and laid a finger gently over her lips when she would have interrupted. 'But I know you're still not ready for that, and I don't have ice in my veins. However many promises I made I know I couldn't keep them if we were married and living together. So I'm going to make you a promise and I want you to make me one in return.'

'If I can,' she whispered.

'I promise I will never force you to do anything you don't want to do, or frighten you, or make you uncomfortable. You only need to tell me and whatever it is, I will stop, but please, please try not to tense up and freeze every time I touch you when we're alone. I shall try to leave you alone on condition that you will tell me when you feel ready to take things further – even if it is only a kiss or a hug. We'll take one step at a time and I give you my word I shall never take advantage or go further than you wish. Will you promise to come to me when you're ready?'

'Y–yes,' Ruth said softly.

'If ever there is anyone else I hope you would tell me truthfully?'

'I can't imagine ever feeling as much at ease with any man as I feel with you, Lint,' Ruth said. 'I do like you so very much, but – but it wouldn't be fair to – to let you think I could marry you and be a proper wife. Maybe I am frigid, maybe there is something wrong with me as Fred said . . .' She shuddered. 'I only know I never want to feel such – such revulsion again. I'd rather live alone for the rest of my life.'

Lint saw her shudder and drew her gently into his arms. He made no effort to kiss her. He simply held her close to his heart and stroked her hair soothingly, as though gentling a frightened filly. Ruth was aware of his growing desire, but she felt no fear of Lint.

When they said goodbye at her door his parting words were a reminder of her promise: 'You will make the first move, Ruth? You will come to me when you're ready?'

Ironically, she had been disappointed when he hadn't kissed her goodnight. Deep down she knew she was not really frigid where Lint was concerned.

She stared unseeingly at the table top in the Bengairney kitchen. So far she had never mustered the courage to move their relationship along. Sometimes she was afraid Lint's patience would run out and he would find another, more suitable woman to marry, a woman without the encumbrance of a ten-year-old daughter.

'You were miles away,' Megan said, pushing a mug of coffee towards her. 'Ruth, how would you feel about us meeting up one evening, just the two of us. Maybe to see a film?'

'Why yes, if that's what you'd like to do, Megan?' Ruth couldn't hide her surprise. 'So long as the weather stays decent. After all, we're into December.'

'It doesn't have to be a film,' Megan said, her mouth tightening. 'We could meet for a meal. Anything you want so long as I get out for an evening.'

'Oh Megan . . . You do seem so very unhappy lately. And Steven doesn't look on top of the world, either. I thought you would both be blissfully happy at Bengairney. It's everything you wanted.'

'We thought it was, b–but . . .' Megan's face crumpled and she hid her head in her hands.

In a flash Ruth had pushed back her chair and hurried round the table to put a comforting arm around her. 'Tell me what's troubling you, Megan,' she urged. 'Are you still suffering from the effects of the miscarriage?'

'No. Yes. I mean, it's since then. Steven doesn't seem to want me any more.'

'That's not true, Megan. I've never seen a couple who cared so deeply for each other. When you were in hospital he didn't care a jot for the farm or even his animals until he knew you were going to be all right.'

'Then why doesn't he want to make love any more? And last night he went out for the evening without me. He never would have done that before.'

'Before the miscarriage? Is it still affecting you? I mean, are you . . .'

'I'm fine. I've been all right for ages, but he's never wanted to make love since I came out of hospital. It makes me feel . . . I feel unclean.'

'Oh Megan, that's nonsense. I don't suppose Steven realizes what they do in hospital, but even if he does he's not squeamish about anything. Nothing would stop him loving you. You must be imagining things.'

Megan compressed her lips and remained silent. She knew what she knew and there had to be a reason why Steven didn't want to love her any more.

The next time Ruth saw Lint she confided in him about Megan and Steven.

'I know I can trust you not to gossip about them, but I'm so worried. They both look unhappy.'

'I haven't seen them for a while, but even if I do see them it's impossible to interfere between a man and wife. They're both very proud. They would resent it.'

Much later on that evening, Lint returned to the subject. 'The only thing I can think of which might hold Steven back from making love to his wife is the doctor's warning. We both know he would do anything to ensure Megan's safety.'

'What sort of warning?' Ruth asked.

'The doctor advised Steven she shouldn't have any more babies for at least eighteen months. Steven told me the doctor had warned him that it would be his responsibility if he valued Megan's good health and welfare. At the time the doctor felt Megan was too distressed by the loss of the baby to trouble her with anything else. Maybe Steven has never discussed it with her. I remember him asking me if I thought condoms were one hundred per cent safe.' He frowned, trying to recall what he had said in reply.

'I doubt if they could be guaranteed absolutely safe – I suppose that's what I told him – but the risk would be very slight, especially now Megan seems to have recovered.'

The following week Steven had arranged to sell three of his newly calved heifers at a pedigree sale at Castle Douglas. They were good animals and he was anxious to reduce his loan to the bank. He, Megan and Joe had spent the previous day grooming and clipping them.

'We'll not shampoo their bodies in this cold weather. I don't want to risk them getting a chill when they're so newly calved. We'll wash their tails and feet.'

Tom Green arrived with his lorry before Steven had finished his breakfast. He grinned as Steven rushed out to load them.

'You said I'd to be early so you'd get a good place for them at the market and time to brush them up.'

'That's exactly what I want. Thanks, Tom. I'll follow on in my van in a few minutes.' He turned to look at Megan. 'I expect I shall be away most of the day, but I think you're right about the Jessie cow. She looks as though she might calve today. I've told Joe to keep an eye on her but I wish I could have been here.'

'You can't be in two places at once,' Megan said philosophically. 'You're not expecting her to give any trouble, are you? I mean, it's not her first calf, or twins or anything.'

'No, this is her second calf. There's no reason why she should have any bother, but she is the best cow we have and I'm hoping for a heifer calf this time. I wouldn't like to lose it. She's the last of the Jessie family unless we get a heifer calf or two out of her.'

'I'm sure Joe will watch out for her, but I'll have a look myself when he goes for his dinner.'

'Would you, Megan? I'd feel happier if I knew you were watching her, but I know it's difficult with Tania following you everywhere, and in this cold weather. If you're in any doubt, phone for the vet. I'd rather pay his bill than lose her calf, even if it is another bull. We might rear him as a stock bull to keep the Willowburn bloodline going.'

Megan always thought Steven seemed to have a sixth sense where the cows were concerned. Her father said it was good stocksmanship, inherited from his father. Whatever it was, she was not surprised when she dressed Tania in her warm coat and hat and took her to the calving shed at lunchtime. Sure enough, the cow was getting up and lying down restlessly, then pressing and getting up again. She should calve soon, Megan thought, probably before Joe returns from his dinner when she's so uneasy.

'Come on, Tania. We'll eat up our dinner then we'll come back and look at Jessie again.'

'Jessie nice cow,' Tania said.

'Yes, she's Daddy's favourite cow.'

Tania ate up her meal without fuss, eager to go back to see Jessie. There was still no sign of a calf. They met Joe coming back early from his own dinner.

'Has she calved?' he asked eagerly, but Megan shook her head. 'She has been up and down all morning. She should have calved. I think something not well for her. Boss said she is special.'

'Perhaps we should feel her, Joe,' Megan suggested. 'I'll stand Tania in the next pen. You can watch Joe through the spars, Poppet,' she said, lifting the little girl into an adjoining pen where she would be safe. 'Now, Joe, if you can get a halter on her I'll steady her from behind and I'll stay beside her while you feel her. Can you manage that or do you want me to feel her?'

'Oh no, Missis Megan. I will feel for feet and head as Boss showed me many times before, but . . .' He looked troubled. 'But if anything wrong I will not know how to make it right.'

'She may be all right and just needing more time,' Megan said calmly. Between them they got the cow tied with a halter and Megan stood at her side, holding her against the gate and murmuring soothingly while Joe soaped his hand and arm and felt inside her.

'One foot here, and it is front foot,' he said with satisfaction, 'and head all right.' He felt around with a frown of concentration. 'Can't feel other leg,' he muttered. He withdrew his arm, rinsed it and stripped off his shirt in spite of the cold day. Then he felt again, pushing his arm into the cow up to his armpit. 'I think I feel other front leg. It is like this.' He curled his arm back behind him to demonstrate. 'We need Boss. He knows how to get other leg forward to let her calf come out all right.'

'It seems a long way down,' Megan said, considering. 'I doubt if I could reach it to get the foot up. I'll phone for the vet, Joe. We'd better be safe than sorry, and she'll not calve until the leg is forward and in the right position. It could be ages before Steven gets home, and she keeps on pressing. I'll phone now.'

She lifted Tania in her arms and ran to the house. They had never needed a vet since they moved to Bengairney, but they had discussed which one they would use and had decided on the firm which Mr Turner had always had. Megan knew her father had great respect for Mr Fisher's skill.

The vet had a small office adjoining his house. A girl answered; she asked what was wrong and made a note of the farm.

'Bengairney? Ye havena been there long,' she said. 'I'll send a vet right away.'

Megan replaced the receiver with a feeling of relief, glad the vet was not out on call at one of the other farms.

The girl turned to the young man who had been flirting with her. He had started with the practice three weeks ago and he kept grumbling that Mr Fisher only gave him odd jobs to do, like feeding the pets who were there to reduce their weight or recovering from a minor operation.

'Here's a call you could go to, Mike. It's the folk frae Bengairney. My Dad says he's an army man so he'll not ken much about calving cows. Probably the calf will only need a pull. It'll be a chance for you to show how clever you are.' She grinned at him. She knew Mr Fisher didn't trust him to attend anything important yet. Although he had wonderful exam results, he'd had little practical experience. His parents lived in the city and he had never even owned a pet.

'An army man did you say? He'll be all blow and bluster with a plum in his mouth, I expect. And he'll know damn all about cows.' He grinned confidently.

Betty, the receptionist, liked to gossip. 'My Dad would have liked to rent Bengairney for ma oldest brother,' she said, 'but nobody had heard old Mr Samson was giving up. He reckons this man's army cronies must have pulled strings with the laird. It was a woman on the telephone, so maybe they have a housekeeper. They'll not be used to farm life.'

# Seventeen

The car came speeding into the farmyard. It stopped with a screech of brakes and tyres, sending dust and mud flying everywhere. Joe had to jump out of the way. At his side, Shandy began to bark at such a disturbance.

'I'm the vet,' the young man announced, climbing out of the mud-spattered vehicle. He eyed the collie dog warily. 'Can't you control him? Does he bite?'

'No, we got fright with your car. You come too fast. Lie down, Shandy, good boy.' Joe patted the dog's soft head. 'I take you to the calving pen. I already have bucket of clean water there for you.'

'You're a foreigner,' the young man said, almost accusingly. His eyes narrowed. 'Where are you from?'

'Germany,' Joe called over his shoulder, hurrying towards the sheds where Jessie was now lying stretched out and giving intermittent presses and groans as she tried in vain to give birth to her calf.

'A POW, I suppose,' the young vet said with contempt.

'I am free man now. Mr Caraford is my employee . . . Beg pardon – my employer.'

'That's queer for an army man, keeping you here.' He shrugged. 'I suppose he's killed plenty of your lot, though, and—'

'The cow need help soon,' Joe said, cutting him short.

'I expect she just needs a pull.' He followed Joe into the shed. 'I see there's a foot there already.'

'Only one foot. The other foot is back like so . . .' Again Joe bent back his arm to demonstrate the cause of the trouble, but Mike Crabbe threw him a scathing glance. Joe flushed. He had seen that look before. It clearly said 'what could a German POW know about anything?'

'I work for Mr Caraford since war finish. He show me many things. I know this problem. You will feel yourself . . .'

The young vet scowled and ignored Joe as he pulled on his waterproof smock. He got out two cords and assembled some sort of pulley with hooks and ropes. He looped one cord securely around the foot which kept peeping out each time the cow pressed, then sucking in again as she relaxed.

'The boss – he push the calf back to get room to manu . . . manvor – to get other foot up,' Joe said urgently. 'Other foot not there,' he repeated desperately. 'Can't pull one foot only . . .'

Mike Crabbe straightened and glared at Joe. 'Where is your bloody boss?'

'He is at market . . .'

'It's a pity he didn't take you with him and sell you there. He's away. I'm here. Don't try telling me what to do.' He made no effort to roll his sleeves far enough to feel inside the cow. When the other foot was not within easy reach he looped the cord around the calf's neck.

'No!' Joe hissed, his eyes widening. 'You kill it.'

'I expect it's dead already.'

'No. Calf still living when you arrive. See . . . the tongue. It still there moving. It need help to get foot up. You can't pull head . . .'

'Why don't you run on back to Germany or keep quiet,' the irate vet said in exasperation. He attached the other ends of the cords to the hooks on the pulley. Joe gasped in horror as he tightened the tension without even waiting for the cow to press.

'You tear . . .' Joe turned and ran to the house to get Megan. 'You must come. Vet not listen. He strangle calf and he – he pull, pull, pull.' Joe was almost sobbing in distress as he tried to catch his breath.

'I'll come,' Megan said, staring at Joe in disbelief, 'but I can't leave Tania alone. I must get her coat and hat. Go back, Joe. I'll come.'

When Megan reached the shed with Tania in her arms, the head of the calf was out and clearly strangled by the cord now tight around its neck and one foot.

'Oh no!' She gasped out loud.

Mike Crabbe glanced round. 'Get out of here! This is no place for women.'

'This is Missis Boss,' Joe said.

'You've killed the calf. Are you wanting to kill the cow as well,' Megan demanded. 'Don't you realize the leg is turned back? The shoulder can't get through.'

'What would a bloody woman know about such things?' Mike

spat at Joe. 'I don't care who she is, get her, and her howling kid, out of here. Then give me a hand to pull the calf out.'

'No, no,' Joe said. 'You tear cow more still . . .'

'Who's the bloody vet here?' Mike demanded, beginning to realize he had made a grave error of judgement. He was unsure what to do about it, but he was not going to admit it. It was too late to push the calf back to straighten the leg now the head was out, but he remembered that was what the textbooks advised.

'Well you're no vet, that's for sure,' Megan flared angrily. 'You're worse than a butcher.' She was trying to comfort Tania and hide her head against her chest to prevent her seeing the half-born calf and all the mess and blood, but she felt like snatching away the pulleys and beating the arrogant young vet about the head. No wonder Joe was so upset. 'You've already killed the calf and you're halfway to killing the cow,' she said furiously. 'The only thing you can do now is be a butcher and cut up the calf to get it out.'

By way of reply Mike Crabbe gritted his teeth and gave an almighty wrench on the pulley, and another and another. The cow gave an unearthly groan, then lay flat out, panting for breath. The sweat had beaded on Mike Crabbe's brow, but he gave another yank and the calf slithered on to the straw.

It was plain to see what the problem had been. Megan felt sick at heart. Her father or Steven would have known how to manipulate the calf and get the leg forward. Now they not only had a dead calf, but they would be lucky if Jessie survived. And even if she did, it was unlikely they would ever get her to have another calf. She turned and left the shed, jerking her head at Joe to follow her.

'I shall call back this evening to check on the cow,' Mike Crabbe called after them. 'She may need an injection.' Neither of them answered.

Outside the shed Megan blinked away her tears. It had been a bad day's work.

'I can't believe that fool is a trained vet.' She daren't think what Steven would say. She knew enough about animals to know the cow would be badly torn inside and would more than likely die. She looked at Joe's white face. Although he was a grown man, she could see he was struggling to control his emotions. 'Leave him. A bucket is all he deserves to wash in. Come on inside, Joe. I'll make you a cup of tea.' Normally the vet would be invited inside to wash with hot water, or at least given a bucket of hot water and a clean towel, followed by the offer of a cup of tea after such a task. She felt too churned up to consider the arrogant young vet.

It was after four o' clock and the December day was fading fast when Steven arrived home. He was later than he had expected, but he was whistling merrily. He had had a satisfactory day all round. The heifers had made more money than he had dared to hope, and almost as important, their type and condition had been noticed by some of the well-known breeders at the sale. More than one man had asked if he would have any more to sell at the next pedigree sale and expressed interest in buying from him in future. It was a good start. On the way home he had made a detour via Annan and called in at Bradleys. Jimmy Kerr had seen his van and come to meet him, taking him through to the shop premises.

'This is Mr Anderson, manager of the retail side,' he said, introducing him to a small, dapper man in a suit and tie. 'This is Steven Caraford who wants the Hoover for his wife's Christmas,' Jimmy said with a grin. 'At least he does if you can give him a reasonable discount. He's a good customer on the machinery side,' he added encouragingly. 'Pays on the dot. None of this a bit each week.'

'In that case I'll see what I can do for a cash sale,' Anderson said. 'The electrical goods are upstairs. If you'll follow me?' There were two models, but Steven knew nothing of such things so he took Mr Anderson's advice, which seemed to please him for he gave a good discount.

Well pleased with his day's work, Steven called on Chrissie to ask her to keep the vacuum cleaner until Christmas eve. John was just coming in from work so Steven stayed to tell him about the day's trade and share a cup of tea.

'Now I'd better get off home,' he said as he drained his cup. 'Megan and Joe will have started the milking, but it's not so easy watching both Sammy and Tania when there's only two people milking as well as carrying the milk to the dairy. Usually Samuel goes with Joe to take the milk and to feed the calves. He thinks he's helping, but when he and Tania are together you never know what mischief they'll get up to.'

'Aye.' Chrissie smiled. 'I remember fine what it was like, taking Sam and Megan to the byre when they were wee.'

'I think Willowburn Jessie might have calved, too. She was uneasy when I left this morning. I told Megan to send for Mr Fisher, the vet, if she thought there was any problem. We've never needed him yet so I havena met him myself.'

'You'll not go far wrong with Mr Fisher. He's a clever man with a lot of experience, and he's reliable. His father was a farmer but he had two uncles who were vets. He took over the practice from one o' them. Mr Turner got on well with him. Mind you, his practice has grown since the war, with farmers keeping more animals. I think he employs an assistant these days.'

'Yes he does,' Chrissie said. 'Mrs Anderson told me he had a really decent young vet for eighteen months, then he decided he wanted to widen his horizons and he's gone to Canada for a year.'

'Oh well, I'll get away home and see what's going on,' Steven said cheerfully, stifling a yawn.

'Up early getting the heifers ready, were ye, laddie?' John Oliphant grinned.

'Yes, and so was Megan. We were up at four to milk them first and give them time for an extra feed and grooming before the lorry arrived.'

'It sounds as though it paid off,' John said approvingly.

Megan and Joe had started the milking and the two children were playing on a pile of hay in an empty stall when Megan carried a pail of milk across to the dairy. Her heart sank when she heard the van drawing into the yard. Steven would feel as sick at heart as she did herself when he saw the dead heifer calf and his favourite cow lying prone on the straw. She and Joe had done their best to prop Jessie up with sheaves of straw to prevent her from blowing up, as cows did if they lay flat for long, but she was a very sick animal with her sunken eyes and dry nose. Even five-year-old Samuel could see she was dying.

'Is Jessie going to die, Joe?' she had heard him asking. She went to meet Steven as he climbed out of the van. She could see by his expression that he had had a good day, and before she could say anything he pulled her into his arms, swinging her off her feet and kissing her firmly on her parted lips before releasing her. It was just the sort of greeting she had longed for lately, just like they used to be, and her eyes filled with tears at the thought of the news she must give him. The smile died from Steven's face.

'What's wrong, Meggie? Are the children all right?'

'Yes, they're fine. It's Jessie . . .' She began to explain, but he was already striding towards the calving shed. She followed. 'If only I'd insisted on Mr Fisher coming in person,' she said. 'I didn't know he had an assistant. He was such an arrogant young man. He wouldna listen to Joe, or to me.'

'Dear God!' Steven exclaimed when he saw the dead calf lying in a corner of the shed and the prone cow. He bent to examine her more closely. His face was pale. 'He's as good as killed them both . . .' he muttered.

'I know . . . He – he said he would be back this evening to check on her.'

'Any fool can see what the problem was with the calf. Surely to God he could have managed to get the other foot up?'

'Joe said he didn't even try, and he had already warned him what was wrong. Joe himself could have made a better effort, but . . .'

'I know, Megan, I know, lass. I told you to get the vet if there was a problem. I should have had more faith in Joe. I'd better get changed and come to the milking.' He squeezed her shoulders. 'I'll not be many minutes, and at least you and the bairns are all right.'

The days were at their shortest and the farmyard was in darkness long before Joe went home after the milking was finished. Megan had taken the children into the house to prepare the evening meal. Although the byre and the dairy at Bengairney had electric lights, none of the other sheds were wired for electricity. It was an improvement Steven planned to put before Mr Griffiths the next time the land agent came round. He pulled his flat cap lower against the biting wind and lifted the lighted Tilley lamp from its hook before going for a last look round the calves and other young animals, all snug and fed now in their sheds. He was heading towards the calving shed when he saw lights turn off the road. A car came speeding into the yard and skidded to a halt. At Steven's heels, Shandy growled and pricked up his ears as Mike Crabbe jumped out. He had given his boss an edited account of his afternoon's work and explained he was going back to check on the cow, making himself out as a conscientious and caring young vet, knowing Mr Fisher would approve of such an attitude. His eyes settled on Steven with the lamp.

'A bit behind the times, aren't you?' he nodded at the Tilley lamp. 'I've come to check up on a cow I calved this afternoon.'

Steven's mouth tightened but he led the way in silence.

'Mmm,' he muttered when he saw the animal stretched out and looking very seedy. He turned back to Steven. 'I'd like a word with your boss, my man,' he said arrogantly.

'I am the boss,' Steven said shortly, striving to curb his anger.

'I want to see the owner. He's an army man, I heard.'

'I'm not interested in what you heard,' Steven said coldly. 'I'm the only boss or owner there is. And I'm not interested in your opinion either because it's not worth a curse from hell. You made a bad job of trying to sort a simple enough problem this afternoon and you've succeeded in killing one of our best cows.'

'She's not dead. I was going to suggest giving her an injection of vitamins.'

'She'll be dead within the next couple of hours so you needn't bother, and you needn't bother sending me a bill either because I shall refuse to pay it. You can tell Mr Fisher this is my first and last dealing with his firm. Now get off my premises and don't come back.'

'You can't treat me like one of your soldier boys!' Mike Crabbe retorted indignantly. 'And you can't believe a word of what that bloody German told you.'

'That bloody German knows more about calving cows than you'll ever know at the rate you're going. I don't need Joe, or my wife, to tell me what a moron you are. It's plain to see when I look at that calf. As for all this rot about an army man, let me tell you I fought for my country during the war, but I was milking cows when I was ten years old, so don't bring your opinions and prejudices here. Now get out of my sight.'

'It's dark . . .'

'Frightened of the shadows, are you?' Steven held up the lamp to light him to the car. 'Don't forget to tell your boss what I said about his bill. If you don't tell him I shall. I should be sending the bill to him for letting the likes o' you loose on a damned fine cow.'

When he had gone Steven leaned against the wall of a shed, trying to regain his composure. He couldn't remember when he had last felt so angry, or so sick at heart. Of course he knew some animals died; farmers had to accept losses, but this had been a needless waste of a fine animal, and one of his best cows at that. His earlier joy in the day's work had evaporated. He was tired and hungry. Wearily he pushed himself away from the wall and headed towards the lighted windows of the house and his wife and children. At least he still had them.

It had been a long and eventful day for both Steven and Megan, and once the children were tucked up in bed and asleep Steven made a last look round, then they were glad to fall into bed too. Tired though they were, neither of them found sleep came easily. Steven turned over, then back again for the umpteenth time.

'Can't you sleep either?' Megan asked softly, and put out a hand, searching for the warmth of him.

'No, I can't help thinking what an arrogant cub that young vet is. I told him I wouldna pay any bill or use that practice again.'

'I felt the same,' Megan said unhappily. 'He was nasty to Joe. If only I'd known Mr Fisher kept an assistant I should have asked for him to come in person. It's all my fault.' She shuddered. 'By the time I got out there it was too late to stop him. It – it was awful.'

'Ah, Meggie, it wasna your fault.' He turned towards her and drew her into his arms. 'Don't blame yourself over that.'

'But I do. I should have been out there . . .'

'I doubt if he'd have listened to you any more than he listened to Joe. He has a lot to learn about more than veterinary science.' His hand was stroking the silky soft skin of her forearm as he spoke. 'Sick though I feel at losing the last of the Jessie cows, it would be a million times worse if I lost you.'

'Me? You wouldn't lose me. Nothing like that would happen to me.'

'Not if I can help it,' Steven said gruffly, trying to stifle the desire that the feel of her soft warm body always awakened in him.

Megan allowed her hand to stray down over his flat stomach and further. 'Oh Steven . . .' she whispered, with a world of yearning in her voice.

'God, Meggie, don't you know what you do to me, just curling in to me the way you do, so soft and warm? It's more than I can bear sometimes. Don't tempt me any more . . .' He caught her hand tightly in his and drew it back up to his chest.

'D–do I still tempt you, Steven?' she asked uncertainly. 'I thought you didn't f–fancy me since – since the miscarriage.'

'Fancy you? Megan, I'll always fancy you, probably until the day I die, even if I live until I'm ninety. In fact I hope I do to make up for all these months when I've had to resist you.'

'I–I don't understand . . . If you – if you want me, why must you resist? I want you too.'

'God knows how much I want you, but after the doctor's warning that I mustn't get you any more babies for at least eighteen months, I only have to remind myself how near I came to losing you. If Ruth hadn't been here and got you there in time . . .' He shuddered and drew a hand over his face.

'I–I didn't realize it was as serious as that,' Megan said slowly. 'I know I felt pretty groggy for a while and they kept putting blood into me, but the doctor said there had been some sort of complication. Anyway, it doesn't mean that would happen again, Steven . . .?'

'Maybe not, but it's not a risk I want to take, Meggie.' His arms tightened around her. 'I love you more than anything in the world. Not all the cows on earth would be worth having if I didn't have you.'

'Oh, Steven . . . I've been so miserable. I thought you kept turning away from me because you couldn't fancy me since the miscarriage.'

'I wish I didn't fancy you!' Steven confessed. 'It's hell holding you in my arms then turning away from you.'

'But I feel perfectly well! I've – I've wanted you to love me for months. And I've been so miserable because I thought you didn't want me. Then – then the other night when you went out on your own, I thought – I thought . . .'

'What did you think?'

'That you were looking for other company,' Megan admitted in a small voice.

'I went to see Jimmy Kerr.' Steven laughed. 'No great attraction there, my love. I wanted to ask him a favour.'

'Oh? What sort of favour?'

'Now that would be telling,' Steven teased. 'It's a secret.'

'Oh you . . .' Megan tried to punch his chest, but he caught her hand and held it fast. She rolled on top of him. 'I don't think there'd be any problem even if we did start another baby, but surely we can risk it with the condoms . . .?' she whispered in his ear, and wriggled against him until he groaned for release.

'They're not a hundred per cent safe . . .'

'I'm not worried about that. I'm as healthy as I've ever been. Honestly, Stevie. All I need is you to love me . . .'

Steven needed no persuading.

The following morning Mike Crabbe made a point of arriving early at his boss's house. He knew Mr Fisher was always up early and in the small annex he used as a surgery cum office cum store. He answered the night calls himself, as well as any early morning ones, and he planned the day's work. Mike was in no doubt Caraford had meant what he said about telling his boss why he would not pay the bill and he wanted to explain his side of things first before Betty arrived. Although she and her family lived on a remote hill farm, they seemed to know all the gossip for miles around and he knew they would make the most of this story if they got wind of it. His life wouldn't be worth living amongst Fisher's clients. None of them would trust him. He was still seething at the lack of respect he had received at Bengairney, and him a qualified vet. Still, he knew the cow would be dead by now and he had made a mess of his first attempt at a difficult calving.

Mr Fisher stared down at the notepad in front of him as he listened and his mouth tightened. He had too much experience of men and animals to swallow young Crabbe's version of events. He screwed his eyes shut as the flow of well-rehearsed sentences came to a halt, then he opened them and raised them to the ceiling.

'Lord give me strength,' he muttered. 'So that's why you went back last night? You knew you'd made a damned mess.'

'I – er, well I didn't think it was right that I should listen to that German fellow. What would he know?'

'More than you, apparently. Now listen to me, young Crabbe. This is the second big mistake you've made – and this one is serious – and you've not been here a month yet. You may have passed all your exams with top marks and flying colours, but in this job it's practical experience and a good dose of common sense you need, and right now I reckon you don't have either.' He saw the angry flush on the face of his assistant. He didn't take kindly to criticism, but he'd need to get used to it.

'I didn't get an opportunity to apologize . . .' he muttered.

'Apologies willna be much good to the man when you've killed his cow! Apart from losing money for him, and for me, it sounds as though you've lost me a new customer. Didn't I tell you the first day you were here that you had to watch carefully, go slowly, and never attempt anything on your own unless you've actually done it under my supervision. Oh I know you thought I was giving you all the menial tasks, but the small animals side of the practice brings in half my income. I only let you do them if I'm sure you can't do much damage.'

'Does Betty need to know about this?' Mike Crabbe muttered.

'She'll not hear it from me. I'm not exactly proud of having an assistant who is incompetent – not to mention arrogant.' Fisher gave a wry grimace. 'But I've no doubt it will get around the countryside sooner or later. I'm often amazed how efficient the grapevine is. Stories lose nothing in the telling, so be warned. And don't be surprised if some of the farmers refuse to let you treat their animals.' Fisher sighed heavily. 'Do you think I can trust you to take any phone calls until Betty arrives? I'll go through and have my breakfast and then I reckon I'd better pay a visit to Bengairney and see if I can smooth this army fellow's feathers. Is he the sergeant major type?'

'He looked like a farm labourer to me.'

Before he set out, Mr Fisher made a telephone call to Murdo Turner at Martinwold, one of his longest standing customers. He liked to know who was who and a bit about them.

'Good morning, Murdo. I'm looking for a bit of information before I make a call which may prove rather tricky. Am I right in thinking that your land shares a boundary with Bengairney land?'

'Yes, we do neighbour at the top side, but only for a short distance at the northern point. Why? There isn't a TB outbreak, is there? Not foot and mouth? God forbid that we—'

'No, no, nothing like that. I didna mean to alarm you. I wondered if you'd met the new tenants there yet?'

'Steven? Of course I know him. Anyway, they've been there six months now. Why?'

'Yesterday was the first time they've needed a vet, or it was the first time they've called my practice anyway. It was the wife who called.'

'Well I shouldn't think she would call anyone else. After all, you're the nearest vet to them and her father always had a good word o' you.'

'Is she local then? I thought it was some sort of army man who'd got Bengairney – or at least that's the tale Betty Halbin had. Mind you, her and her brothers dinna always get the right story.'

'Well Steven was in the army during the war. He didn't want to go, but he didna have much choice. He was a sergeant before he finished. His father was Eddy Caraford of Willowburn.'

'Caraford? Willowburn? Surely that can't be right?'

'Why ever not?'

'You remember young Iain McNaught, my last assistant?'

'Of course I do. He was a grand young vet. I'm surprised you let him go now you're not getting any younger, and you've no lads of your own wanting to carry on. You're as bad as me.'

'I'd no option. He wanted to see a bit of the world before he settles down. I've promised to make him a partner if he comes back from Canada. Anyway, I had a letter from him a few weeks ago telling me where he'd been. One of the local vets had been taking him round before he moves on to his appointment further east. On one of the first farms he visited he said he'd met a Scotsman who came from this area. He told Iain he was a Caraford from a farm called Willowburn. He said he was planning to return to Scotland but he's been ill and he had some sort of treatment to finish first. They went out for a drink together before Iain moved on to take up his new post.'

'I see,' Murdo Turner said slowly. 'It's a small world. I suppose it could have been Fred Caraford. He was Eddy's elder son, by his first wife. I believe he went to America or Canada when the war finished. I think he married a land girl. Well, I wonder what Steven will think to him returning.'

# Eighteen

Murdo Turner was temporarily side-tracked at the possibility of Fred Caraford returning to Scotland. Where would he consider his home to be these days?

'Anyway, Patrick, why did you want to know about Steven Caraford?' He listened as his old friend explained the previous day's fiasco.

'You know I value my reputation. I could slaughter young Crabbe. He had brilliant exam results, but I don't think he'll ever be any use except for something in animal health administration. I'm thinking of going down to talk to Mr Caraford to see if I can make peace. He said he'd never use my firm again and he wouldn't be paying any bills either. I can't blame him for being angry, but gossip spreads and it's easy to lose a good reputation.'

'Steven is a good stockman and he can't afford losses like that at this stage, but I don't think you'll find him unreasonable once he's had time to calm down.'

'I hope not. I don't like bad blood. Did you say his wife is a local lass?'

'You know his wife well enough. She's John Oliphant's lassie, Megan.'

'My God! Of course I remember wee Megan. She did brilliantly at the Academy then trained as a school teacher, didn't she? I wondered what had become of her. No wonder she was furious with Mike then. He said she'd called him a butcher.'

'Did she now? I don't envy you your task then, Patrick. It sounds as though you have a lot of feathers to smooth.'

'So it seems.' Fisher grimaced. 'Thanks for the information, Murdo. Give my regards to your wife.'

Megan pulled Samuel's blue school cap firmly down on his head. He looked smart each morning in his grey school shorts and pullover, his knee socks pulled up and newly polished shoes; by the time he returned he was a scruffy urchin. She made sure his coat was buttoned up before she gave him a hug and sent him off to school. When he had first started she and Tania and Shandy had accompanied him each morning, but on the third day he had announced, 'I'm a big boy now and I'm going to go to school with Davy and Rick.' The two older boys came from the cottages further up the road and they had arranged to wait for him at the road end. Further along they met a brother and sister from a neighbouring farm and the five children walked to school together. Shandy had been Samuel's shadow ever since he was born, and the faithful collie still accompanied him as far as the farm road end, which was no more than five hundred yards or so, then with a wag of his tail he turned around and trotted back.

As Megan stood watching from the doorway she saw Samuel draw in close against the garden wall with Shandy pressed to his side. A car was drawing into the farmyard. They were not expecting any early morning callers. She watched as the driver wound down his window.

'Hello, young man. You're looking very smart. Are you on your way to school?'

'Yes, I am.'

'What is your name?'

'I'm Samuel Caraford. Who are you?'

'My name is Mr Fisher and I'm a vet. Is your daddy in?'

'Are you the man who killed Jessie?' It was more an accusation than a question, and Patrick Fisher sighed. Out of the mouths of babes and sucklings. It would be all round the village school by lunchtime and round the parish by night. They hadn't a hope of keeping his stupid assistant's negligence to themselves. He'd better see what he could do to make his peace with the Carafords. He'd worked hard to build up a reputation for skill and reliability, but it didn't take many bad mistakes to lose customers.

Megan recognized the gleaming mop of blond gold hair as belonging to Mr Fisher, and she took Tania by the hand and went across to the byre to warn Steven. He accompanied her back to the house as Patrick Fisher got out of his car and came to meet them.

'Well, Megan, it's a long time since I've seen you and I'm more sorry than I can say that it has to be in these circumstances.'

'So am I, Mr Fisher,' Megan said coolly. 'This is my husband,

Steven Caraford – Mr Fisher.' The two men eyed each other warily, but when Fisher held out a hand in greeting Steven shook it firmly.

'This is a bad business at any time, Mr Caraford, and it's worse when you're a new customer, and a young couple working hard to build up your stock. How do you dispose of your dead stock?'

'We send them to the kennels for the local hunt. I telephoned this morning but they havena been lifted yet. You'd better come and take a look.' Steven's expression was grim, but at least Fisher had not tried any flowery talk with him. He hated insincerity. He led the way to the calving shed and the dead cow and calf. Megan went back into the house with Tania.

Fisher stared at the calf then swore fluently. 'The problem was so obvious! That young fool gave me a garbled tale . . .' He broke off, shaking his head and frowning. 'I'm the fool for taking him on. He might be clever but he hasna an ounce o' common sense. I knew by the second day I had him he'd never be any use in my practice. I was out on a call when Megan telephoned yesterday. He must have thought he'd show me he could manage the more important jobs. He resents me giving him trivial tasks. Not that any of this helps you, and it's my responsibility.'

'Nothing you say can bring her back to life,' Steven said sternly. 'I meant what I said. We shall not be paying a bill for calling you out.'

'I shall not be sending you one, but as you say, neither can I bring back the animal, nor can I replace her.'

'No, you certainly can't do that. She was the last of that particular line from my father's breeding.' Steven shrugged. 'I've often heard other farmers say when they've lost an animal it was their best one, but in this case it's true.'

'Aye, I believe you,' Mr Fisher sighed, 'and I wouldna blame you if you stick to your guns and refuse to have us back.'

'I certainly would not!' Steven exclaimed, then more calmly, 'Well, I wouldna have your assistant near the place however desperate I might be, but Megan's father had a good word of you, yourself.'

'I'm pleased to hear that, for John was a fine stockman. I expect you or he would have managed this yourselves if you had been available.'

'Yes, that's what makes it worse. I was selling heifers at Castle Douglas yesterday and you can't be in two places at once.'

'No, I often wish I could divide myself in two,' Mr Fisher agreed. 'But I would like you to give me another chance at least, and I guarantee not to let Mike Crabbe come near Bengairney again. I'm hoping to get my last assistant back in a year's time, and if he agrees I've promised to make him a partner so there will be some continuity in the practice. What do you say? Will you give us another chance?'

Steven looked him in the eye then nodded slowly. 'I reckon most men deserve a second chance – so long as you keep that arrogant young cub away.'

'I'll do that. I know it doesn't cover the cost of a fine animal, but to show goodwill I'll come and inject your first twenty heifer calves with S-nineteen. You do vaccinate against abortion, don't you?'

'Yes, that's one chance I never take,' Steven said with feeling, remembering his shaky start after his so-called brother had sent him infected animals. He looked at Mr Fisher then held out his hand. 'Right you are. Now you'd better come in for a cup of coffee and catch up with Megan. Did you know her mother was seriously ill two years ago?'

'Yes, Mr Turner told me that's why John had decided to give up the dairying. Murdo was really sorry to lose him. He's had a few changes since. How is John?' They chatted amicably as Steven led the way to the house.

Megan had always liked Mr Fisher, and her father had great respect for him as a vet. If he managed to smooth things over she knew Steven would bring him back to the house for coffee. If not, they would go to another vet in future. She poured milk into a saucepan and set it on the rib in front of the fire to be warming, but her thoughts were on last night and the way Steven had loved her. She gave herself a mental hug. The worst of troubles could be managed so long as they had each other. They had always been able to find comfort in each other's arms and it was wonderful to return to a loving relationship. Mr Fisher would find Steven a little easier to deal with this morning than he might have done, she thought with a tender smile.

★    ★    ★

Ruth had been busy both during and after school in the run up to the end of term, with rehearsals for the infants' nativity play, and the older children's carol service. When she and Avril eventually spent a Saturday at Bengairney, she knew at once that things had changed. Christmas preparations apart, there was a happy, expectant atmosphere in the house, and both Megan and Steven looked more relaxed and content than she had seen them since they moved from Schoirhead. Her heart rejoiced for them.

Megan had now sorted out the small sitting room off the kitchen where she and Lint had stored Mr Samson's extra chairs and other oddments. 'I've used the carpet from our sitting room at Schoirhead,' Megan said, 'and our old sofa. Come and look, Ruth.'

'Oh my, this is cosy,' Ruth exclaimed. The fire was burning brightly behind a substantial fireguard, and the three children had their toys and games spread around the room and were playing happily.

'Avril is a proper wee mother,' Megan said affectionately as she watched her patiently teaching Tania how to dress her doll. 'Come on,' she added softly, 'we'll leave them to it and enjoy our coffee in the kitchen, in peace.'

'So?' Ruth said, smiling, 'I can tell things are back to normal with you and Steven – all those tender glances and secret smiles,' she teased. 'I assume you no longer have a desire to go out to the cinema on a cold December evening?'

'No I haven't. I was so silly. Steven went to see Jimmy Kerr the evening he went without me. He said the reason was a secret, but he still hasn't told me what it was.'

'You don't look bothered anyway.' Ruth chuckled. 'I suspect you have more important things on your mind these days.'

'Oh yes. Really, Ruth, married life is so wonderful. I'm sure you and Lint would be just as happy as we are. Don't you think you could . . .?'

'Don't – don't say any more, Megan. Sometimes I long for the sort of relationship you have with Steven, but I can't get rid of the fear that I could never give Lint the sort of love he would expect and deserve from a wife. It's only what any married man has a right to expect. Please let's not talk about it.'

'All right, Ruth. I'd just like to see you both as happy as we are. Is Lint still as busy?'

'No, things are a bit easier. They have a new junior surgeon who started a fortnight ago and Mr Higgins has returned to work part time, more on a consultancy basis than to perform major surgery, and only on condition that he can have Lint as his assistant with a view to him taking over eventually.'

'Well that's very good, isn't it?'

'Yes, it means a rise in salary and it's almost certain Lint will be the chief when Mr Higgins retires completely. I think he has some sort of heart complaint. Anyway, Lint says he's hoping to be here for Christmas dinner by one thirty if that's still all right?'

'Of course it is. Does he want to stay overnight or is he keeping house at Langton Tower for the Palmer-Farrs again?'

'No, they're not going south this year. Lint says he'll return to Carlisle that evening so he will be available if there are any emergencies.' Ruth chewed her lower lip thoughtfully, then she said hesitantly, 'I didn't like to mention this before, but now that I see you're so happy again, I may as well tell you. Katherine Palmer-Farr is expecting a baby. She says it's all down to Samuel and Tania and how much she enjoyed them while you were in hospital.' Ruth looked at her uncertainly. 'Do you – do you mind, Megan?'

'Mind! Of course I don't mind.' Megan smiled. 'In fact I'm delighted for them. I know everybody thought I was unhappy because I'd lost the baby – and I was at first, and I suppose I shall always feel there's a wee empty space in my heart, but I was far more unhappy because I'd convinced myself Steven no longer loved me. I know now how stupid I was. He was only trying to protect me. I didn't know that's what held him back, of course. Anyway, I believe nature has its own way of telling us things, and I hope we shall have another baby sometime so please pass on my congratulations to the Palmer-Farrs.'

'I will.' Ruth beamed. 'Katherine will be pleased. She's longing to discuss things with you and ask your advice, you being another young mother and all that, but she was afraid it would be rather tactless. Douglas thinks she should go to hospital to have the baby, but she would like to stay at home.'

The first Christmas at Bengairney was a happy affair, with everyone gathered around the large dining-room table which Mr Samson had left behind with his assortment of chairs. It was the first time Megan had used the dining room and she was dismayed when she lit the fire on Christmas Eve to warm up both room and chimney for the following day. It smoked everywhere and in the end Steven had to do an emergency chimney sweep; Megan was still cleaning away the soot and dusting at nine o'clock that evening.

'We have to make sure the chimney is clean so Father Christmas can get down, haven't we, Mummy?' Samuel said anxiously. 'It will be all right now, won't it?'

'Of course it will, sweetheart, but Father Christmas might not come at all if you don't go to bed and fall asleep.'

In the end everything had gone well, and Megan was delighted, and a little overwhelmed, with Steven's thoughtful gift of a vacuum cleaner.

'You've started something now, lad.' John Oliphant grinned. 'You know I shall get no peace unless Chrissie gets one next Christmas, don't you?'

'Oh you don't need to wait until Christmas,' Chrissie said, with tongue in cheek and eyes sparkling. 'My birthday in June would do just fine. It would save you having to help me lift and beat the carpets.'

'Aye, well, there's that,' John Oliphant conceded with a laugh. 'See what a lucky man you are Lint, with no wife to pester you.'

'Oh I don't know about that.' His eyes rested on Ruth. 'I wouldn't mind buying half a dozen electric cleaners if I had a wife as good as you and Steven.' Everyone laughed, but Ruth's cheeks grew pink.

Lint had bought her a lovely ruby necklace of her own, with matching earrings and bracelet, but when he had given them to her he had bent and kissed her cheek and whispered, 'I only need permission to give you the ring now.' From time to time he reminded her gently that he wanted her for his wife. So often she was tempted to say yes, but always something held her back. She was terribly afraid of being a disappointment to him, but she knew he would not wait forever.

Towards the end of March Mr Turner called in at Bengairney to see whether Steven had any spare lambs.

'We've a ewe lambed during the night and she laid on one lamb and hung the second. We're nearly finished lambing so we have no spares, and she is a good ewe with plenty of milk.'

'We had one lambed triplets this morning,' Steven said. 'You can have one of them. We've three pet lambs as well, but I daren't let you have them all; Samuel and Tania would never forgive me. You could take the youngest of them, though. It's been on the bottle a couple of days. The others have been bottle fed for about a week.'

'I'll give one of the triplets and the youngest pet lamb a go,' Mr Turner said. He was bundling them into a small crate in his van when he turned to Steven. 'How's Fred getting on in Canada? Do you ever hear from him?'

'Nope,' Steven said. 'As far as I know Mother has never heard a cheep from him since the day he left Willowburn, but I don't think anybody is sorry.'

'No, I suppose not. Ah well, I'll get off home and see if we can get these two lambs fostered on.' It was the first time he had seen Steven since his conversation with Patrick Fisher. He had considered mentioning Fred's intention to return, but he had no desire to unsettle anyone. If Fred had wanted to keep in touch with his family he would have done so.

May 1955 seemed to arrive without warning for Steven and Megan.

'In many ways it's hard to believe we've been at Bengairney a year,' Megan said, 'and yet it has been an eventful twelve months.'

'It has,' Steven agreed, 'and we've still a lot to do, but apart from losing the baby and you giving me the worst fright of my life, Meggie Caraford, we've had a better year than I expected.'

'I agree. I'm glad Samuel has settled well at school and he's made friends. He keeps pestering to visit his neighbours already. I reckon he's going to be a sociable young man when he grows up.'

'Aye, he has his mother's fetching smile and a wicked glint in his eyes.' Steven grinned. 'Apart from the children, though, all the heifers we've had to sell have brought a good price and helped to lessen the bank loan, and Mr Griffiths has promised to install electric lighting in the rest of the sheds and put some plugs in the house for you. I was amazed when he mentioned plans for a new dairy at the end of the byre, with a built-up churn stand outside. I wouldn't have dared ask him for that. He's hoping it will be finished before he leaves, but he says if it's started it will have to go ahead whether his successor approves or not. I think he has done his best for us. My father always thought he was a good agent.'

'It will save a lot of time carrying milk as we do at present,' Megan reflected. 'We've been so lucky.'

'I know, but this time I want to take the greatest care of you, Meggie . . .' He drew her back against him and reached round to stroke her stomach.

'Don't worry, Steven. I feel really well this time. I'm certain everything will be fine. If you remember I was sickly and out of sorts right from the beginning last time.'

'Even so, we must not take any risks. I've spoken to Jimmy Kerr and he's going to keep his eye out for a little car. It will be more reliable than the van.'

'It said in the paper the government are going to build new motorways, whatever that means. It sounds as though people will all drive one way on one road and come back the other way on another road. I don't know if I shall like that.'

'That's only from Yorkshire to London and from Birmingham to Preston,' Steven said. 'It's a lot busier down there. We shall be all right here.'

'Can we afford a car, do you think? Do we really need one? All the groceries are delivered, and we have a butcher and a baker twice a week. I've never had so many deliveries.'

'I expect they're all trying to get more business since the rationing finished. How is Mrs Palmer-Farr? Is she still in hospital?'

'Yes, Mum went in to see her yesterday. She says the baby is beautiful. They're going to call her Rosemary Lavender, but it will be another ten days before they get home.'

'Rosemary Lavender Palmer-Farr?' Steven echoed and burst out laughing. 'The poor wee thing will have a job learning to spell her name.'

'I know. I don't suppose they've considered that.' Megan smiled. 'Christianna is bad enough. We shall have to teach Tania her proper name before she goes to school.'

'Yes, I suppose so. I hear Samuel's friends call him Mule.'

'That's because Tania called him Muel before she could say

Samuel. You always called my brother Sam although he was christened Samuel.'

'We all called him Sam, even your mother and father.'

'I know. It was Dad who started it, or so Mum says.'

'Did you know Joe's wife has started going out to clean? She does two half days at Langton Tower for the Palmer-Farrs and an afternoon at a farm down the road. Joe's bought her a bicycle to get there. I think we should ask her to help you on two mornings a week, Megan. After all, you have all your hens and the eggs to clean and pack, as well as helping with the milking most days. And you'll have three children soon.'

'Oh I don't know . . .' Megan said. 'I like my house to myself.'

'I know, sweetheart, so do I, but I don't want you overdoing things.' He flushed and looked uncomfortable.

Megan eyed him shrewdly. 'You've already arranged it, haven't you?' she flashed accusingly.

'I did mention it to Joe,' he admitted. 'But, Meggie, it's only because I don't want you to take any risks this time.'

'Steven Caraford, you're getting as fussy as my mother,' Megan declared, trying to maintain a stern face.

'I know.' He nuzzled her neck affectionately. 'We both love you to bits.'

Steven had been mowing hay all day, so he was hot and tired by the time he came back to the farmyard to start the milking. Megan was bringing in the cows from the field and swishing a small elderberry branch in an effort to keep the flies at bay. Shandy walked sedately on the other side of Tania, who toddled along singing songs known only to her in her high child's voice. The cows didn't seem to mind; they continued their slow, ambling pace, swishing their tails at the persistent flies. Honeysuckle perfumed the air as they passed and bees hummed drowsily as they flitted amongst the pink and white roses. Megan was filled with contentment.

'I've left tea on the table for you, Steven,' she called as they entered the yard. 'If you'll take Tania inside with you I'll be getting the cows tied up in the byre.'

'All right. Come on, my angel.' Steven hoisted Tania on to his shoulders, a perch she adored as her chubby hands fastened around his bristly chin.

'By the way, there's a letter addressed to you on the dresser, Steven. It has been forwarded from Schoirhead, but it looks as though it has come from abroad originally.'

'I'll open it while I'm drinking my tea, but I don't suppose it can be that important. We've been away from Schoirhead for over a year now.'

Steven swallowed down his first cup of tea in one long drink to quench his thirst and wash away the dust and pollen of the hayfield. He poured himself another cup and spread a scone with Megan's freshly made strawberry jam. It smelled delicious and he took a large bite before he slit open the thin envelope and drew out a single flimsy page.

Dear Mr Caraford,
You will not remember me, but I used to be a land girl for your parents at Willowburn. I came to Canada with your brother Fred. We planned to get married but we never did make it to the altar. I still see Fred but he has been ill. He says the treatment for sick people is free in Britain since the war, so he has decided to return to Scotland. I told him he ought to let somebody know, but neither of us knew where Mrs Caraford went to live after Willowburn, or whether she is still alive. Fred only remembered the name of your smallholding as he was ready to leave. He told me what it was. After I had waved him off I decided I would write to you myself. I think the ship takes about six days to reach Britain but I am sending this by air and I hope it reaches you before Fred arrives. I don't think he will have much money left so he will need somewhere to stay.
Regards
Edna Wright

Steven gasped and his mouth tightened into a thin line. He read the letter again.

# Nineteen

Steven stuffed the letter into his trouser pocket. He didn't mention it to Megan until after they had eaten their evening meal and the children were in bed.

'Goodness me!' Megan gasped as she read it. 'I wondered why you were looking solemn and preoccupied. It sounds as though he is expecting to stay with your mother – or even with us?' She gulped. 'I can't believe he's coming back.' Her eyes widened in dismay. 'Ruth! Oh Steven, we shall have to warn her.'

'She'll be at school during the day, and she does have her own separate apartment, thank goodness, but things will certainly be uncomfortable for her.'

'It will be awful, absolutely awful, the way she feels about him.' She clapped a hand to her mouth. 'I've just remembered – Samuel starts his summer holidays on Monday, so Ruth and Avril will be on holiday too.'

'That will make things more difficult.' Steven frowned. 'Especially when Avril is so used to running around with my mother.'

'Difficult? That's a massive understatement. Ruth will be devastated. She never wants to see Fred again – and he's sure to guess Avril is his daughter if he's smart enough to reckon up the date of her birthday.'

'I hadn't considered that aspect,' Steven said, 'but I'm not having him here. I wouldn't trust him anywhere near you, Meggie.' He pulled her closer and kissed her neck and then her mouth. 'I'd hoped we'd seen the last of Fred,' he muttered. 'We must warn my mother. By the sound of this letter he could be here any time. It depends how long it took to reach us.'

'It's too late to phone tonight. Your mother will never sleep for thinking about it and worrying about Ruth. We'll telephone first thing in the morning. She will have to prepare Ruth. If only there was somewhere she could stay out of the way until Fred moves on.'

'If he moves on,' Steven muttered grimly.

'Surely he can't expect to stay with your mother? Not after the way he behaved?'

'You don't know Fred. He's as thick-skinned as an elephant, but without its memory. He's quite capable of convincing himself we all owe him a debt of some kind instead of the other way round.'

The following morning Steven telephoned Hannah and explained about the letter being sent on from Schoirhead.

'So you see, Mother, he could arrive any day. Megan is terribly worried about Ruth.'

'And so am I,' Hannah said. 'Can I speak to Megan? Or is she taking Samuel to school?'

'No, he takes himself. He's excited because this is the last day. Ruth will be on holiday too tonight. She could come and stay here, but this will probably be the first place Fred will come. He'll probably go to Schoirhead and get directions from there.'

'That's true,' Hannah said slowly. 'But Jimmy Kerr knows where I live.'

'I doubt if Fred would speak to Jimmy after that fiasco with the tractor when he tried to sell it to Jimmy's boss and got caught out. I'll hand you over to Megan. I need to get on with the haymaking. I'll let you know if we can think of any way to help Ruth.'

'Hello, Megan. I never expected this. I don't know how I shall break the news to Ruth,' Hannah said anxiously. 'She'll not want to stay here, but I don't know where else she could go. There would always be a risk of her running into Fred.'

'Sometimes I think it might be better if she did see him and slay the ghosts which seem to haunt her,' Megan said diffidently.

'You may be right,' Hannah agreed, 'but unless Fred has changed completely, I wouldn't trust him not to claim Avril if he realizes he is her father, or use her as a pawn of some kind.'

'Yes, that would be a worse complication,' Megan agreed. 'Why oh why did he have to come back and upset everybody? Steven tossed and turned last night. I know he's worried about Fred returning. He says it's not easy to turn somebody out if they're family, and he doesn't want you to be worried or used.'

'It isn't Steven's worry. He doesn't owe Fred anything,' Hannah said grimly. 'It's the other way round, but Fred will never see that. Anyway, Megan, if he turns up on your doorstep will you keep him there for a few hours and let me know so that I can warn Ruth?'

'Of course I will, but if he plans to stay with you I think Ruth and Avril should come here. At least they wouldn't see so much of him.'

'Thank you, Megan, you're a good lassie,' Hannah said with some relief, but she knew it was not a solution and she was certain Ruth would want to get as far away as she could. Yet she had no family left in the Lake District; in fact she had no one closer than second cousins.

Megan put the phone down then picked it up again and telephoned her mother to give her the news.

'Ruth and Avril would be safer with us than with you,' Chrissie said slowly, mulling things over as they chatted. 'Even if Fred knew we'd moved he wouldn't know where we live. I'll discuss it with your dad and let you know what he says, but I don't think he'll mind. The trouble is I reckon Ruth will be afraid to go into town or anywhere away from the house in case she runs into Fred.'

'It will be a nightmare for her. Even Steven's mother is afraid he might use Avril as a pawn if he discovers she's his child.'

'Better if he never meets Avril then. It's a lovely morning again. I think I'll walk over to the Tower gardens and talk to your dad before he starts working with the bees in the orchard. I'll telephone you this afternoon.'

Chrissie was heading across the drive towards the walled garden in search of John when Lint drove up in his car.

'Morning, Chrissie. It's a lovely day. How are you keeping?'

'I'm fine. I'm looking for John.'

'I'll park the car and come with you. He's going to show me what to do with the beehives this afternoon, but I got away earlier than I expected and I'm not due back at the hospital until Monday morning.' He gave a boyish grin. 'It feels good to have two whole days of uninterrupted leisure again.'

John Oliphant looked up as they approached.

'Hello, Lindsey, you're earlier than I expected. What are you doing here, Chrissie?' He grinned. 'I didn't think you were that keen o' the bees?'

'Oh I don't mind them if I'm kitted out as you men get kitted, but I didn't come to see the bees.' She explained about Megan's phone call. 'So I said Ruth and Avril could come to stay with us if you agree? Fred Caraford isna likely to call on us, and we all think it would be better if he never hears of Avril's existence. Even Hannah thinks that.'

Lindsey Gray had stood beside her in silence, frowning. He knew as well as anyone how much Ruth dreaded ever meeting this fellow again. It seemed impossible for her to put that episode of her life behind her, and seeing him again would bring it all back.

'I have a better idea,' he said before John could reply. He explained about his mother keeping a furnished apartment for his sister and her family. 'They went back abroad three weeks ago and she misses the twins dreadfully for weeks after they've been. Avril's cheerful young company would be the perfect antidote for her if I can persuade Ruth to stay with my parents in Gloucestershire. They'll be getting their school holidays soon.'

'They start on Monday. The term finishes today. They're a bit earlier up here than they are in England.'

'And when does Hannah expect this fellow?'

'That's the problem, we don't know.' She explained about the address and the letter needing to be forwarded. 'He could be here any day. Megan is afraid Ruth might panic and do something desperate.'

'Well there's nothing anyone can do until Ruth gets home from school. Do you think Megan could persuade Hannah Caraford not to mention any of this to her until I get there myself and offer my solution?'

'I think Hannah will be eternally grateful to you, Lint,' Chrissie said warmly, 'if you're certain your parents willna mind? Hannah has always had a liking for Ruth, and since she and Avril came back she treats them both as family.'

'Can I leave it with you then, Chrissie? There's no point in me going down to Ruth's until she gets home from work, and I'd like to see how John handles these bees.' He smiled at her and his blue eyes crinkled. 'This sort of thing makes the perfect contrast to my work as a surgeon and the hothouse atmosphere of the hospital. I reckon the countryside must be in my genes.

I'm keeping my eyes and ears open for a house in the country with a large garden. It will have to be near enough to the Border for me to travel to work, though.'

'We'll keep our ears open for you then.' Chrissie smiled. 'I'll telephone Megan and leave you to get on with the bees. We all like Ruth so we'll do anything we can to protect her and Avril.'

'It would be an excellent solution,' Hannah said with relief when Megan phoned her. 'I know Ruth is very independent, but I think she will be desperate enough to grasp any solution, and at least she trusts Lindsey. Like you, I'm afraid she may panic when she hears Fred is on his way back to Scotland. At least it would give me time to discover what plans he may have.'

Ruth was astonished when she arrived home and saw Lint's car parked in the drive. She was much later than usual because she liked to leave her classroom tidy and remove all her personal belongings and teaching aids before the long summer break. Avril had hung around supposedly helping while waiting for a lift home. She was both sad, because this was her last day at primary school, and excited because the holidays had begun. She bounced out of the car and ran to Hannah's house. She was as much at home there as she was in their own wee apartment, and she always welcomed Lint's visits.

Hannah had already agreed on a strategy to keep Avril with her long enough to allow Lint to explain the situation to Ruth on her own.

'You're just in time to demolish this gingerbread man before Lint eats him,' Hannah greeted her with a smile, 'and then I have a surprise to show you outside.'

'Ooh, what can that be? You haven't found Minnie, have you?' For a moment the light died out of her bright brown eyes and she looked sad. Minnie was one of the bantams which Megan and Steven had given her for Christmas; she had been missing for at least a fortnight and they had concluded she had been taken by a fox, although they were conscientious about shutting them in at night.

'As a matter of fact Minnie has returned all by herself. She has been hiding.' Hannah didn't mention the brood of tiny chicks the wee bantam hen had produced. That would keep Avril occupied outside while Lint and Ruth talked next door.

Ruth popped her head round the door. 'Is Avril interrupting?' she asked.

'No, not at all,' Hannah said with a smile. 'In fact she'll be staying a while, I think. Come and have a cup of tea before you unload the car and all the school paraphernalia. I expect you're as ready for the holidays as the children, Ruth?'

'I'd certainly appreciate a cup of tea,' she said, smiling happily at them both, unaware of the news which Lint was about to impart.

When Hannah and an excited Avril went outside, Lint turned to Ruth. 'Let's go next door if you've finished your tea, then we shall not be interrupted. I've a proposition to make to you.'

'Oh?' Ruth eyed him warily.

'Come on.' He grinned. 'And remember you promised to trust me at all times,' he added, and she noticed there was a serious look behind his smiling eyes. She guessed he and Hannah had arranged this time for them to talk – but what about? A small frown creased her brow and her brown eyes looked up at him anxiously.

'Avril is so like you, Ruth, except she doesn't have your lovely black hair.'

'No, Hannah says her real grandmother had that same golden brown hair with a slight tendency to curl. But what is it we have to discuss, Lint?'

He took a deep breath and began to explain that Fred was on his way home from Canada.

'Fred? Coming back? Oh no! No!' Lint was dismayed at the way the colour drained from her face. She stared up at him. 'Tell me it's not true,' she whimpered. She began to tremble, and when Lint drew her close she offered no resistance, in fact she clung to him and he could feel her reaction.

'We don't know exactly when, or what his plans are, but apparently he didn't get married when he left Willowburn and he is coming back on his own.' She was shaking visibly now and Lint's arm tightened while he stroked her silky hair with his free hand in firm, soothing strokes. At least she trusted him now, and he liked the way she burrowed against his chest like a small animal seeking refuge.

'Steven had a letter from the woman, Eve or Edna Wright,

I think she's called. It had been forwarded from Schoirhead so
Fred will probably go there and then to Steven's, but it sounds
as though he is intending to visit Hannah and it's possible he
means to stay with her,' Lint said gravely, trying hard not to panic
Ruth any more than she was already.

'No! No, I couldn't bear it!' Her eyes were wide, dark pools
of distress as she looked up at him, and his arm tightened protec-
tively.

'Listen, Ruth, we all know how much this upsets you and we
all want to help. Chrissie and John Oliphant have offered to have
you and Avril to stay with them, as it's unlikely Fred Caraford
will visit there, or even know where they live, but no one knows
how long he plans to stay or what he intends to do and you
can't stay cooped up in the house all day for fear of running into
him. Avril would wonder what was wrong.'

'He mustn't see Avril. I never want him to see her. If he asked
her how old she is, or – or . . .'

'Precisely,' Lint said, his mouth tightening. 'It's not a risk we
should take – at least not until we see what sort of man he's
turned out to be.'

'Not ever!'

'All right, Ruth,' Lint said soothingly. 'So this is what I suggest
we do. Remember I told you my mother keeps an apartment
ready for my sister? Well, they went back abroad three weeks ago.
I would like you to pack away all your personal belongings, like
photographs and things, and bring all yours and Avril's summer
clothes. You can stay down in Gloucester for the summer, or at
least until we find out what this fellow intends to do. There's no
reason why he should be in here, but it would be better if he
didn't know you have been here. Hannah agrees with me. It seems
she doesn't trust him any more than you do and it's obvious she
would do anything to protect both you and Avril.' He hadn't
given her time to interrupt, and now he looked down into Ruth's
stunned white face and saw that hope was beginning to take the
place of fear in her dark eyes.

'But your mother . . . She will not want to be lumbered with
two strangers . . .'

'The apartment is even more separate than this, so you needn't
see each other if you don't want to, but I'm certain my mother

will enjoy having you both. She's missing the twins terribly. She always does when they leave. This time they have left two pet rabbits behind so Avril will probably help her look after them. She has a dog and at least three cats. She doesn't keep hens, but she does still ride and she has her pony at the stables about half a mile away. She will probably give Avril a few riding lessons if she is still as mad about ponies when she's had a go.'

'It sounds as though Avril would love it,' Ruth said slowly, 'but can you be certain your mother wouldn't mind?'

'Positive. I telephoned her this afternoon and mentioned the possibility of you coming. She's delighted. As for my father, he'll probably not even notice you're there. Although he's retired he reads more about bacteriology now than he ever did at medical school.'

'I–I don't know what to say . . .'

'Trust me, Ruth. I don't like to see you so upset or worried and I know you'd be safe down there. It may not be for very long, but you can stay the whole summer if Avril is enjoying it. I shall come down to see you whenever I get a long weekend.'

'Will you? Will you really, Lint?' She looked at him eagerly and his heart lightened. He liked the feel of her soft body pressed so close to his. He was sorely tempted to kiss her, but he knew he wouldn't stop at one kiss and Ruth reminded him of a frightened fawn.

'If you could pack up your things this evening I could drive you down tomorrow and drive back on Sunday. I'm off this weekend.'

'Pack now? B–but . . . so soon? And surely I must drive my own car down there?'

'You'll not need it. They keep a little runaround for Yvonne. It is insured and licensed for another month so you may as well use it. I'll ask Katherine to come down with me tomorrow and drive yours up to Langton Tower, if you agree? They have a huge garage and it's better away from here so he doesn't ask questions or begin to wonder.' Ruth nodded, but she was gnawing at her lower lip and he felt the tremors which she seemed unable to control. He drew her closer and stroked her hair while she took time to consider all the implications.

'Do we really need to leave so soon?'

'Well I'd like to drive you there myself and it will be a fort-night before I have another free weekend.'

'And . . .? What are you not telling me, Lint?'

'Well, we're not sure when Fred Caraford is due to arrive. We don't know how long the letter has been on its way. He was travelling by ship, so I imagine he must arrive within the next few days.'

'I see . . . How shall I break the news to Avril?'

'I'll go round and tell her now. I'll say it's a surprise holiday and convince her of all the delights in store. Hannah will back me up. She's as keen to know you're both safe as I am. As we all are. I'm certain she'll be happy down there.' He tilted her chin and looked deeply into her eyes. 'I'm the only one who will be unhappy. I don't like you being so far away, Ruthie.'

'Oh Lint . . . I–I don't want to be so far away from you either . . .' She looked surprised by her own admission, but she lifted her arms and kissed him of her own accord. He would not have been human if he had not returned the kiss with interest. They clung to each other.

'Mummy!' Avril burst in, making them draw hastily apart. She began to giggle.

'I–I was just thanking Lint because he has arranged a surprise holiday for us, Avril. He will tell you all about it but we need to get ready so we can leave tomorrow.'

'Leave tomorrow? But what about my bantam chicks, Mummy? They're so tiny and fluffy, and – and . . .'

'I know, sweetheart, but the hen will never let you near them until they're bigger. That's why she ran away and hid her nest until they hatched, and they'll still be here when we come back. Granny C will look after them.'

'Come on, Avril,' Lint said, stepping away from Ruth regret-fully. 'We'll go and ask Granny C what she thinks and I'll tell you all about the two pet rabbits who are simply dying for a girl like you to pet them and cuddle them. I haven't seen them yet, but I know one of them is pure white and soft except for the black bits on his big floppy ears.' He imitated two big ears and pulled a face, making her laugh, and Ruth flashed him a grateful glance as he went on to tell Avril about his mother keeping her own pony and maybe she would get a ride.

The following morning Ruth telephoned Megan.

'I didn't get to bed until after two this morning so I'm glad I haven't to drive all the way to Gloucestershire. I've packed a lot of my personal belongings in the boot of my car and Katherine is taking it to Langton Tower until we come back. I'm so nervous, Megan . . .'

'You'll be fine. Lint's family sound lovely and not at all the interfering kind.'

'It's so kind of them to have me. I don't know what Lint has told them.'

'I think he'll leave it to you to tell them as much or as little as you want to, Ruth,' Megan said sympathetically. 'Fred has upset everybody. Steven is not sleeping well. I suppose it's difficult to forget how spiteful and selfish Fred was before he went away, and we've no idea what his plans are.'

'I know. I think Hannah feels the same.' She shuddered. 'I'm glad I shall not be here. Lint says we can stay all summer if we want. Surely he'll have gone back before the end of the school holidays?'

'I certainly hope so, for everyone's sake,' Megan said with feeling. 'Steven and Joe are working at the hay today so I've promised to make a picnic and take Samuel and Tania to the field to eat our lunch with him and Joe and the other two men.'

'It's beautiful weather for haymaking. I wish I could be there to help too, except . . .'

'I know, but I'm relieved to know you will be far away and Avril will be safe, Ruth. Try not to worry. We'll keep in touch. I'll write to you, or I'll phone if you have a number of your own. I'll tell you if we have any news. Please try to relax and enjoy yourself.'

Just after midday Megan set off to the hayfield with a basket of food and a can of tea. Samuel ran on ahead and three-year-old Tania plodded sturdily at her side, her small face half hidden by her cotton sun hat. Megan breathed in deeply. She felt a wonderful sense of well-being as she looked around at the fields which she and Steven now farmed. In the distance the low rolling hills looked purple in the heat haze, in contrast to the fresh green of the grass and fields of corn which had not yet begun to ripen. Above them the sky was a vast expanse of cerulean blue, with delicate white wisps of cloud floating lazily in the still air. Her spirits soared to match the heavens. Last year at this time she had been so miserable, now it felt good to be alive.

They all gathered round to enjoy the food, and the children ate twice as much as they would eat at the table.

'That's always the way.' Steven laughed. 'I remember my mother saying if she made a picnic for Sam and me she needed twice as much bread.' The men were all grateful for the gallon can of tea and they drained it dry. Samuel and Tania would have stayed to play all day in the sweet-smelling hay.

'We've spent all morning putting it into neat haycocks,' Steven said, 'now you two are spreading it around again. Just wait until you're a bit bigger. I shall get a fork made specially for the two of you and set you to work.'

'I wish I was big enough now, Dad,' Samuel said, trying to make his scrawny arms bulge into muscles.

'Aye, and when you are big enough you'll be wanting to go off with your pals instead of working,' Steven said dryly.

The sun was high in the sky and they were hot and tired by the time Megan and the children got back to the house. She was glad she had let the fire go out to keep the kitchen cooler. She was ready for a sit down. She hoped Tania might be persuaded to have a nap too, and with any luck Samuel would be content to play with the new toy tractor and trailer which Joe had made for him and painstakingly painted to match his daddy's. They never locked the door and she pushed it open with her shoulder while hanging on to the basket in one hand and the empty gallon can in the other. She almost dropped the lot in shock as she headed straight for the kitchen. There was a man stretched out in the old armchair on the other side of the fireplace. Her heart thumped erratically. Tania clung to her skirt and hid behind her, sucking hard on her thumb. Samuel eyed the still figure suspiciously.

The last time Megan had seen Fred Caraford had been at his father's funeral. She barely recognized the gaunt, bald-headed man who lay in the chair. The pale, yellowish skin was stretched tightly across his broad cheek bones and the bridge of his nose. His teeth looked too big now for his shrunken features. She gasped aloud.

'You'll be wee Megan then?' His voice sounded weak and weary, not at all as she had expected.

'Fred?' she asked uncertainly.

'That's me. The black sheep returned.' He grimaced.

'H–how did you get here? I didna see a car . . .'

'I got a lift to Lockerbie and hired a taxi.'

'I see. Would you like a cup of tea?'

'No thanks.' He sighed heavily. 'I seem to be off tea these days.'

'I have a jug of lemonade in the pantry,' Megan offered tentatively. She had never known Fred Caraford well, but she knew he had been a terrible bully to her brother Sam, and to Steven, although they had both been five years younger than him. Looking at him now he looked twenty-five years older than Steven.

She watched him hesitate, then he said politely, 'A cup of milky coffee would be good if it's no trouble?' He looked at the ashes in the range, then his eyes moved to the slight swell of her stomach.

'It – it's no trouble. Steven bought me a small electric cooker. It's in the scullery. It has three rings. I can easily heat some milk.'

'Thanks. I seem to live on milky drinks these days.'

'Would you like a sandwich? Or a scone and cheese perhaps?' Megan was nothing if not hospitable, however unwelcome her visitor might be. She had been brought up in the ways of most country people.

'No thanks. I couldna face anything to eat.'

'Maybe you'll feel better when you recover from the journey if you're a bad sea traveller. Do you intend to go back the same way or has the sea sickness put you off ships?'

'There's nothing wrong with the liners, but I'm not going back.'

# Twenty

Ruth had barely put the phone down after speaking to Megan that Saturday morning when Lint arrived to whisk her and Avril away. Avril was torn between excitement at all the things Lint had promised she would see and do, and her reluctance to leave the brood of new bantam chicks.

She hugged Hannah tightly. 'I wish you and Samuel and Tania could come too,' she said tearfully.

Ruth was white-faced and heavy-eyed. She had worked long into the night, packing and sorting her belongings and locking things away. Even when she did go to bed she had been plagued by dreams.

Lint had brought Katherine with him. She promised to drive slowly and take care of the car as she hugged Ruth warmly.

'You'll love it down there and I know Aunt Adeline will make you welcome. She'll enjoy having Avril around, she loves children.' She gave Lint an arch look. 'She still hopes Lindsey will present her with a whole brood of grandchildren.'

Ruth gave a wan smile and thanked her. Now she was packed up, all she wanted was to get on the road.

It was a long journey, but Lint was familiar with the road and his car was large and roomy. They stopped at a country hotel for lunch and then he insisted they should stretch their legs by taking a short walk beside the river before embarking on the second half of their journey.

'I telephoned Mother again this morning.' He grinned at Ruth. 'She sounds as excited as Avril. My sister, Yvonne, insisted on having a fridge in the apartment. When mother saw how good it was she got one too. It sounds as though she has enjoyed stocking them both up ready for your visit. She said she would have a light meal ready for us when we arrive as she expects you will both be tired.'

'It's terribly kind of her, Lint. I don't know how I shall ever repay her. Or you . . .'

'Don't you, Ruth?' His voice was gruff. He took her hand in his and intertwined their fingers as they strolled on the narrow path. Avril was dancing along in front, throwing pebbles into the water one minute and lying on her stomach looking for fish the next. 'She will probably sleep after the big meal she ate.' Lint grinned. His expression then sobered. 'And you look as though you haven't slept for a week yourself. I don't mind if you want to curl up and snore your pretty head off, you know. I'm used to this journey.'

'I don't snore!' Ruth said indignantly. 'At least I don't think I do,' she added uncertainly.

'One day I hope to be able to tell you whether you do or not,' Lint said, and although he was smiling down at her she glimpsed the yearning in his eyes and her heart gave a little jump.

'I think I'm falling in love with you,' she whispered, almost to herself. 'If only I could be certain I would be a proper wife . . .'

'This time away from familiar surroundings will give us an opportunity to really get to know each other,' Lint said, his heart soaring at her confession. 'Although I can't stay this weekend I shall try to get some time off to spend with you. I have worked a lot of extra hours when Mr Higgins was off and while we were short-staffed. I'm due some leave.'

As they drove steadily south both Ruth and Avril fell asleep. Lint was content, knowing they were both at ease with him. He believed in fate and in making the most of an opportunity when it was presented to him. He was genuinely sorry Ruth was so upset about Fred Caraford's return, but if it gave him a chance to help her get things in perspective he would be eternally grateful. They had come a long way since the first time they met, when she almost struck out at him in blind panic simply because he was a stranger and they were alone in the byre at Martinwold.

Ruth wakened soon after they passed through Stow on the Wold. She stretched and yawned then realized where she was.

'Oh Lint, I'm so sorry. Have I been asleep for ages?'

'Don't worry about it.' He grinned and patted her hand. 'It will have done you a world of good. My guess is you didn't get much sleep last night?'

'No, I didn't. Where are we now?'

'Heading towards Burford, but we're almost here.' They were

speaking in hushed voices since Avril was still sleeping. Ruth scrabbled in her bag to find a comb and a tissue to wipe her hot face, feeling both apprehensive and excited.

'I feel as though a heavy weight has been lifted from me,' she confessed, 'even if it is only temporary. I promised to telephone Megan and give her the telephone number of the apartment so she can give me any news. I don't suppose she'll have anything new to tell me for a few days, though. I'll wait until tomorrow evening, then I can tell her how we're settling in.'

'Yes, I expect I shall be seeing John Oliphant when I'm up at Langton Tower so he will pass on any news of Fred Caraford's arrival – that is, if he turns up. He may have changed his mind.'

'The countryside is beautiful round here. I love the warmth of the yellow Cotswold stone.' Lint didn't know whether she had changed the subject deliberately or not, but he was happy to go along with it.

'I hope you'll not be disappointed in my family home,' he said. 'Remember it was a farmhouse at one time and it's quite old.' He remembered Natalie had made no secret of her disappointment. Apparently she had expected a small mansion house.

'I think people make a place into a home, rather than the bricks and mortar,' Ruth said slowly.

'You're probably right, except for those people who look for opulence and grandeur.'

On the outskirts of a pretty village Lint turned the car into a short drive, and there before them was a large yard with pots of brightly coloured flowers in front of a long rambling old house with a pink rambler rose climbing up one side of the door.

'This is the back of the house really, but everyone comes in this way,' Lint explained. 'You go up the side to the front entrance but it's rarely used except for picnics in the garden.'

Before he had drawn the car to a halt they saw a collie dog coming forward to investigate, and she was followed by two collie pups.

'Oh look!' Ruth exclaimed. 'Aren't they adorable. You didn't tell us there were puppies as well.'

'I didn't know.' Lint grinned. In the back Avril stirred and stretched.

'Are we there?' she asked, smothering a yawn.

'Yes we are, and look out there, sweetheart.'

'Puppies! Oh, Mummy, how super-duper-wonderful.' She bounded out of the car and moments later was crouched beside the puppies while their mother looked proudly on. In the open doorway Lint's mother stood, smiling in welcome. She was of medium build, and in spite of the hot weather she was wearing a fine tweed skirt and a blue cotton blouse, open at the neck. Her hair was still more brown than grey, worn in a thick coil at the back of her head. Her skin was tanned and it was obvious she was used to being outdoors.

'I'm so pleased to see you,' she said, taking both of Ruth's hands in hers and drawing her into a cool hallway. 'Lint was not at all sure he could persuade you to come until this morning.'

'It's very kind of you to have us,' Ruth said almost shyly. 'I do hope we shall not be a nuisance.'

'I know you will not, my dear. Lint knows very well what sort of company I like. And as for Avril . . .' she turned to look at her, 'you're just the young person I'm needing to help me with my animals.'

'I am?' Avril's eyes sparkled in anticipation. 'Lint said . . . er, Uncle Lindsey said—'

'Eh there, Madame Avril, I thought we'd agreed my best friends call me Lint,' he interrupted with a grin. 'And yes, I'm sure you can see the rabbits, but not until we've had a quick wash and some tea. I'm parched and hot and sticky.'

'Of course you are.' His mother smiled. 'I'll show you to the bathroom, Ruth, my dear. Lindsey has his own room. After we've eaten he can show you where you will be staying while I take Avril to see my animals.'

The meal was a simple one with thick slices of cold roast ham and chicken with an assortment of fresh salads, most of which Adeline Gray had grown herself with the help of an elderly gardener who came when she needed him. This was followed by generous ladles of strawberries and raspberries with lashings of thick cream and thin, melt-in-the-mouth shortbread biscuits in the shapes of various small animals, including cats and dogs and rabbits. Avril was thrilled and Ruth knew Lint's mother had made this special effort for her daughter and her heart warmed towards her.

'Where's Father?' Lint asked. 'Isn't he joining us for tea?'

'He went down to the village green to watch the cricket. You know he never remembers when it is time to eat, dear. He's probably helping the team to celebrate in the pavilion if they've won – and he was expecting they would win today.'

'This is lovely,' Ruth exclaimed in delight when Lint took her to see the apartment she and Avril would use. 'It's like an extension to the house.'

'I suppose that's what it is in a way. I believe the stables or a cowshed adjoined the house at some time. My parents had the building converted when they realized Yvonne would be abroad so much of the time. They both wanted to see her and the children when they do return to this country and it seems to suit both ways.'

'No wonder. The kitchen is so compact and modern and it even has an electric washing machine as well as the fridge. I may never want to leave all this luxury.'

'In that case I shall have to apply for work down here.' Lint grinned. 'And there was me looking at houses within travelling distance of the hospital.'

'Are you seriously looking, Lint?'

'Yes. I'd like a place of my own so that I can settle down now that I've got promotion, with prospects of more when Mr Higgins retires. I'm not rushing into anything but I've looked at one or two. I fancy a farmhouse, or something similar in the country, with a large garden or a small paddock.'

'I see.' Ruth chewed her lower lip and moved towards the rest of the rooms. 'The bedrooms are beautifully furnished and the beds are made up already. I brought sheets and things.'

'I thought we had a large load.' Lint grinned. 'I'll help you carry them in, then I thought we might go for a walk, if you're not too tired? I need to leave after an early lunch tomorrow, but I'd like to show you the village and the surrounding area.'

'But Avril will—'

'She'll be fine with Mother until we get back. I see she's to sleep in the twin bedded room and you in the double bed. The bathroom is between the two but it has a shower as well as a bath. That was Yvonne's idea, and I'm sure she was right. I like a shower myself. She gets a lot of ideas with travelling so much.'

The living room ran almost the length of the extension, except for the kitchen at one end.

'There's even a television,' Ruth said in awe. 'I may have a problem getting Avril to leave such a delightful place.'

'I doubt if the television would make her want to stay, but some of Mother's pets might, especially when she sees Moonbeam.'

'Moonbeam?'

'Mother's horse. She's a silvery grey. Rather too big for Avril, but I'm sure Mother will put her up and lead her round a time or two.'

'But I don't expect your mother to entertain either of us, Lint.'

'Don't worry. She'll probably set you both to work helping her in the garden or doing the shopping.'

'Oh I would enjoy that.'

'Yes, I believe you would,' Lint mused, carrying in a large suitcase and setting it beside the double bed.

It was a beautiful evening and Ruth enjoyed strolling through the village with Lint, past the village green and the small cottages with their mellow stone and chocolate box roses around the doors, all opening on to the street. There was a post office and a grocer's shop, and on the opposite side of the street a butcher, a greengrocer and a baker. Further along they came to the village pub with people sitting outside.

'We could go in for a drink if you feel you've walked far enough?' Lint offered.

'I'd rather carry on walking, I think.'

'Good.' Lint smiled and took her hand in his. 'I thought we'd carry on past the church at the end of the village, then there's a track which leads round the back where all the cottages have their gardens. It will take us through a small wood and past the stables where mother keeps Moonbeam. Eventually we'll come out at the far side of our own garden.'

'Full circle? That sounds lovely.'

'It is a lovely part of the country, I admit, but so is southern Scotland and many parts of Cumberland.'

'Yes, there's beauty everywhere if we bother to look for it,' Ruth agreed. 'At least that's what my father always believed, but Westmorland is very beautiful anyway.'

'I'm sure he was right and he sounds a wise man. I wish I'd met him.'

'Yes, I think the two of you would have got along very well.'

'Never mind, I'd be quite content with his daughter!' He smiled and cast her a sideways look which brought the colour to her cheeks.

When they returned, Avril was getting into her pyjamas and Adeline Gray was preparing her a drink of hot chocolate. As soon as she saw them Avril flew into Ruth's arms,

'Oh Mummy, Mummy, there's so much to see. You'll never believe it . . .' She hugged her tightly around her neck, then she moved to Lint and gave him the same exuberant hug as well as a big kiss on his lean cheek. 'Thank you for bringing us to such a lovely, lovely place,' she said. It was the first time Avril had treated him as she might have treated her own daddy and he was touched. Over her head his eyes met Ruth's, then he smiled and kissed Avril's petal-soft cheek.

'You're welcome, Poppet, after all, you're my best girl. Would you mind if I steal your mummy for another half-hour?' He turned to his mother. 'If it's all right I'd like to introduce Ruth to Father, then I shall be ready for bed myself. I've a long drive back tomorrow and I don't want to be late or overtired.'

Lint's father was sitting by the window in a small room almost completely lined with books. He was tall and slightly stooped, but Ruth didn't think he looked his age, which Lint had told her was sixty-four. He had a thick thatch of silvery grey hair and the same lean jaw and mobile mouth as his son. Although he looked serious, there was a twinkle in his eyes as he greeted Ruth.

'I hope you will enjoy your stay with us, my dear. You will never believe how much you cheered your mother, Lindsey, when you telephoned. It was far better than any medicine I could have produced.' Ruth knew it was his way of welcoming her and making sure she didn't feel such a nuisance, and she was grateful.

As soon as Ruth and Lint entered the apartment Adeline stood up from the bed where she had been telling Avril all the things she would be able to do during her stay at Berrywold. She smiled at them both.

'Do tell me, dear, if there's anything you need, but I'll say good-night for now and hope you sleep peacefully.'

'Thank you. I'm sure I shall. Goodnight.' Lint did not go with her as Ruth had expected. Instead he drew her down beside him on the long settee.

'I wish I didn't have to return so soon, Ruth, but I'll get back as soon as I can. Meanwhile, I hope you feel secure down here. Even if that fellow learned you had been staying in Scotland, or discovered you have a child, he would never find you here.'

'No, I know. I do feel safe here. I'm sure we shall both enjoy being here. And Lint . . .'

'Yes?'

'I'm sorry you have to go back too. I really enjoyed our walk this evening, and I think your parents are lovely.'

'So you might miss me a bit then?'

'I shall miss you a lot.' She leaned forward and kissed his cheek, and then more bravely a soft kiss on his mouth. For a moment his arms tightened around her, but he was determined to let Ruth come to him in her own way, in her own time, and he was beginning to hope that time might not be too far away, if only that beast of a man who had haunted her for so long would get himself back to Canada without her ever needing to see him.

On Sunday morning they all walked to church then returned for a cold lunch before Lint set off on the long drive back. Although his parents were standing at the door with Avril, and in spite of his resolution, he drew Ruth closer.

'I need something to sustain me for two whole weeks,' he whispered in her ear before planting a lingering kiss on her mouth. He jumped into his car and drove away with a final wave through the window and a little toot-toot on the horn. His father looked at Ruth with a twinkle in his eye and Adeline smiled at her heightened colour. There was nothing brash or overconfident about Ruth Vernon, and she'd already guessed this was the young woman Lint hoped to marry. Secretly she had been worried when she had first heard Ruth had a child, with no mention of a father, or of being widowed, but almost from the moment she had looked into her pansy brown eyes and seen the vulnerable look on her face she had known they were going to be friends.

Later that evening Ruth telephoned Megan to give her the telephone number to the apartment.

'Is it a lovely place to stay, Ruth? Do you like Lint's parents?'
Ruth did not miss the anxiety in her tone.

'He's arrived, hasn't he?'

'Yes. He came yesterday. I was so relieved Lint had insisted on
getting you away so quickly. I thought he was rushing you, but
now I'm glad. But Ruth, you didn't say, are you going to be all
right there?'

'The apartment is really lovely and it has more conveniences
than I'm used to having, including a television and a washing
machine and fridge. Lint's parents are delightful people and his
mother is wonderful with Avril. She has promised to take her to
the local stables and give her a ride on her own pony tomorrow.
Did he say how long he was staying?'

Megan knew by the abrupt question that Fred was uppermost
in Ruth's thoughts, in spite of the rosy picture she had painted.

'Megan? Did he say when he was going back?' Ruth prompted.

'Er, not exactly. Steven drove him down to stay with his mother.
I never knew Fred very well myself, but I always knew he was
a bully and lazy and selfish, but he was so quiet when he arrived
I couldn't believe it. I hadn't seen him since his father's funeral
and he didn't look like the same person. He's so thin. He looks
ill, very ill.'

'Megan . . . please don't try to persuade me that a leopard can
change his spots,' Ruth said bitterly. 'If he looks ill he probably
had a bad journey.'

'You could be right. We shall hear more when he's been with
Granny C for a day or two, but Steven thought she was shocked
by Fred's appearance too. I think she was quite prepared to shut
the door in his face if he'd arrived making demands or trying to
bully her. Steven hasn't slept well for several nights. I think he
felt his mother might need protecting in some way.'

'I hope he doesn't stay long for everyone's sake,' Ruth said
flatly. 'I'm more grateful to Lint than ever now I know he really
is there.'

'I'm sure you are, Ruth. I promise I will keep in touch and
let you know if there's any news.' She couldn't bring herself to
tell Ruth that Fred had no intention of returning to Canada.

'Maybe we should let Lint tell her,' Steven said when Megan
put the phone down. 'He seems to know how to handle Ruth.'

'I hadn't the heart to tell her myself, but I wouldn't be surprised if Ruth hands in her notice and looks for a teaching post in another part of the country when she realizes Fred intends to stay.'

'In that case the sooner she knows the better,' Steven said with a frown. 'I wouldn't blame her. I was dreading his return myself. I can't believe the change in him, but I don't suppose it will last once he gets used to being back. He was talking of looking for work on the way to Mother's. I suspect he's running out of funds, but that's nothing new,' he added cynically.

# Twenty-One

When Hannah saw Fred her heart sank like a stone. All her instincts told her he was ill, seriously ill. He would not be returning to Canada anytime soon. She had felt angry and resentful at the news of his return; she had never expected to feel compassion. On Monday morning she suggested taking him to the doctor's surgery to enquire about registering him as a patient under the National Health Service. Fred offered no objection. It seemed to take a great effort to get himself up and into his clothes in time to reach the doctor's before the surgery hours ended.

When he had gone to bed that evening she telephoned Megan.

'I think Fred is a very sick man. He didna say if the doctor offered an opinion, but he is making him an appointment to see a specialist at the infirmary. I thought I had hardened my heart against him, but when I see the way he is I canna turn him away, Megan. Do you understand, lassie?'

'Ye—es, I think so. I was shocked when I saw him too.'

'Do you think Steven will understand?'

'I don't know. He is more concerned about the effect on you. So long as he doesn't try bullying you or wanting money I don't think Steven can object.'

'I have a feeling Ruth may never forgive me,' Hannah said unhappily. 'I'm thinking of telephoning Lint to ask him to break the news that Fred plans to stay indefinitely. She may want to look for a job in another area. Avril is due to change to secondary school anyway.'

'I think that would be a good idea.'

Lint was glad Hannah had confided in him, and that she was willing to leave Ruth to his discretion.

'I would prefer to break the news to her face to face. I've put an offer in for an old farmhouse between Canonbie and Langholm. I think it's time I had a pad of my own and it's near enough for me to travel to work in Carlisle. If I get it there will be plenty of space for Ruth and Avril to have rooms, so you needn't worry about them being homeless.'

'Langholm? But that would be a long way for Ruth to travel to work.'

'Not as handy as staying with you, Hannah, but not impossible, and I wouldn't be surprised if she decides to change schools.'

'Who could blame her? I feel I'm letting her down,' Hannah said unhappily.

'Don't worry about it. I'm sure you must have guessed how I feel. If I had my way I would marry Ruth tomorrow and adopt Avril officially as my own daughter. That way she would be completely safe, but I don't want Ruth to marry me as a means of protecting her child.'

'Of course you don't, Lint. No man would want that, but I don't think Ruth would agree to it anyway. She would have to love a man very much before she would consent to marry him after her experience with Fred. I shall never be able to forgive him for that, even though I do feel some responsibility towards him as he is now.'

Early the following morning Lindsey Gray telephoned his solicitor and asked him to increase his offer for the house by five hundred pounds.

'Five hundred pounds! Are you sure about that, Mr Gray? I believe it needs quite a bit of work doing.'

'It's exactly the sort of place I have in mind and I mean to have it,' Lint said firmly.

Steven telephoned his mother each evening to see how she was coping, and he visited her more often than usual. He was dismayed at Fred's increasing lethargy and his tendency to sleep most of the time.

'He has no appetite to eat either,' Hannah said. 'He has an appointment to see a visiting specialist next week. I shall drive him there myself. I'd like to speak to him too, but Fred is an adult and I'm not even his mother.'

Lint planned to go down to Gloucestershire at the weekend, so he telephoned Megan for the latest news before leaving. She told him the name of the specialist Fred was to see.

'He's based in Edinburgh,' he said in surprise. 'He specializes in cancer patients, I think. The doctor must suspect something like that.'

'I think you would too if you saw him. Steven's mother thinks he's seriously ill, either with cancer or depression, but he doesn't seem to be taking any medication.'

'No wonder he plans to stay in Britain. I shall have to break the news to Ruth for certain then when I'm down there.'

He had planned to set off early the following morning, but after a few hours' sleep he wakened. It was two in the morning and he was longing to see Ruth. He knew he would not sleep again. He washed and dressed, made himself some toast and coffee and set off. The roads were quiet and his spirits soared as the miles sped by.

Adeline Gray had taken Avril to the stables with her the first Monday morning she was at Berrywold. She put her up on her own horse to lead her round the paddock, explaining the rudiments of holding the reins correctly and how to sit in the saddle. Adeline never allowed anyone to ride Moonbeam, and Donald and Holly Hastings, owners of the stables, came to lean on the railings to watch.

'That child could have a natural seat for dressage,' Holly remarked. 'I wonder who she is and how she got round Adeline.'

'I don't know, but Moonbeam is a bit big for her if she's a beginner. She'd look well on Chezzie if Adeline is thinking of bringing her for riding lessons.'

Later they all chatted together and Holly offered to teach Avril about caring for horses and give her a half-hour's riding lesson each day in return for helping with the daily cleaning out, grooming and feeding. Avril jumped at the chance.

'You will need to get your mother's permission first,' Adeline warned, smiling at her eager young face. 'And it is an early start in the mornings.'

'Yes, I expect my helpers to be here by seven, but you can tell your mum I insist on all my pupils wearing a riding hat,' Holly said. 'I usually have at least one schoolgirl or boy to help me during the holidays. I had Bessie for three years, but her parents have taken her abroad to visit an aunt so I'm without anyone at present.'

'Oh I do hope Mummy will say yes,' Avril repeated over and over on the way home.

'Can you ride a bicycle?' Adeline asked.

'Yes. I have a bicycle at home.'

'Well then you could borrow one of the cycles belonging to the twins. They're for boys, but I'm sure you'd manage and it would save time in the mornings.'

So on that Saturday morning two weeks later, Lint was driving into the yard at Berrywold shortly before seven o' clock as Avril was setting out for the stables. He saw Ruth waving from the door, still dressed in her nightgown and a light wrap. Grinning widely he stepped out of the car, greeted Avril with a smile and a cheery wave, then headed straight for Ruth. He gathered her up in his arms, swinging her off her feet in his joy at seeing her again. She seemed every bit as delighted to see him, judging by the way she flung her arms round his neck and gave him one of her quick butterfly kisses. They were becoming endearingly familiar.

As his mouth lingered on hers he became aware of the softness of her body pressed close to him through the thin material of her garments. Ruth sensed his stillness. She realized how flimsy her clothes were and colour flooded her cheeks.

'I – I didn't expect you until afternoon, Lint. I'm sorry I'm not dressed, but if I don't make Avril eat breakfast she would go without any.'

Lint was silent, smiling down at her, and she saw his eyes were fixed on the neck of her lacy nightgown. 'I'm not sorry,' he said, his voice deepening with desire. He held her gaze steadily then bent his head and kissed the soft white vee at the neck of her gown, gently pushing it lower still.

Ruth gasped softly and clung to him as his hands moulded her against him. 'I've missed you so much, Lint,' she said huskily.

In answer he found her mouth again and this time his kiss was searching, questing, while his hands moved over her body, pressing her ever closer. Ruth responded hungrily to his kisses. She had no doubt how much he desired her, even though she had had another man's child.

'Teach me to love, Lint,' she whispered as he moved his mouth to her neck and to her earlobe, and back again to her mouth. For a second he didn't think he could have heard correctly, but when he lifted his head she repeated her plea and her eyes were dark with desire.

Lint did not hesitate, even as he struggled to curb his own passion. He must not spoil this opportunity, this most precious of moments. He must not rush her or awaken frightening memories. He had waited so long for this moment; Ruth must never regret giving herself to him. He lifted her up in his arms, while his lips hovered close to hers, murmuring endearments. He laid her gently on the big double bed where the rumpled sheets still bore the familiar scent of lavender. Ruth was never quite sure when Lint had cast off his own clothes. She only knew that he was awakening wave after wave of desire and giving her a greater pleasure than she could ever have dreamed possible.

Afterwards they lay close, with his arms around her and her head against his chest. Outside the birds were whistling merrily in the trees. There was no need for words. They belonged to each other completely – a union of body, mind and soul. After a little while Ruth's fingers tentatively explored the hairs on his chest. Such a small gesture but one she had never dreamed of doing with any man before. Her hand moved lower and she felt Lint's stomach muscles clench with renewed desire, just as her own had done earlier. She laid her cheek against his and smiled as her fingers continued their exploration. He groaned softly.

'I have awakened an enchantress,' he said huskily.

'Don't you like that?' Ruth asked, half smiling but with that familiar note of uncertainty.

'I adore it, and I shall adore it even more if I'm permitted to reciprocate.'

'Oh!' Ruth gasped as he proceeded to do exactly that. Her cheeks flushed and her eyes were bright.

'Again, my darling?' he whispered against her mouth.

'Yes – oh yes . . .'

Sometime later Lint said, 'Shall we try the the shower? Together?' He saw Ruth's teeth catch her lower lips and the familiar blush colour her cheeks. He was filled with exultation. She was still shy with him, but they had crossed the chasm which had kept them apart. He smiled tenderly. 'I love you so much, Ruth,' he said softly, laying an arm around her shoulders and drawing her with him to stand beneath the exhilarating spray of water.

It was after ten by the time they had dressed and eaten break-fast, but there was a glow about Ruth which no make-up in the world could provide.

'You must be terribly tired, Lint, after driving through the night,' she said with compunction.

'I don't feel in the least bit tired, and I would drive through a thousand nights for such a reward.' He laughed softly at the sight of her swift blush.

'Your parents will know you're here. They'll have seen the car.'

'I'm sure they will know where I am, if not exactly what I've been doing – though knowing Mother she may very well guess.'

'Oh no!' Ruth gasped in dismay. 'You don't really think she would?'

'It doesn't matter if she does. How soon will you marry me, Ruth? You will marry me, my darling, won't you?' It was Lint's turn to look uncertain.

'I will marry you, Lint, if you're sure that's what you want?'

'It is what I want more than anything in the world. I have waited a lifetime for this, my darling Ruth. I want to marry you as soon as it can be arranged.'

'We can't have a white wedding,' Ruth said wistfully. 'I wouldn't feel right, but I would like a small wedding in church.'

'I'm sure that can be arranged,' Lint said triumphantly, and came round the table to lift her in his arms again as his mother tapped on the door and popped her head inside.

'Oh, I'm sorry. I didn't mean to disturb you,' she said, backing out again.

'You're not. Come in, Mother. We have some news for you.'

She looked from one to the other and began to smile. 'As if I couldn't guess, and about time too.' She came to Ruth and hugged her tightly. 'You've accepted him at last, my dear?'

'Y–yes.'

'I'm so glad. I wish you both all the happiness in the world. I do hope Avril will be pleased. She's a lovely child.'

'We shall have to talk to her first,' Lint warned. 'I would like to adopt her officially if she, and you, are willing, Ruth?'

'I should be very happy with that,' Ruth said. 'Avril adores you so I think she will be happy too, but we must ask her, of course.

At eleven she's neither child nor teenager. In many ways she's so sensible and reliable, but emotionally she's still a child.'

'Yes, I agree,' Adeline said. 'Tell her I shall be delighted to have her for my granddaughter.'

'You're so very kind to both of us,' Ruth said with a happy sigh.

'Where would you like to be married? It would be wonderful if you were to be married in our local church where Lindsey was christened, but I know the Carafords have been like family to you, Ruth, so I do understand if you feel you should be married in Scotland.'

'That's something we have still to discuss,' Lint said, his expression serious now. 'There's still things I have not had time to tell Ruth . . .' He looked at his mother.

She smiled. 'I shall leave you to talk some more. Avril will be back by midday. Do you want me to give her lunch?'

'Thank you, but the sooner we tell her our news the better.' Ruth smiled. 'Otherwise she might guess. I feel so happy I'm sure everyone must know.'

'Very well, I'll see you later.' Adeline hummed a merry tune as she went back to tell her husband the news.

'I have two bits of news to tell you, Ruth. Fred Caraford does not intend to return to Canada at all . . .'

'What? No, oh no, he can't possibly mean to stay.' The colour had drained from her face and Lint went to put a comforting arm around her shoulders, but she shrugged him away, her eyes wide with dismay.

'Please listen to what I have to tell you, Ruth, because Hannah is in a dilemma and it's important you should understand. I have not seen Fred Caraford myself, but both Megan and Hannah think he is seriously ill – so ill that Hannah feels she can't close the door in his face, although she can never forgive him for what he did to you.' Ruth was staring at him, her eyes wide and dark; myriad expressions passed over her face. 'He has to see a specialist and from what I've heard it sounds as though he may have cancer. Apparently he is not eating and he has lost a lot of weight. Even Steven is astonished at the change in him.'

'I don't care how ill he is, or how much he has changed, I never want to see him again!'

'I can understand that, sweetheart. It is another reason why I should be happier if we have the banns called down here and plan our wedding for three weeks from now before the school holidays end. I'm hoping you will resign from your teaching post, and as my wife you would have no reason to return to Hannah's, except to collect the rest of your belongings.'

'No, I suppose not. Why oh why did he have to come back.' Ruth's voice shook. 'I was so happy.'

'I hope we shall still be happy. We must shut him out of our lives and forget about him, however callous that might sound about a dying man.'

'You really think he is dying?' Ruth asked, her face registering shock.

'I can't say for certain but Hannah thinks so.'

'What was the other news?' Ruth asked flatly. 'Surely it can't be bad too?'

'No, at least I hope you'll think it's good news. I have put an offer in to buy a house. It's in the country between Langholm and Canonbie. It's an old farmhouse with some outbuildings and two small paddocks, but it needs a lot of repairs and improvements. It looks a bit like Bengairney did before it was cleaned up and lived in. If I get it I had thought you and Avril could share it, although it would have been quite a distance to travel to your work at Annan. Now −' he smiled − 'now you will not need to travel anywhere, except as far as my bedroom.' There was a wicked glint in his eyes and Ruth blushed as he had known she would. He was anxious to take her mind off Fred Caraford. 'Avril will be going to secondary school and you and I will be busy doing up our very own home − at least we shall if they accept my offer. I shall know next week. Even if they don't, we'll look for another house far enough away from Fred Caraford, but near enough for you to meet Megan or Hannah whenever you wish.'

'Dearest Lint, you think of everything.' She moved round the table and burrowed into his arms, laying her cheek against his chest while he stroked her hair. 'Do you mind if I talk to Megan before we make any plans for a wedding. I would like to have talked to Hannah, too. She has been like a mother to me, but I never know whether she will be free to talk or whether he will be listening.'

'Telephone Megan and tell her our news. She could ask Hannah to phone you when it's convenient.'

'All right, I'll phone now before Avril is due back. I'd like you to be present when I tell her.'

'Can we invite Katherine and Douglas to our wedding?'

'Will they want to come with such a young baby? If they can't we could have a house-warming celebration later in the year and invite them all then.'

'That's a splendid idea, Ruth. Mind you, I shall agree to anything so long as you don't make me wait too long to make you my wife.'

Megan was delighted with the news. 'I knew it was only a matter of time,' she said triumphantly. 'Of course I'd love to be there, but that's not as important as you getting married soon. I'm sure Granny C will say the same. As you say, we could have a lovely celebration if Lint gets the house he wants.'

'I know, it's just that you've been such a good friend, Megan. I would have loved to have you for my maid of honour.'

'You know how happy I would be to be able to do it too, dear Ruth, even if I shall probably look like a tent by then.'

'In three more weeks? Did I say Lint would like us to be married before the school holidays end?'

'Only three weeks!' Megan squeaked. 'How romantic, Ruth. I will phone Granny C now and I'm sure she'll phone you tonight when Fred is asleep. Mind you, he seems to sleep most of the day, too.'

Adeline Gray insisted on making lunch for them all as soon as Lint and Ruth had broken the news to Avril. 'You two love-birds would never get anything ready anyway,' she chuckled.

Avril looked from Lint to Ruth and back again, her brown eyes wide with excitement as she took in what they were saying. 'Does that mean you will buy Mummy a gold ring?' she asked. 'All the other mums at school wear a gold ring to prove they are real mummies.'

Lint chuckled, but when he looked up he glimpsed the sadness in Ruth's eyes. 'I shall buy your Mummy a real gold ring and give her my name. If you like I will buy you a gold ring too with your initials on, but you will wear it on a different finger.'

'Oh yes please, I'd like that.'

'When I give your mum a gold ring she will change her name to mine so she will be Mrs Gray. Would you like to change your name too and become Miss Avril Gray?'

'Could I do that? Is that right, Mummy?' She turned her eager little face to Ruth.

'Yes, if you would like that, darling. Lint would like to adopt you officially and I would like that very much. We shall be a real family.'

'Yes! Yes, I would like to be a real family like Samuel and Tania. Do you think I could have a wee brother and sister, too?'

'We'll have to see about that, darling,' Ruth said, unable to control her hot cheeks or meet the laughter in Lint's eyes.

'Meanwhile,' he said soberly, 'if I get the house I am hoping to buy, Avril, you can choose one of the puppies and we'll take it to our new home with us.'

'Oh thank you, thank you!' She beamed. Then her young face grew sad. 'It will be awful when I have to say goodbye to Chezzie. I really love him and Holly says he loves me too. Shall we be able to come back here for holidays so that I can ride him again?'

'I'm sure we shall,' Lint said firmly. 'After all, you'll not only have me for a father, you will have a new grandma and grandfather. I know my mother has always wanted a granddaughter.'

'Speaking of your mother, Lint, we're already late for lunch,' Ruth reminded him.

# Twenty-Two

Hannah telephoned that evening and her congratulations and good wishes were warm and sincere.

'Of course I would have loved to be at your wedding, Ruth, whether it was here or in Gloucestershire, you know that, but most of all I'm delighted that life is working out for you at last, and for Avril too. I like Lint and I'm sure he will make a good father.'

'I'm sure he will too. We both understand how tied you must feel just now.'

'I'm afraid I do, dear, but I don't think it will be for many months and I feel I owe it to my cousin Eleanor to look after her son in his hour of need, even though I know he has not deserved anyone's care.'

'You're very good and forgiving. I know my father would have expected me to forgive, but I can't.'

'I understand, my dear. You go ahead and make arrangements for your wedding down there and then you can come to see me as Mr and Mrs Gray.'

'I would have liked Megan and Steven to be at my wedding,' Ruth said with a sigh. 'They are such good friends to me, but I know I'm fortunate to have Lint's family. They are being so kind to me, and to Avril. She's fallen in love with a horse called Chezzie and I fear we shall have a few tears when she has to say goodbye after another three weeks of seeing him every day.'

'Yes, I feel I know all about Chezzie from the two long letters I've had from Avril. She writes beautifully. She has also told me about the two rabbits and the puppies. I'm so pleased she is enjoying her stay down there.'

When John and Chrissie Oliphant heard about the wedding they were delighted.

'I like them both so much. I'm quite sorry they will be getting married down there.'

'I know,' Megan said. 'So am I in a way, but with Fred staying with Steven's mother it makes sense. Ruth would have liked me to be her maid of honour, but she understands it's impossible.'

'Is it impossible, Meggie?' Chrissie said. 'What do you say to John and I moving in here for a few days to look after the children and do the milking? You know your father would take the greatest care of Steven's cows and I think he would enjoy it.'

'Oh . . . I don't know about that, Mum. Wouldn't it be too much for you?'

'We'll see what your father and Steven say when they come in from wandering around the cows in the field. After all, the haymaking is finished and the sheep are all clipped. I don't think the oats will be ready for harvesting in three weeks, do you? Anyway, you'll only be away a few days.'

'It would be lovely if we could manage it,' Megan said pensively, 'and I know Ruth would appreciate us being there for her.'

When the men came in John had no hesitation about agreeing to look after things. 'Joe is a capable man now,' he said. 'He knows the ropes and he's conscientious. It's not as though I'd be on my own. I'll bet old Ben will be looking in to see if I'm making a good job,' he grinned. 'He was here everyday when I was milking, before you moved in.'

'Yes, I reckon he would. He comes up most days and does a few odd jobs, or has a talk to Megan and the bairns.' Steven looked at Megan. 'Maybe we should ask Evelyn to come in every morning to lend a hand, then the children wouldn't tire out my favourite mother-in-law.'

'Your *only* mother-in-law, I hope,' Chrissie said with a smile. 'That's very considerate of you, Steven. If it makes you both happier about leaving us I'll agree. It will do the pair of you a world of good to get away on your own for a few days before the next wee one arrives in November.'

'Evelyn will be happy with that,' Megan agreed. 'Now that I'm getting to know her better I've discovered there are two things she craves. The first is a baby of her own to love, and the second is she's saving up to try and persuade Joe to swap his motorbike for a wee car and she wants to learn to drive.'

'Both worthy enough goals,' Chrissie said. 'At least she doesna mind working.'

'I'm beginning to feel excited,' Megan said. 'Can I go and phone

Ruth now and tell her we'll be coming? I shall have to get a dress. I wonder what colour? I think Ruth is having a dress and jacket in shell pink, and Avril can't decide what colour she wants yet. Lint's mother had her measured for a pair of jodhpurs and Ruth says she wears them at every opportunity, but she is really excited about being a bridesmaid and carrying a posy.'

'I'm sure she is. It would be nice if you both wore the same colour,' Chrissie said. 'It's a pity Ruth is not here or she would probably have made you a dress to camouflage your bump.'

When Megan telephoned with her news, Ruth was over the moon.

Lint took the telephone receiver. 'She's so happy she's laughing and crying at the same time,' he said. 'Seriously, Megan, we're both very grateful to you for coming and to your parents for making it possible. I'll hand you back now. I'm leaving in half an hour so don't let Ruth change her mind when I'm not here beside her.'

'I don't think there's any fear of that, Lint. I've never heard her so happy and so positive about everything. You deserve a big hug from me too.'

'I can't wait!' He laughed. 'I expect I shall be seeing you when I'm up at the Tower. I only hope my offer to buy Eskriggholm will be accepted or we shall be searching for a house to rent.'

'When will you know?'

'By Wednesday or Thursday. Bye for now, Megan.'

Ruth volunteered to make a dress for Megan before she had time to mention getting one to fit. 'I know how well you suit pale lemon with your colouring, and Avril would suit that too with her golden brown hair. I'll see what she says. Let me have your measurements and I'll make a nice floaty style with a seam beneath the bust. Later on you will be able to draw it in with a sash, or I'll add some seams for shape, if you still want to wear it.'

'But isn't your sewing machine still at Granny C's, Ruth?'

'Yes, but Lint's mother says I can borrow hers. I may need to get used to it, though. It's electric. Oh, Megan, I can't tell you how happy I am that you're coming.'

After Megan put the phone down she went back to the living

room. 'Ruth never mentioned Fred once. I think she's so happy and full of plans he's gone right out of her mind.'

'About time too,' Steven said. 'I feel sorry for him now, seeing him the way he is, but he was never worth all the anguish he caused.'

Lint and Ruth visited the vicar before Lint set off back to Carlisle. The banns had been arranged and a date fixed for their wedding.

'All we need now is to find out whether we shall have a house to live in,' Lint said wryly.

'Shall we postpone the wedding if you don't get it?' Ruth asked with an impish smile.

'Indeed we will not! We'll live in a caravan if necessary . . .' Then Lint saw her smile and grabbed her, swinging her off her feet. 'You're not getting rid of me that easy.' He kissed her long and deeply, then sighed. 'I wish I didn't need to go but I must earn my crust. I shall soon be a family man with an expensive wife to keep,' he teased. Ruth opened her mouth to protest and saw the laughter in his eyes.

'I'm so happy, Lint,' she said softly instead.

It was very late when Lint telephoned to say he had arrived back safely, but Ruth had waited up.

'The roads were busy and it was a slow journey,' he explained, 'but guess what? There was a letter from the solicitor waiting for me. We've got the house! All it needs is my signature and to arrange the money. I shall make an appointment tomorrow as soon as his office is open.'

'Oh Lint, that's wonderful.'

'Mmm, I hope my wife and daughter will not be too disappointed at the sight of it . Wife and daughter – I like the sound of that. Seriously, Ruth, will you go into town and pick some colour schemes for our bedroom and for Avril's. Let her choose, whatever colours she wants. I want her to be happy too.'

'All right, if you're sure?'

'I am. I'll get a decorator in. We need a clean room to sleep in, but there's five bedrooms to choose from as well as an attic so you can take your choice later. Everything else will have to wait until you can tell me what you would like to do. I think we shall enjoy planning our home together, don't you?'

'Yes, I'm looking forward to it. When we worked at Bengairney together I almost envied Megan and Steven, and now it really will be our home.'

'The outbuildings have been well maintained, but I think we may want to knock down a wall or two at the back of the house, so we shall be living in a bit of a muddle for a while. Will you mind that, Ruth?'

'Of course not. It will be our very own home when we're finished.'

'I'm glad you agree, but I've arranged a few nights away before we settle down to the hard work. Mother will take care of Avril. We'll enjoy a touch of luxury, sweetheart, while I make wild and passionate love to you.'

'I hope there's no one listening in,' Ruth said breathlessly. Just hearing Lint's voice sent a tingle of desire right down to her toes. Only a few weeks ago she would never have believed she could feel like this. 'I do love you, Lint,' she said softly.

Adeline Gray took Ruth to one of the most exclusive shops in town to choose her wedding outfit, and they both agreed when she tried on a deep rose-coloured dress that it suited her better than the pale shell pink she had intended to buy.

'With your shining black hair and fair skin it suits you beautifully, Ruth,' Adeline said in admiration, 'and I insist on buying it for you. I shall leave the hat and gloves to you. It is a delight to me to have Avril, in fact I'm going to miss her cheerful young company badly when she leaves. My morning rides have given me twice as much pleasure since she has been able to accompany me, and she has such a lively, enquiring young mind. I hope you will let her come to stay with us sometimes for holidays?'

'Of course, if it is what you want,' Ruth said huskily. 'You have been so very kind to us, and you have never asked any questions about her father.'

'No. I know you will tell me when you feel ready to talk, but meanwhile I'm content seeing you and Lint so very happy together. I'd begun to despair of him finding the girl of his dreams. Now he has and my prayers have been answered.'

They found a frothy pink hat and gloves in exactly the same shade, but the material for Megan's and Avril's dresses was a rich cream silk rather than the pale lemon Ruth had suggested.

'Will your friend mind?'

'Oh no,' Ruth smiled. 'Megan could wear almost anything with her vibrant colouring, and she is genuinely happy that Lint and I will be together at last. I thought my world was at an all-time low when my father died and I was literally homeless with having to move out of the vicarage, but I have found so many kind friends through Hannah. I hope you will meet before long. Maybe when we have made our house habitable you will come to stay?'

'My dear, I should love to do that.'

Megan and Steven arrived the night before the wedding and Lint arrived soon after. Avril was excited at seeing them again and she insisted on taking Megan to meet Chezzie, the beloved pony.

'I shall be really sad when I have to say goodbye to him, Auntie Megan,' she confessed. 'But Mrs Gray says I can come to stay with her for my holidays, and Holly will make sure he's always here for me to ride.'

'I'm sure she will, Poppet,' Megan said, 'and you will be taking one of the puppies home with you, I hear. Have you decided which one yet?'

'It's hard to decide, but I think we are taking Bimbo and leaving the girl puppy with Mr and Mrs Gray. Lint says they will be my grandparents after the wedding and I shall be Miss Avril Gray and Mummy will be Mrs Gray and she'll have a gold ring like the other mums at school.'

'I think it's wonderful all these things have happened, don't you?'

'Oh yes. I shall have a daddy too.' Her smooth brow creased in thought. 'I asked Mummy once where my real daddy was, but she said she didn't know so maybe he's in heaven.'

Katherine and Douglas Palmer-Farr and their baby had arrived when Megan and Avril made it back to the house, and Avril was enchanted with the tiny infant in the wicker cot.

The wedding went off perfectly. Ruth looked radiantly happy. Her heart almost turned over at the sight of Lint in his dark suit and pristine white shirt. She was more used to seeing him in scruffy flannels and an old tweed jacket or pullover when he was not at the hospital; he looked so handsome she could scarcely believe this man would soon be her husband. She smiled shyly at him as Steven led her down the aisle to give her away.

There were hugs and kisses all round as Lint and Ruth drove away amidst swirls of confetti. Ruth had insisted she did not want an engagement ring until they were truly married. She had not forgotten that Lint had once been engaged to Natalie Turner and she had thrown the ring back at him.

'I don't want anything to go wrong for us,' she said. Now, sitting beside him in the car, she gazed down at the plain gold wedding band which seemed to mean so much to Avril, a fact she had never suspected until recently, and beside it Lint had slipped on the ring he had wanted to give her for some time: a ruby with a diamond on either side. It matched the jewellery he had given her at Christmas.

Megan and Steven thanked Adeline Gray and her husband for their hospitality.

'We have decided to leave now that the bride and groom have gone,' Steven said. 'We intend to have a leisurely journey and stay a night on the way home. We are enjoying the break, and time on our own, too.' Megan blushed as she caught his eye. They felt like a honeymoon couple themselves, in spite of having their third child on the way. They were as much in love as ever.

Too soon for Avril the day arrived when they must all head north for their new home and she had to say goodbye to Chezzie. She got up extra early so that she could cycle to the stables to say goodbye and feed him one last apple as a treat. Holly saw her from the window. She was surprised and dismayed, and she watched as Avril headed straight for Chezzie's stable. Avril didn't really want to see anyone because she knew she might cry and she was much too grown-up now to cry in public, but the stable was empty. She stared at the empty box, still bearing traces of Chezzie's bedding. She moved along the boxes but the usual ponies were still in, including Moonbeam. She turned at Holly's footsteps.

'I came to say goodbye to Chezzie,' she said, 'but he's not in his box.'

'I know dear, he . . . er, he had to go away this morning. The lorry came very early. I'm sorry you've had a wasted ride over.'

'He's gone in a lorry?' Avril stared at her with wide accusing eyes. 'B–but you promised! You said he would always be here when I came for my holidays . . .' Her chin trembled as she struggled for control. Suddenly she made a dash for her bicycle, jumped on and pedalled furiously away, the tears pouring down her cheeks. They had sold her beloved Chezzie and she hadn't even said goodbye. They had all promised he would be there for her when she came back again. When she reached the little wood she jumped off her bike and ran into the trees. She flung herself on the soft ground and sobbed as though her heart would break. Eventually she knew she had to get up and go, but she no longer cared where they went or what they did. Back at the house she ran to the bathroom to wash her face, but she couldn't eat any breakfast. She felt she would choke with grief. Where had Chezzie gone? Would he have a good home, or would his new owner be cruel to him like Black Beauty in her favourite book?

Neither Lint nor Ruth guessed where Avril had been. They put her silence and lack of appetite down to her sadness at leaving after such a happy summer. Even when Bimbo scrambled into the back of the car beside her and tried to lick her face she couldn't summon a smile, and she almost burst into tears all over again when Adeline Gray kissed her goodbye and told her to come back again soon so they could go riding together.

They stopped for lunch, but even then Avril only picked at her food and her eyes looked heavy and dull. Ruth guessed she had been crying and she knew now why she had heard the odd little sniffs in the back of the car.

'Cheer up, Avril,' Lint said, as he filled a bowl of water to give Bimbo a drink before they resumed their journey. 'See how he's wagging his tail. He must be happy to be going with you to his new home and I'm sure you'll like it too. We shall have just as much space as there is at Berryhouse.'

'Yes, and we'll go to see Granny Caraford soon and collect your bantams and the wee brood of chicks,' Ruth said. 'Lint has asked a joiner to make them a pen to keep them safe from the fox.'

'They'll not be fluffy chicks any more,' Avril said flatly, but she added more brightly, 'Granny C said in her letter they had grown feathers like their mother. One of them is a cockerel and she said he is going to be a handsome bird with green feathers in his tail.' That was the end of her conversation, and it was almost a relief when she fell asleep.

'I do hope she will not be silent and unhappy when we arrive,'

Ruth said. 'She's been through a lot of upheavals in her young life, but I never remember her being so quiet or looking so sad.'

'Don't worry, sweetheart. I'm glad she got on so well with my mother, but she'll soon settle down when she's had a look around. I have a nice surprise for you both.'

'Can I guess what it is?' Ruth asked.

'No, you must wait and see.'

Ruth guessed it was the newly decorated bedrooms and she doubted if Avril would be excited by such things. She hoped Lint would not be too disappointed by her reaction or lack of enthusiasm

She would have one more hurdle to cross herself. She had agreed they would all go to Hannah's in a day or two to collect the rest of her belongings and Avril's bantams. She accepted that Fred Caraford really was seriously ill. The specialist had told Hannah he had had radium treatment for lung cancer while in Canada. For a while he had thought he was better, but it had already spread and it was now affecting his bones. Although she had no desire to see him again she no longer felt afraid. She had Lint now, and he was sure it would be better for Avril to meet him, if only briefly.

'One day she will ask questions about her real father,' he said gravely. 'There is no need for her to know the details. You can truthfully say he went to Canada and that she met him once before he died. I had a chat with Steven when they were down. He says Fred is on morphine pills for the pain. It's doubtful he will ever think he might have fathered a child, and we need have no fears that he would try to claim her.' All this was true, but Ruth knew her own strength came from Lint and knowing she was loved and cherished by him.

Avril wakened as they were crossing the Border into Scotland, but instead of taking the usual route west Lint turned north towards Canonbie and Langholm.

'That's Netherby on the other side of the river,' he said. 'You know the poem about Young Lochinvar, Avril? He seized the lady he loved and galloped away with her on his horse.' Ruth was dismayed when she turned to look at her daughter and saw her eyes were full of tears. Mention of Young Lochinvar's horse had reminded her of Chezzie, and she would never see him again.

Shortly afterwards they turned off the road on to a minor road and then on to a track leading up a hill to a small farmstead sheltering against the brow of the hill and with a view of the river and the woods down below. They climbed stiffly out of the car and Bimbo barked and danced with delight at being free again.

'Avril, you could go and see the sheds over there and see which one you would like for Bimbo to sleep in.'

'Can't he sleep in the house?' she pleaded. 'Everything will be strange for him here and he'll miss his mother and his sister.'

'We—ell, I suppose he could for tonight, so long as you clear up any puddles he makes,' Lint said gravely, 'but take him for a walk to see the sheds anyway.' He led Ruth inside the house which was to be their new home. Minutes later they heard a squeal of delight and Avril came flying into the house, her face wreathed in smiles.

'Chezzie is here! Oh, Mummy, Chezzie is here! Right here at our house. How did he get here? Can we keep him?' Ruth looked from her daughter's radiant young face to Lint, who was trying to hide a smile of satisfaction.

'I believe he travelled in a lorry up the road early this morning,' Lint said.

'So that's why his stable was empty when I went to say goodbye!' Avril exclaimed.

'Did you buy Chezzie from the stables specially for Avril, Lint?' Ruth asked seriously.

'Yes, after some persuasion. Now he's your own horse, Avril. You can be like Grandma Gray and keep him yourself, but you will have to groom him and feed him,' he warned. In answer Avril threw herself into his arms and hugged him.

'You're the best daddy in the whole world!' she cried. 'Now I really do have a proper family, with a pony and a dog and a Mummy and Daddy.'

Over her head, Lint and Ruth exchanged contented smiles.